"*Dangerous Waters* is a bumpy ride through a devastatii _ powerful events and resolute characters. Radclyffe gives us the strong, dedicated women we love to read in a story that keeps us turning pages until the end."—*Lambda Literary Review*

"Radclyffe's *Dangerous Waters* has the feel of a tense television drama, as the narrative interchanges between hurricane trackers and first responders. Sawyer and Dara butt heads in the beginning as each moves for some level of control during the storm's approach, and the interference of a lovely television reporter adds an engaging love triangle threat to the sexual tension brewing between them."—*RT Book Reviews*

"*Love After Hours*, the fourth in Radclyffe's Rivers Community series, evokes the sense of a continuing drama as Gina and Carrie's slow-burning romance intertwines with details of other Rivers residents. They become part of a greater picture where friends and family support each other in personal and recreational endeavors. Vivid settings and characters draw in the reader…"—*RT Book Reviews*

Secret Hearts "delivers exactly what it says on the tin: poignant story, sweet romance, great characters, chemistry and hot sex scenes. Radclyffe knows how to pen a good lesbian romance."—*LezReviewBooks Blog*

Wild Shores "will hook you early. Radclyffe weaves a chance encounter into all-out steamy romance. These strong, dynamic women have great conversations, and fantastic chemistry."—*The Romantic Reader Blog*

In **2016 RWA/OCC Book Buyers Best award winner for suspense and mystery with romantic elements** *Price of Honor* "Radclyffe is master of the action-thriller series…The old familiar characters are there, but enough new blood is introduced to give it a fresh feel and open new avenues for intrigue."—*Curve Magazine*

In *Prescriptioi*   ll town with
colorful charac   Flann's little
sister, Margie, ;   `his romantic
drama has plen

2013 RWA/New England Bean Pot award winner for contemporary romance *Crossroads* "will draw the reader in and make her heart ache, willing the two main characters to find love and a life together. It's a story that lingers long after coming to 'the end.'"—*Lambda Literary*

In **2012 RWA/FTHRW Lories and RWA HODRW Aspen Gold award winner** *Firestorm* "Radclyffe brings another hot lesbian romance for her readers."—*The Lesbrary*

Foreword Review Book of the Year finalist and IPPY silver medalist *Trauma Alert* "is hard to put down and it will sizzle in the reader's hands. The characters are hot, the sex scenes explicit and explosive, and the book is moved along by an interesting plot with well drawn secondary characters. The real star of this show is the attraction between the two characters, both of whom resist and then fall head over heels." —*Lambda Literary Reviews*

Lambda Literary Award Finalist *Best Lesbian Romance 2010* features "stories [that] are diverse in tone, style, and subject, making for more variety than in many, similar anthologies...well written, each containing a satisfying, surprising twist. Best Lesbian Romance series editor Radclyffe has assembled a respectable crop of 17 authors for this year's offering."—*Curve Magazine*

2010 Prism award winner and ForeWord Review Book of the Year Award finalist *Secrets in the Stone* is "so powerfully [written] that the worlds of these three women shimmer between reality and dreams...A strong, must read novel that will linger in the minds of readers long after the last page is turned."—*Just About Write*

In **Benjamin Franklin Award finalist** *Desire by Starlight* "Radclyffe writes romance with such heart and her down-to-earth characters not only come to life but leap off the page until you feel like you know them. What Jenna and Gard feel for each other is not only a spark but an inferno and, as a reader, you will be washed away in this tumultuous romance until you can do nothing but succumb to it."—*Queer Magazine Online*

Lambda Literary Award winner *Distant Shores, Silent Thunder* "weaves an intricate tapestry about passion and commitment between lovers. The story explores the fragile nature of trust and the sanctuary provided by loving relationships."—*Sapphic Reader*

Lambda Literary Award winner *Stolen Moments* "is a collection of steamy stories about women who just couldn't wait. It's sex when desire overrides reason, and it's incredibly hot!"—*On Our Backs*

Lambda Literary Award Finalist *Justice Served* delivers a "crisply written, fast-paced story with twists and turns and keeps us guessing until the final explosive ending."—*Independent Gay Writer*

Lambda Literary Award finalist *Turn Back Time* "is filled with wonderful love scenes, which are both tender and hot."—*MegaScene*

Applause for L.L. Raand's Midnight Hunters Series

The Midnight Hunt
RWA 2012 VCRW Laurel Wreath winner *Blood Hunt*
Night Hunt
The Lone Hunt

"Raand has built a complex world inhabited by werewolves, vampires, and other paranormal beings…Raand has given her readers a complex plot filled with wonderful characters as well as insight into the hierarchy of Sylvan's pack and vampire clans. There are many plot twists and turns, as well as erotic sex scenes in this riveting novel that keep the pages flying until its satisfying conclusion."—*Just About Write*

"Once again, I am amazed at the storytelling ability of L.L. Raand aka Radclyffe. In *Blood Hunt*, she mixes high levels of sheer eroticism that will leave you squirming in your seat with an impeccable multi-character storyline all streaming together to form one great read." —*Queer Magazine Online*

"Are you sick of the same old hetero vampire/werewolf story plastered in every bookstore and at every movie theater? Well, I've got the cure to your werewolf fever. *The Midnight Hunt* is first in, what I hope is, a long-running series of fantasy erotica for L.L. Raand (aka Radclyffe)."—*Queer Magazine Online*

By Radclyffe

The Provincetown Tales

Safe Harbor

Beyond the Breakwater

Distant Shores, Silent Thunder

Storms of Change

Winds of Fortune

Returning Tides

Sheltering Dunes

Treacherous Seas

PMC Hospitals Romances

Passion's Bright Fury (prequel)

Fated Love

Night Call

Crossroads

Passionate Rivals

Unrivaled

Rivers Community Romances

Against Doctor's Orders

Prescription for Love

Love on Call

Love After Hours

Love to the Rescue

Love on the Night Shift

Honor Series

Above All, Honor

Honor Bound

Love & Honor

Honor Guards

Honor Reclaimed

Honor Under Siege

Word of Honor

Oath of Honor
(First Responders)

Code of Honor

Price of Honor

Cost of Honor

Justice Series

A Matter of Trust (prequel)

Shield of Justice

In Pursuit of Justice

Justice in the Shadows

Justice Served

Justice for All

First Responders Novels

Trauma Alert

Firestorm

Taking Fire

Wild Shores

Heart Stop

Dangerous Waters

Romances

Innocent Hearts

Promising Hearts

Love's Melody Lost

Love's Tender Warriors

Tomorrow's Promise

Love's Masquerade

shadowland

Turn Back Time

When Dreams Tremble

The Lonely Hearts Club

Secrets in the Stone

Desire by Starlight

Homestead

The Color of Love

Secret Hearts

Short Fiction

Collected Stories by Radclyffe

Erotic Interludes: *Change Of Pace*

Radical Encounters

Stacia Seaman and Radclyffe, eds.:

Erotic Interludes Vol. 2–5

Romantic Interludes Vol. 1–2

Breathless: *Tales of Celebration*

Women of the Dark Streets

Amor and More: Love Everafter

Myth & Magic: Queer Fairy Tales

Writing As L.L. Raand
Midnight Hunters

The Midnight Hunt

Blood Hunt

Night Hunt

The Lone Hunt

The Magic Hunt

Shadow Hunt

Visit us at www.boldstrokesbooks.com

UNRIVALED

by

RADCLYffE

2021

ISBN 13: 978-1-63679-013-8

This Trade Paperback Original Is Published By
Bold Strokes Books, Inc.
P.O. Box 249
Valley Falls, NY 12185

First Edition: May 2021

Credits
Editors: Ruth Sternglantz and Stacia Seaman
Production Design: Stacia Seaman
Cover Design by Tammy Seidick

Acknowledgments

The twelve months during which this book was conceived and written—February 2020 to February 2021—were some of the most challenging in my life, and probably for the majority of the people in the world. In the twelve years I spent as a medical student and then a surgery resident, we had a saying: *You can do anything for a month*, when we would be assigned to a service or a rotation that for one reason or another we did not want. But we knew there was a beginning and an end to our time there. COVID-19 changed the timeline to one of open-ended uncertainty, which is much harder to endure. Even now we cannot see the finish line—if there will ever be a hard line that says "the end"—but we are at least moving toward a place where we can live and work together again. I'd like to thank the people who have made these past months not only endurable, but productive and even enjoyable—for time is the one commodity I do not wish to squander: Sandy Lowe, who works and plays beside me every day while keeping BSB not just moving, but moving forward; my friends and colleagues who support, encourage, and share the journey, Eva, Jenny, Paula, and Molly; the amazing team of friends and colleagues at BSB, Ruth, Cindy, Toni, Carsen, Stacia, Susan, and so many others too numerous to count; our readers everywhere who support and inspire us; and my wife, Lee, for endless patience and faith.

I hope you enjoy this one. Read it in good health, hope, and happiness.

Radclyffe, 2021

CHAPTER ONE

West Mount Airy, Philadelphia, PA
July 1, 5:03 a.m.

A dilapidated red Volkswagen Bug careened around the corner and missed T-boning Declan's shiny new black Range Rover by an inch. Dec caught the blur of motion out of the corner of her eye just in time to yank the wheel to the left. The big SUV swerved across the road and bounced up onto the grassy lawn of a pale yellow West Mount Airy Victorian, narrowly missing the low stacked-stone wall that marked the entrance to the drive. White-knuckling the steering wheel, her vision blanking out and sweat bursting from every pore, she gasped against the crushing pressure in her chest. Couldn't breathe. Her arms trembled and her midsection cramped as if she'd been punched. Sirens blared. Help was coming. They'd be here soon. Hurry. Have to hurry.

Screams echoed the piercing cry of the sirens.

The screams were hers, in her memory.

Just a memory.

Dec fought her way through the fog of remembrance. Air flowed into her lungs, and the stampeding thunder of her heart slowly settled. Reality returned and her vision cleared.

She took another breath, and then another. The sirens still wailed, but they weren't coming for her this time. Glancing in her rearview mirror, she checked that the road was clear and carefully backed out onto the narrow residential lane. The hospital was two blocks ahead, and though she hadn't driven this route in almost ten years, she could have navigated with her eyes closed. The trees along the way were taller, the slate sidewalks fronting the three-story single Victorians a little more uneven from the ravages of winter frost, and the cars parked in the driveways a little more upscale than in the past, but all the same, she knew this place. Nothing essential had changed, except her.

She'd almost reached the medical center when a string of rescue vehicles overtook her. She pulled over, allowing them to pass, and followed them past the big sign indicating Trauma Admitting—that was new—down the drive to the ER entrance. When they screeched to a halt in front of the wide double doors, she swung around them and darted into an empty staff parking slot. Whoever *D. Abrams* was hopefully wouldn't be too upset that she'd taken their slot. On still-trembling legs, she climbed out just in time to see a ragtag quartet of women pile out of the red Bug a couple of parking places away. The small brunette who jumped out of the driver's side led the pack toward the ER with the speed and grace of a gazelle and, from what Dec could make out as she grabbed her shiny new laminated ID from the Range Rover's center console, was wearing a ragged gray tank top, flip-flops, and…boxers? A lanky brunette in jeans and a rumpled shirt along with two blondes hurried along behind. Suddenly, the lithe blonde in the sleeveless pale green shirt and sage capri pants sprinted around the others and made it to the ER doors first.

Another ambulance tore into the emergency area, and Dec had to jump out of the way to avoid being sideswiped. She landed awkwardly on her right leg, and the swift stab of pain shooting from her hip reminded her she wasn't who she used to be. As if being here wasn't reminder enough. Shoving the thoughts aside, she headed for the rear of the first ambulance in line. The back doors swung open and the EMTs—a male and female in navy blue pants and shirts, each looking about thirty and fiercely focused—slid the stretcher out, letting its folding legs open as they eased it to the ground.

"What's the situation?" Dec asked the one closest to her.

"Multiple car accident on the Schuylkill. They're still extracting the injured."

"How many are we expecting?" Dec jogged along beside them, ignoring her burning hip.

"Hard to tell. At least eight cars were involved, most of them with multiple passengers."

"All right. What's the status—"

"What have you got?" a young guy in wrinkled green scrubs, whose name tag read *A. Armand, MD, Emergency Medicine*, yelled as he rocketed out the ER doors.

The female EMT replied, "Restrained male driver. Closed head trauma, alert but disoriented in the field. Fractured left humerus and left lower extremity, hypotensive to seventy systolic, pulse one thirty, responded to fluid resuscitation."

"Bracketing injuries," Dec said to the resident. "That means chest and abdomen may be involved. Make sure you get a chest X-ray and abdominal ultrasound as soon as you get the lines in."

"Who are you?" Armand said.

Dec tapped the ID hanging from the pocket of her pale blue Oxford shirt. "ER attending. Get going."

The young guy's eyebrows rose, but he said, "On it," and disappeared inside with the patient.

When Dec turned around, three more ambulances began disgorging patients. A redhead in sky-blue scrubs ran over to her.

"I'm the ER charge nurse. Donna Carlisle." She spared a glance at the line of rescue vehicles. "God, I hate July first. A house full of newbies and *this*. Please tell me you're staff?"

"Yep," Dec said.

"Are you triaging?"

"I can unless you need me inside," Dec said.

"We've got plenty of residents, but we're light on staff right now. Dr. Blake is directing inside."

"Then I'll triage. Can you get me a couple of residents out here?"

"Got it." The nurse frowned, staring at Dec as if trying to place her. "Who are you again?"

Distracted, Dec didn't reply and the nurse didn't wait for an answer. Just as well. Sometimes Dec wasn't sure she knew the answer to that question.

❖

"Holy crap," Zoey Cohen said as she scanned trauma admitting. The three trauma bays were full, and two of the regular cubicles they usually used for less acute patients also held injured. PAs, techs, nurses, and residents hurried back and forth, edging around instrument carts and skirting a portable X-ray machine that appeared to somehow have stalled in the middle of the floor. She turned to Emmett McCabe—ex-friend-with-benefits, still best friend, and soon-to-be chief resident—reigning monarch of the surgical residents. "What are we doing? I'm supposed to be going to transplant."

"Not for two more hours." Emmett shoved an unruly lock of dark hair off her forehead and turned to Dani and Syd. "Dani, you'll be senior on the trauma service starting today, so you run it." She pointed to a stack of yellow cover gowns. "You might want to put a little more on, first."

Grinning, Dani shrugged into the gown to cover her boxers and tank top and pulled booties over her flip-flops, saying at the same time, "Syd, you're now a senior neuro resident, so go do neuro. Emmett and I will handle the gen surg stuff."

"Got it," Syd said, casting her new girlfriend Emmett a sideways smile that looked sweet and hot at the same time before hurrying away.

Dani rolled her eyes and Emmett smirked.

"Where do you want me?" Zoey slipped into a cover gown and looked from Emmett to Dani for direction. July was always weird as everyone shuffled into their new roles, one year closer to finishing, but still the same people they'd been the day before. Sort of. She might not know a lot more than she had twenty-four hours before, but she had a whole new set of responsibilities and a whole new crop of junior residents who expected her to know all and keep them out of trouble. So, yeah, more things than her on again-off again, no strings-no demand sex life had changed.

Dani said, "You're still general surgery, so go grab a patient and get to work."

"I'm headed outside," Zoey said quickly. "Everybody in here is covered."

She spun around and headed for the door before anyone could object or grab her to assist somewhere. She didn't want to assist. She wanted to be in charge. She wanted Emmett's job when the year ended. And that meant lots of cases. Big cases.

"Trolling for the best cases?" Emmett called as Zoey sprinted away.

"They all need docs, right?" Zoey replied over her shoulder. Sure, she was looking for the most interesting cases, but those patients were also going to be the ones who needed attention the most. That was the good thing about surgery. The sickest people were always the most challenging.

She bolted outside and jerked to a stop. The parking lot was chaos. A clutch of ambulances that had just delivered the injured stood off to the side with engines idling, waiting for their EMT crews to return, and several more perched in front of the entrance, light bars flashing, sirens blaring, radios blasting call signs and emergency dispatches. Medics guided stretchers onto the ground, pausing in their headlong rush only long enough to shout a status report to the closest ER staffer. Zoey's gaze traveled to a slim brunette in a pale blue shirt and skinny, tailored black trousers, who stood in the center of the wailing vehicles, surrounded by a surreal aura of calm. The rising sun glinted on the blue-black of her collar-length hair and reflected in shooting sparks of silver off the buckle of her narrow black belt. Whoever she was, she seemed to know what she was doing—at least, the two ER residents orbiting in her wake as she assessed and directed focused on her as if she was the sun to their moons. Zoey understood why. Something in the woman's confident stance and the preternaturally quiet expression, despite the pandemonium, imposed order on the insanity.

Zoey recognized authority when she saw it and sprinted in that direction.

"We're getting full inside," Zoey said as she edged into the woman's orbit, "so we might need to set up a field unit out here."

Zoey caught her breath as the woman spun to face her. She was striking and might have been called handsome—hell, she *was* handsome—despite the faintly raised pink scar that crossed her forehead from her hairline to her left eyebrow, where it thinned down to a pale white line that interrupted the sweeping curve of her dark brow. The scar did nothing to detract from the arch of her cheekbones and the long line of her jaw or the faint hollow above the strong bones. A shock of dark hair dipped down onto her forehead, and she probably could've covered most of the scar with it had she chosen to, but apparently, she hadn't.

The scarred brow rose in question. Her eyes were very dark. Could eyes actually be black? Zoey didn't think so, but she couldn't see any hint of brown either. No flecks of gold or green or anything except deep, mesmerizing midnight on a starless night.

"Declan Black," the woman said when Zoey remained tongue-tied. "ER attending. You are…?"

Her voice was low and full, not friendly as much as assured. Dark honey with a hint of liquid smoke.

"Zoey. Zoey Cohen. Senior surgery resident…fourth year."

"Good. I'd rather not try treating anyone out here, so let's get them assessed ASAP. Take the next one over there, see what we've got. Anyone who needs immediate intervention, get them inside. Otherwise, hold them back for now."

"I'm on it," Zoey said, finally getting her legs to move. As she turned away, Declan Black's face remained imprinted in her mind, the way a dream sometimes did behind closed lids.

In the next instant, the only thing on her mind was the woman on the gurney being pulled from the rear of the nearest rescue van. An ET tube protruded from the corner of her mouth, and the medic clambering down beside the stretcher methodically squeezed an Ambu bag attached to it, breathing for her. A cervical collar obscured most of her lower face, but the MAST trousers encasing her lower body suggested she was hemodynamically unstable.

"Run it for me," Zoey said, leaning over to check the woman's pupillary responses. A long scalp laceration running just behind her hairline oozed blood. The MAST trousers provided compression in the lower extremities to force blood back into the circulatory system. Good in cases of shock, but not recommended for head injury. Her pupils were sluggish, but equal and reactive. No sign of unilateral bleed at least.

The medic reported her vitals and added, "Unrestrained back seat passenger, ejected from the vehicle, unconscious at the scene. Hypotensive, multiple extremity fractures, unable to assess the C-spine. Breath sounds diminished on the right. She's had three liters of Ringer's already, and we're just keeping her pressure above sixty."

"Hold up a second." As their pace slowed, Zoey quickly listened to the woman's lungs. "She's got no breath sounds on the right now." She slid her fingers over the few inches of throat exposed below the cervical collar, searching for the trachea. She finally was able to palpate it. Deviated far to the left.

"She's got a tension hemothorax. She's going to need a chest tube right away. Let's go."

She grabbed the side rail and shoved the gurney toward the entrance, the first EMT with the Ambu bag running opposite her and the second behind them steering. When they hit the main trauma unit, she couldn't see an empty bay and pointed to a space along the wall. "Over there."

"What have you got," the smoky-smooth voice asked from behind her. Zoey'd only heard it once, but once was enough never to forget it. Declan Black had followed her in.

"Hemopneumo, most likely," Zoey said, looking around for a PA or resident to assist. A harried-looking second year resident in the signature ER baby-blues raced by. "Hey, Alan, can you get me a chest tube tray stat."

He looked over his shoulder without slowing down and yelled, "In a minute. Dr. Blake needs the ultrasound machine right now."

"Don't have a minute," Zoey muttered, rapidly running through the trauma assessment protocol, one eye on the BP monitor. "Damn it—her pressure's bottoming out. We have to get a tube in. I'll go find a chest tube set."

"Have you got a cutdown tray?" Declan said.

"Yeah, right up here." Zoey reached up to the shelf along the wall and pulled down an intravenous cutdown tray. It didn't have much in it, a few hemostats and basic instruments for inserting IV catheters in deep veins. She started to hand it to Declan, who shook her head.

"That'll do. Let's get a hole in her."

"What about a needle thoracostomy?" Zoey said. "It'll be quicker."

"Not if there's blood in there. It'll clot off in a second." Declan's tone was cool and calm, almost conversational. Not like they were in the midst of a critical situation. "We're going to lose her pulse in about twenty-five seconds. Your call."

"All right, all right." Zoey slammed the cutdown tray onto a silver Mayo stand that she dragged over with one arm. She knew how to do this. Chest tubes were usually an intern's job. Only not when the patient was seconds from arresting. Beside her, Declan Black unhurriedly opened the cutdown tray, and just those few calm seconds steadied Zoey's racing pulse. "I need gloves."

"Here." Declan peeled back the outside wrapper paper and held out a sterile pair. "Seven and a half, right?"

Zoey looked at her. "Yeah."

She'd find time later to wonder just how Declan Black knew that. While she yanked on the gloves, Declan cut open the patient's clothes with a scalpel and swabbed the right side of her chest along the outer aspect of her breast with Betadine. "All set."

"Anterior axillary line, fifth intercostal space?" Zoey said, gripping a new blade. She knew that too, but she wouldn't have a second chance. And she wasn't too proud to check.

"Sounds good to me. Don't be dainty."

Zoey made the incision two inches long in the midspace between the two ribs. The patient was unresponsive and thankfully wouldn't feel much, if anything at all, of what she was doing. "Can you hand me a—"

"Here's a Kelly." Declan slapped an oversized hemostat into her palm.

"Thanks," Zoey muttered and poked the clamp through the thin layer of muscle between the ribs and into the patient's chest. A gush of maroon fluid liberally sprinkled with clots flooded out. She jumped back, not in time to avoid getting soaked, and swore under her breath. "I really liked these pants."

Declan laughed. The dark ripple of sound caressed Zoey's overheated senses. "Nice work. Pressure's coming up."

Zoey turned to her, flushed with success, and caught the briefest flare of heat in Declan's eyes before the flames were abruptly extinguished.

"Hand her off to someone to finish the workup, and head back outside," Declan said.

"Right. Than—" Zoey halted midword. Declan Black was gone, as quickly as a shooting star winking out midflight, leaving a mix of wonder and disappointment behind.

CHAPTER TWO

W ho was that?" Dani asked as she edged up behind Zoey at the counter where she was quickly entering notes into the patient's chart.

"Who?" Zoey said distractedly. She'd handed off the woman with the chest trauma—unidentified as of yet—to the admitting ICU resident and needed to document the chest tube procedure before she could get back outside to find her next new patient.

Dani snorted. "Tall, dark, and sexy—the one working with you just a few minutes ago."

"She's not that tall," Zoey said. Declan was a few inches taller than her, and that put her at maybe five ten, which wasn't that tall. Tall enough for her to need to look up just a little to see Declan's eyes, those eyes that still fascinated her. She'd have to look up to kiss her too. Zoey blinked at the image that came out of nowhere. Her kissing Declan Black? Now there was a totally out-there idea. Kissing women she hardly knew—okay, knew not at all—wasn't usually her first thought. Although now that she *did* think of it, maybe it was. Her housemates were her best friends, and she never pictured them as bed partners— except for Emmett McCabe, of course, who was now and forever off-limits. The other women in her life, not that there were many, were usually super casual, time-limited acquaintances. The kind of almost-strangers who she knew by sight and, when she bumped into them at the bar after a shift or in the OR or the ER, prompted her to imagine a quick and simple fling. Who had time for anything more? Who *wanted* anything more, with all the complications being a resident brought with it? Broken dates and zombie bedmates took a toll on even the most solid relationships, let alone ones just trying to get off the ground. Who wanted *that* hassle? So if a little twinge in the back of her mind said *you do* every now and then, she'd learned to ignore it.

Nothing about Declan Black said casual, just the opposite—intense, complicated, captivating. So Dr. Not-Right-for-Me.

Nope, no kissing Declan Black.

"She's tall *enough*," Dani said, "and I notice you didn't say she wasn't sexy."

"I hardly had time to notice that," Zoey said, knowing she sounded irritated and not really knowing why. "I was in the middle of a trauma alert, remember?"

"So? She's hot," Dani said. "I'd do her, or let her do me, anytime."

Zoey finally gave Dani her full attention. Dani Chan, half a head shorter than her, small boned and tight bodied, was super attractive with her perfectly proportioned features and her jet-black hair and that little bit of tiger tattoo peeking out from underneath the V of her scrub shirt. Anybody would look twice at Dani if she wasn't their housemate—well, technically their duplex-mate, since Dani shared the other half of the Victorian twin with Syd and Jerry. Dani was also one of the few friends Zoey couldn't afford to lose, and friendship and sex were tricky to juggle.

Declan might look twice at Dani. Dani certainly sounded like *she'd* be looking at Declan.

Zoey's shoulders tightened with a completely irrational flare of jealously. "Can you leave off? I'm trying to get my notes done here."

"So who is she?" Dani said, completely unperturbed in her Dani-like way. Nothing really ever diverted her attention or slowed her down when she had some goal in sight—conquest or surgery case. Once in a while Zoey wondered about that, how driven Dani was beneath her wiseass exterior and why she hid it. They lived together and spent long nights on call together talking, too pent-up to sleep, just waiting for the next page to the ER or some other emergency, but she didn't really know what made Dani tick. She'd prefer, though, that it not be Declan.

"She's a new ER attending. That's all I know," Zoey said briskly, hoping to signal a change in subject.

"Well, she certainly didn't need any breaking in," Dani mused. "That's weird, don't you think? That she just showed up and went to work?"

"She did show up in the middle of a mass trauma alert. What was she supposed to do, sit on her hands?"

"I guess not. But she doesn't act like a newbie, does she? And she's older than most new attendings. So that's kind of mysterious, don't you think?"

Zoey sighed, signed off on the chart, and put it back in the slot with the other tablets where the ward clerks could organize all the info into the electronic records system.

"I dunno, Dani. But aren't you supposed to be running the show?"

Dani grinned and, without blinking an eye, systematically and rapidly summarized the status of every single patient presently in the trauma unit.

"You know," Zoey said, "I sort of hate you."

Dani shrugged. "Can't help it. I was just born that way. By the way, that was a slick pickup on your patient with the pneumo out in the field today. Great job in here too."

And there it was—the reason Dani was one of her best friends. She was competitive, like every other surgery resident in the known universe, but she was also generous and staunchly loyal.

"Thanks," Zoey said. "I love you too."

Dani rolled her eyes. "Go find another one to save."

And then Dani was off to check on the next resident, leaving Zoey pleased and exasperated, which was how Dani often left her feeling.

The chaos in the parking area had settled when Zoey rejoined the other residents and staff who were evaluating the last of the patients. She automatically looked for Declan. When she didn't see her, a strange and unexpected surge of disappointment washed through her. No time to think about that now as a new resident waved to her and said, "Can you check this guy with me?"

Remembering that she was the one the juniors would be looking to for guidance and support, she squared her shoulders and hurried over. She would think about Declan Black later.

❖

"Dec," Honor Blake exclaimed, grabbing Dec by the shoulders and pulling her into a quick hug. "Sorry I didn't catch you when you arrived."

"I don't mind. I figured you were a bit busy." Declan eased out of Honor's hold, the awareness of a woman's body next to hers so foreign she needed a second to register all the odd sensations. Seeing Honor again after so long filled her with the same jumble of conflicting emotions almost everything in her life did these days. Sadness and pleasure had become so entwined that the feeling she was left with resembled melancholy more than anything else. Like the longing she had when she remembered summer days growing up and how easy life seemed then, how simple. Didn't everyone yearn for those endless summer afternoons, where nothing was urgent and everything was possible? She recognized the wish as a trick of memory, accepted the impossibility of going back, and resigned herself to the loss. At least, she was trying to.

"It felt good to be working. In some ways, it just seemed like just another day, almost like I'd never left." Dec smiled because she *was* very glad to see Honor. They hadn't seen each other since she'd left for Dallas, but the years they'd spent together as students and residents forged a friendship that even time and distance couldn't erase. She hadn't expected a job offer when she'd contacted Honor for advice about what to do next with her life, but she hadn't hesitated when Honor had simply said, *Come home.* "I was happy out there."

"Were you," Honor said gently, her piercing gaze tenderly surveying the shaky barricades of Dec's defenses. "I'm glad. We needed you this morning. We're still waiting for the day staff to arrive, and everyone else is overseeing the patients we just admitted. I'll introduce you to the group as soon as the storm settles."

"No hurry. The last of the patients are on their way in now," Dec said. "What do you need me to do?"

"Can you make rounds on the ones waiting for disposition who haven't been seen by staff? Check with the residents and make sure everyone's had a thorough assessment?"

"Sure." Dec surveyed the full house and the bustling throng of residents, PAs, and nurses. She'd been one of them once, but now all the faces were unfamiliar. All except one. Zoey Cohen. She stood out from the others. Draped in the ubiquitous yellow cover gown, a mask dangling around her neck, she might have been just one more rushing body among many, but Dec found her instantly, as if drawn to her by some second sense. Zoey only stood out when you looked at her—at the unusual shade of silver-blond hair, at the delicately sculpted but unmistakably strong face, at the sleek body. Once you saw her, the way Dec had seen her that first moment in the shimmering glow of the breaking dawn, you would never mistake her for anyone else, or anyone else for her. She was too singularly lovely.

And she looked like she had things totally under control. Zoey stood by the patient's bed in the first trauma bay, talking with a husky young guy with tight black curls and a baby-smooth face that looked like it'd never seen a razor. His attention was riveted to her face, and he nodded emphatically at regular intervals. Dec could almost hear his brain memorizing every syllable Zoey uttered. Sponges. Good residents were sponges, soaking up every crumb of wisdom and experience they could before they were all alone on the firing line. Dec had no reason to walk over and talk to her. She chose to interpret the crashing sensation in her midsection as relief and turned away.

❖

Zoey parted the curtains surrounding the cubicle and slid inside. A teenage or early-twenties male, most of his body obscured by the cervical collar, the breathing tube, the Aircast on his right leg, and the multitude of lines and monitors, lay unconscious, his face miraculously untouched and looking somehow peaceful. To someone who didn't know better, he would look like he was merely asleep. She surveyed the monitors automatically, taking in the vital signs by second nature. A resident she didn't recognize in a pristine white coat—ironed, no less—stood by the side of the bed, a slightly wild look in his eyes that morphed almost instantaneously into one of relief when he saw her. She glanced at his name tag. John Quan. Surgery.

Translation: first year, one day out of medical school and now presiding over the care of a multiple trauma victim. She remembered those first days with crystal clarity, the terror and exhilaration that combined to create a near-constant roller coaster of amazing highs and terrifying lows.

"Well?" she said.

"Sorry?" he said with just an edge of that long-remembered fear in his voice.

"I'm Zoey Cohen, your senior resident for the moment. Do you want to present the patient?"

"Oh," he said, nearly jumping to attention. "This is…I don't know his name."

"Then that would be unidentified male." Zoey made a slight come-along gesture with her hand.

"Right." John took a deep breath and, to his credit, visibly got himself together. "Back seat passenger in a sedan, restrained, found unconscious, other occupants dead at the scene." He swallowed. "They had to cut them out."

"Vitals in the field?" Zoey said sharply, glancing again at the monitors. With a history like that, internal injuries were almost a certainty, and sometimes they didn't show themselves immediately.

"Stable in the field with just Ringer's resuscitation."

"Labs?"

"All normal, except first round hemoglobin was 11.5. I…uh…sent off another one just now."

"Good. That might be just hemodilution from the Ringer's, but if he's bleeding somewhere, that will show us. Exam?"

John wet his lips. "Neuro—"

"Start with the basics," Zoey said.

"Right. Lungs are clear on both sides, heart sounds are clear—no murmurs, normal sinus rhythm, abdomen is soft. Obvious fractures of his left upper extremity and right lower leg. Neuro exam…" As John recited the physical findings, Zoey moved around the bed, verifying his findings, listening for any muffling of his heart sounds that might indicate he was developing an effusion or other signs of cardiac or major vascular trauma, palpating his abdomen, looking for rigidity or fullness where there shouldn't be any.

As she worked, she sensed the curtains parting behind her, and someone moved up beside her. Her pulse quickened and she looked up, expecting Declan. Out of habit, she straightened almost as abruptly as her intern had when she saw Quinn Maguire, the trauma chief and the head of the training program. Quinn looked like she'd just come from the OR—she still wore her signature maroon surgical cap covered in soccer balls, a gift from the team she coached—and the faint lines from her mask creased her bold cheekbones. Her hair was black like Declan's, but her eyes were nothing like hers. Gorgeous, but not— Zoey blinked away the image. Indescribable, and what was wrong with her?

"Hi, Chief," Zoey said.

"Everything stable in here?" Quinn asked.

"Yes, but we ought to ultrasound his abdomen all the same. His hemoglobin's borderline."

"Hasn't been done yet?"

"No, we've had acutes that needed doing first."

"All right, see to it, then."

"Got it," Zoey said.

Quinn nodded to the first year. "Dr. Quan."

"Um, yes?" Quan's voice might have squeaked just a little.

Quinn smiled. "Welcome to PMC. Have fun."

Quinn disappeared back through the curtains, and John stared at Zoey. "She knew my name. We just got here today, and there are twenty-five of us."

"She knows more than your name," Zoey said. "You can count on her knowing every single thing you do every day for the next five years. So don't screw up."

"Right." John swallowed. "I'll go find the ultrasound machine."

"Good idea."

John disappeared, and Zoey dug the tablet out from beneath the plethora of lines and paperwork at the foot of the bed to enter her notes.

A woman on the other side of the curtain in the next cubicle murmured in a husky whisper, "Did you see her?"

"Who?" a second woman said.

"Declan."

"Declan?"

"Declan Black. She's back."

"Donna, I have no idea who you're talking about."

"Oh, wait—you haven't been here long enough. She's been gone…goodness, must be almost ten years."

After a pause, not-Donna said, "And? From your tone, there's a story. Hand me the Foley bag, will you?"

"Here." A pause. "She was a student here—resident too. Everyone expected her to join the staff, but her wife—"

Zoey stiffened. *Wife?*

She wasn't usually interested in hospital gossip, although sometimes it was the only thing that broke the unrelenting tension. There was so much of it, with everyone living in close quarters, sometimes never leaving the hospital for days at a time, that usually the constant chatter became just more background noise. Who hooked up with who, who wasn't hooking up with who, and who *might* be hooking up with who. This time, though, every word was as sharp and clear as a heartbeat through her stethoscope.

Not-Donna laughed. "Oh, now I understand. I might have seen her but not noticed. Not being, you know, girl crazy."

"I'm not."

"You so are. So I guess you didn't know she was coming?"

"No," Donna said. "It's not like they tell us who they're hiring. But I'm surprised that Honor kept that one secret. Considering how close they were."

Close? Zoey tried to remember how long Quinn and Honor had been together. Like with all couples who seemed perfect together, it just seemed like forever. But she couldn't make a picture of Honor and Declan, and when she tried, her skin prickled.

"I wonder what she's doing down in the ER?" Donna mused. "Maybe it has something to do with the accident."

"All right. This story is getting deep," not-Donna said. "What happened?"

"I don't know the details, other than she was almost killed. Her wife—"

Honor Blake's distinctive honeyed-steel voice cut in. "Are we ready in here? Transport's on the way to take Ms. Santorini up to the neuro ICU."

"Yes," Donna said brightly. "All set."

The conversation ended, but the words swirled in Zoey's brain. Accident. Of course there had been an accident. There was almost no other way Declan could've gotten a scar like that on her forehead. And she remembered watching for a few seconds as Declan'd walked by. She had the faintest limp. But *wife*?

There was no reason for the sinking feeling that settled in the pit of her stomach, but there it was. She'd indulged a fantasy for a few minutes when she was too busy to remind herself that fantasies never came true, and wishing for something never made it so. Well, she didn't need any more reminding now. Wife? No way.

CHAPTER THREE

PMC Trauma Admitting
6:29 a.m.

Once the critical patients had been moved to the OR or the ICUs, Honor scanned the admitting area to check that all six remaining patients were stable while their workups proceeded. Satisfied, she finally settled at the central station to review the steady flood of lab and X-ray results streaming in.

Her best friend Linda plopped down beside her and blew a lock of blond hair off her forehead with a sigh. The Scooby-Doo cartoon characters on her smock cavorted across her very pregnant abdomen.

"Hi," Honor said.

"Hi yourself. Is that all you have to say?" Linda frowned. "I can't believe you didn't call me. I'm five minutes away, and you know I'm always up since Robin and the monsters hit the ground running at the butt-crack of dawn."

"You practically worked a double yesterday. And you'll be on your feet all day today making sure none of the newbies get into trouble. And," Honor said, holding up a finger to halt Linda's expected retort, "your back is bothering you."

Linda pressed her lips together, not bothering to deny it. "You try carrying a load like this around for an eternity. Your back will kill you too."

"Been there, done that. Twice. So we're in agreement. You work one shift, and you sit every chance you get. Direct, oversee, review— but leave the actual patient care to the staff."

"I don't remember agreeing to that."

"You just did." Honor smiled, her amusement at Linda's attempts to ignore the obvious limitations of her condition turning to pleasure when she spied her wife striding down the hall. Quinn automatically glanced into the occupied cubicles as she passed, and Honor was certain Quinn could have reported every one of their occupants' vital signs by the time she reached the station.

"Am I interrupting?" Quinn asked as she walked behind the counter to join them.

"Only your wife mother-henning me," Linda said.

"Ah." Quinn raised a brow but wisely remained silent.

"How are things upstairs?" Honor asked. She and Quinn had left the house at the same time that morning, both of them wanting to arrive early for new resident orientation. Thank goodness she had, or she wouldn't have been as prepared for the onslaught of trauma victims as she had been, which wasn't saying a tremendous amount. Most of the new house staff, or any of the staff for that matter, had yet to arrive. Shift change wasn't until seven, so none of the day people were actually in the hospital or even on their way. Luckily some of the residents, especially the surgery residents, lived close enough to get there in just a few minutes, and when they'd gotten the alert, they'd shown up in record time. And by some miracle, Dec had arrived early and picked up as if she'd never left. Of course, she wasn't a resident now, and technically she was a brand-new attending—at least here. But Honor wasn't going to pretend she didn't know the truth, even if Dec had asked her to keep her arrival low-key. Low-key in a place like this wasn't really possible—plenty of people would remember her, and some probably even knew the whole story. Since news was the lifeblood of a hospital, a mainstay of keeping the tragedies witnessed every day from draining the soul, Dec couldn't hope to go unnoticed. But Honor'd do what she could to protect Dec's privacy.

Setting worries about Dec aside, Honor added, "We sent quite a few patients to the OR. I'm surprised you didn't close us to trauma."

"We pulled staff in, but we haven't even started the elective schedule yet," Quinn said. "Plus I've got half my senior residents checking the ICU patients you sent up, and the other half down here. We're stretched thin."

"You can take them," Honor said. "Just make sure they sign out to one of mine before they go."

"I'd rather they finish up here." Quinn grabbed a stool and rolled over next to Honor. "We'll have the backlog sorted out soon. Let them finish their workups. If we need them, we'll pull them, as long as everything is quiet down here now."

Honor nodded. "We've still got patients to clear before they go upstairs, but we don't have anything surgical cooking right now."

"You've got a bunch of my first years down here. They doing all right?"

"No one has fainted."

At that, Linda laughed and stood to go. "That might be a record. I'm going to make rounds and check on them."

Quinn grinned as Linda visibly waddled away. "Are you really worried about her or just being careful?"

Honor waited a beat until Linda was well out of earshot. "Not about anything specific. But she refuses to admit this pregnancy is hard on her, probably because she doesn't want any of us to worry, so she overdoes it."

"Maybe," Quinn murmured, tucking a strand of Honor's auburn hair behind her ear, "that's her way of dealing with her own worries."

"I know," Honor said. "But she's high risk, age-wise, and pretending otherwise will not change that. So I plan on reining her in as long as I can, and then I'm sidelining her."

"Let me know when you decide to do that, so I can be somewhere else."

Honor squeezed her thigh. "Coward."

Quinn leaned closer. "We both know which one of us is toughest."

"Depends on the circumstances," Honor said softly. "I can think of a few times when you definitely call the shots."

"Those would be the times when you let me."

Honor laughed. "I'd say we're even on that score."

"Agreed." Quinn grinned. "I'd better get back upstairs. I've got elective cases scheduled as soon as we clear the board of the traumas." She tilted her head as Declan Black walked by with Dani Chan. "Who is that with Dani?"

Honor followed her gaze. "Oh, that's Dec Black. She got here with the first of the rescue vans. She's been outside triaging since then."

"Huh." Quinn regarded Honor with a question in her eyes. "How'd she do?"

"She's solid, Quinn. I knew she would be."

"I don't doubt your judgment in hiring her." Quinn blew out a long breath. "I just don't know if I could..."

Honor stroked the top of Quinn's hand, curled into a fist on the countertop. "I know. Me neither."

Quinn straightened and, without even bothering to look around, kissed Honor soundly on the mouth. "Right. And I'm headed back to work. Let me know if any of my residents screw up."

"Your senior residents really stepped up, Quinn. Every one of them. They're a great bunch." Honor rose. "I've—"

Honor's trauma cell phone rang, and Quinn waited while Honor answered.

"PMC trauma unit." The rushed words assaulted Honor's ears like a jumble of discordant cymbals. "I'm sorry. Repeat that, please."

A few seconds later she ended the call and met Quinn's gaze. "They're bringing the last victim here. They found part of a PMC ID in the wreckage, but they don't have a name."

Quinn stood abruptly. "What department?"

"They didn't say. Probably don't know. At five in the morning, though, it wouldn't be a seven-to-three employee or anyone from admin. It's most likely someone medical." Honor glanced toward the entrance as the sounds of an approaching siren grew louder. "I have to get out there."

"Honor," Quinn said as she jogged beside Honor, "you'll need attending staff to handle this, especially if it turns out to be one of the house staff. They're all friends to one degree or another, and doing the initial eval will be tough."

"I know. I'll direct the triage and resuscitation myself. Declan can oversee everything in here until the other staff arrive and get up to speed."

"I'll see if I can get someone to cover my cases and help out," Quinn said.

Honor slowed as the double doors slid open. "You've got a full

ICU, new house staff, and all your ORs running. Let's see what we have first."

Reluctantly, Quinn said, "All right. But call me as soon as you know anything."

"I will. Go do what you have to do."

Quinn sprinted away, passing Zoey, who turned to stare after her. Honor stepped out into a surprisingly bright, warm summer morning. 6:32 a.m. The flash of red and the screaming siren, usually so familiar as to go unnoticed, filled her with foreboding. She steeled herself against the disquieting sensation. For one fragile second she remembered with crystal clarity that long-ago summer morning when she'd waited with a different ER team for the ambulance that carried Terry. Dec had been here that day too.

"Go inside, Honor," Dec said. "We'll take care of her."

"No." Honor willed the ambulance rushing toward them to go faster. "I want her to know I'm here."

"She'll know, I promise," Dec said.

"They said it was her neck," Honor said, her voice sounding wooden to her ears. "That there was an accident and she'd hurt her neck."

"I know. Kos is on his way."

Honor grasped Dec's arm. "You'll stay, though? Terry knows you. I trust you. Don't let anyone else except you and Kos—"

"I won't. I promise."

The ambulance screeched to a halt, and Dec ran forward to meet the EMTs. Honor ran with her. No one tried to stop her.

One look at the still form strapped to a backboard with sandbags on either side of the pale face turned Honor's legs to jelly, and her stomach heaved. Not just a minor accident. Oh my God.

When she tried to speak, no words came out. When she tried to raise her hand, her arm felt leaden. As if in a dream, she watched, nearly paralyzed, as Linda directed the EMTs and Dec into the procedure room. Two ER attendings, another resident, and as many nurses rushed after them. Finally, Honor followed.

At the threshold, Honor halted, staring at the flurry of activity surrounding her lover. She recognized the routine, but it seemed so out of place with Terry lying there so still. After only a moment, the activity abruptly halted, and Linda materialized from the crowd, a strange look in her eyes. She walked to Honor and took her arm.

"Come over here, honey."

Honor protested when Linda started to draw her away from the room. "No. I have to help. I have to take care of her."

"Honor...Honor, sweetheart, her neck is broken. It must have been instantaneous." Linda's face was white. "There's nothing they can do. She's gone, sweetheart."

"Of course she isn't. That's ridiculous."

"More incoming?" Zoey Cohen asked at Honor's elbow.

Honor jumped, the memories faded, and the present returned with just enough sharp edges to clear her mind. Terry would always live in her heart, but she hadn't thought back to that day for years. Her life now was not that life, and she was not that woman. She looked away from the oncoming ambulance. "Yes. Find Declan Black, and tell her I need her out here."

"I'm free now too."

"Not this time, Zoey. They're bringing in someone who works here. We don't know who. Until we do, it's attendings only."

Zoey's eyes widened. "Who is it? Do we know?"

Honor shook her head. "No, they just found part of an ID. It's a guy—that's all the information I have."

"Jerry," Zoey blurted. "We can't find Jerry. We haven't seen him all morning."

"We don't know *who* it is," Honor said firmly, seeing the alarm rise in Zoey's eyes. With a sinking feeling in her midsection, the EMT's rushed words came back to her. Young Black male. Like Jerry. "I need you to find Declan. Tell her outside, stat."

Wordlessly, Zoey pivoted and sprinted back inside.

Honor focused on the approaching ambulance. No memories assailed her now. Dec was here, but life had changed for both of them since that long-ago morning. Whoever was inside the ambulance was almost certainly someone she knew by sight, if not intimately, and her only priority was to keep them alive. Sometimes circumstances meant she would fail, but she never approached any patient believing this was that time. Not while there was a chance.

CHAPTER FOUR

Dec poured a much-needed cup of coffee from what looked like a brand-new pot simmering on the two-pot coffee maker in the break room. Everyone must've been too busy to even grab their first cup of the day, or the last one of the night. She fished around in the tiny undercabinet refrigerator, found the creamers, and settled at one of the small round tables fronted by trios of straight-backed metal chairs. A sofa sat against one wall, opposite the one with the obligatory television fixed in the center. Mercifully, the sound was turned down, so she could ignore the running tape along the bottom informing her of the world's tragedies and political miasmas.

Funny how this part of the ER didn't seem any different to her than it had a decade before. The trauma bay itself had been expanded, along with the addition of the new turnaround outside with its own drive and parking area. The older parts of the building that had been present since the hospital was first built over a century before still housed the break room and on-call rooms. Other than the shiny new equipment, the absence of X-ray light boards, and new paint, the place looked pretty much the same as it had when she was a student and resident. While she'd been waiting to move back from Texas, she'd perused the information on the staff and facilities available on the medical center's website. Quite a few faculty names she recognized, but a lot more she missed. People moved on. Or, sometimes, people died.

Leaning back, she closed her eyes. Those memories belonged to a different time, when she was a different person. This was a new beginning, or at least a new place to be in her life. If sometimes her journey felt like walking along a narrow road with no clear destination, at least she was going somewhere.

"Dr. Black," Zoey said breathlessly from the doorway. "Honor… um, Dr. Blake needs you outside."

Dec opened her eyes and pushed the coffee away as she rose. "What's going on?"

Even as she spoke, she jogged toward the door. Zoey spun and headed down the corridor toward the trauma unit. Dec was a little taller, with a longer stride, and easily caught up to her. "Zoey? Dr. Cohen?"

"They're sending another patient from the wreck. It's…" Zoey's breath caught, as if she was running at race speed, which she wasn't.

Dec took a closer look at her. Nerves. Her dilated pupils and rapid, uneven breathing resembled nothing of the calm, in-command look she'd had about her just a few minutes before.

"Dr. Cohen," Dec said, putting an edge of command in her voice, "what do we know?"

Zoey glanced at her as she skidded around the corner into the trauma bay. She blinked and visibly steadied. "It's one of us. Dr. Blake says it's one of us, and—"

"Whoa," Dec said, catching her by the arm. "Let the ER staff know what's coming. I'll take it from here."

"I…It might be…"

Dani Chan came trotting over. "What's going on? Dr. Blake asked for PAs but told me to stay inside."

"Trauma on the way," Zoey blurted. "Someone from PMC."

"What the hell?" Dani said. "Who?"

"No one knows. But what if—"

"We'll get this sorted out," Dec said sharply enough that Dani and Zoey stopped in their tracks. "Until we do, you two cover the patients already here. Go."

When Dani and Zoey finally nodded and turned away, Dec bolted through the doors and sprinted over to Honor. "Who is it?"

"I don't know," Honor said as the rescue van screeched onto the ER approach drive and headed their way. "They found a PMC ID, or part of one, in the wreckage."

"Zoey seems to think she knows who it is."

Honor shook her head. "We don't know anything yet, but I don't want the residents out here until we make sure it's not...God, whoever it is, it's going to be tough."

"Maybe you should let me take the lead, Honor," Dec said quietly. Standing beside Honor, watching the strobing lights draw closer while sensing Honor's tension, triggered a sense of déjà vu so strong she shivered. In the next second she shook it off. Being back had pulled the past into the present, that's all.

"I'm fine," Honor said, and sounded it, "but actually, that's a good idea. It would be best if you followed this one all the way through. Anytime an employee comes through here, the curious are everywhere."

"I've got it." Dec stepped out as the van came to a stop and the rear doors popped open.

In an instant replay of the dozen times she'd done that already this morning, she reached for the end of the stretcher as the EMTs passed it out, already scanning the individual strapped down and covered with monitors. Backboard, cervical neck collar, blood-soaked bandages covering much of his forehead and the left side of his face. Left forearm in an Aircast.

"Unidentified male," the EMT said as she hopped down, "extracted from an overturned vehicle, single occupant, restrained, seat belt bruises across the clavicle. BP ninety in the field but falling. Left pupil dilated and unresponsive. Pulse erratic, breath sounds good bilaterally."

"EKG?"

"Some PVCs."

Dec sprinted along beside the stretcher with Honor close behind as the double doors swung back and the bright lights of the trauma bay greeted them. ER staff descended on them, a ring of residents pressing in close behind them.

Who is it, can you see?

It's a guy.

Who?

As they zoomed past the gaggle of residents, Zoey blurted *oh God*, but Dec didn't hear the rest. She had her stethoscope in her ears, checking for breath sounds while she felt his abdomen with the other hand. Diminished breath sounds bilaterally. Tight, moderately distended abdomen. His arms and legs, partially covered by equipment and a thermal covering, were flaccid.

Honor broke away, saying, "I'll notify neuro and ortho. X-ray's here."

"We'll need the ultrasound too. Tell ortho not to rush—they'll have to wait in line until we get him stable."

Once they'd slotted the stretcher into an open unit, ER staff instituted the well-rehearsed protocols of inserting IV lines and tubes, attaching monitoring cables, and drawing blood for gases and labs.

Zoey appeared at the foot of the bed with the ultrasound.

Dec snapped, "I thought I said—"

"It's not Jerry," Zoey said breathlessly. "It's not Jerry, and I'm next up for a patient."

"Do you know him?" Dec asked.

Zoey slid up to the head of the bed opposite Dec. Her mouth tightened. "I recognize him. He's a medical resident. I'm not sure of his name."

Dec spared her a glance. Zoey looked back, gaze unflinching and sure. Solid again. And determined. "All right, ultrasound his belly."

"Got it." Zoey maneuvered the machine the rest of the way to the bedside, exposed his abdomen, and prepared the ultrasound probe.

Dec left the rest of the exam to Zoey and checked the young man's pupils.

Honor stepped inside the curtain and squeezed in beside Zoey. "Ah, damn. That's Tony—Antonio—Ricci. He's a medical resident. Third year, I think. How does it look?"

Dec said, "The right pupil's sluggish and the left fixed. Whatever's going on in his head, it's getting worse. With the asymmetry of his pupillary reflexes, could be anything from a localized bleed to diffuse intracranial hemorrhage. Where's neuro?"

"They're all tied up in the OR," Honor said, "along with their chief resident. They can break someone out in an hour."

"That's not going to work," Dec said. "We need to put in an intracranial bolt now. Who's their senior resident? They should be able to handle that."

"As of today, that's Syd Stevens. She's good, but she can't do it alone. You'll have to talk her through it."

Zoey looked up, surprised. Neuro procedures like that were rare in the ER and never supervised by an ER doc.

"Honor," Dec said with a strange flatness in her voice.

"You're supervising, Dec, and perfectly within legal bounds."

"All right, get her in here."

Honor turned to go. "I'll wake up someone in HR," she said, "get the information on his next of kin."

Zoey completed the ultrasound and said, "He's got some haziness around his spleen. There's a little fluid in the cul-de-sac too."

"Impression?"

"Low-grade capsular tear."

"What's your plan?"

"If it wasn't for the head injury, I'd have a low index of suspicion to explore him, but if he's got a serious intracranial injury, we might need to wait."

"How do you plan to assess his belly?"

"If we can't move him down to CT for a while, I'd do an open paracentesis."

Dec nodded. "Go ahead."

Zoey said to John, the first year who'd slipped in a moment before, "Go find a paracentesis set. You're assisting."

His eyes widened. "Okay. Right away."

Syd arrived and said to Declan, "Hi, I'm Syd Stevens, senior neuro, but I'm new."

"Ever put in an intracranial bolt before?" Dec asked.

"No," Syd said, "although I've seen it done a number of times in the ICU."

"It's not that complicated. Grab some gloves, and let's get started."

Zoey set up her paracentesis tray, her shoulder brushing Declan's as Declan stood opposite Syd at the head of the table, preparing to put in the intracranial bolt. Zoey swabbed the abdomen with Betadine and toweled off a four-inch square just below the patient's umbilicus. John, who apparently was now her official sidekick, stood opposite her, a slight tremor in his gloved hands.

"Where should we make the incision," Zoey said softly, trying not to interrupt what was happening next to her. She was used to multiple teams working at the same time. Surgical subspecialists and general surgeons often worked on trauma patients together. The neurosurgeons would be working on the patient's skull while the chest surgeons took care of punctured lungs and ortho pinned fractured limbs. Zoey'd learned to focus on her own task and not think about what the other surgical teams might be doing. For some reason, it was just a little bit harder to concentrate with the slight pressure of Declan Black's arm against hers. Resolutely, she put the sensation out of her mind, and the questions as to why she even noticed it.

John pointed to a spot just below the lower part of the umbilicus. "Right there."

"Okay. Put a little lidocaine in. He probably won't feel it, but with what's going on in his head, we really don't want to stimulate him at all."

Once John injected the area, she said, "All right, go ahead."

"I'm sorry?" John said.

Zoey raised her eyes. "If someone gives you the chance to do a procedure, don't wait. Do you want to be a surgeon or not?"

Something in his eyes glinted, and she smiled inwardly. *Attaboy.*

"Right." He lifted the scalpel from the tray and made the incision. He didn't hesitate to cut through the skin, another good sign. Sometimes the first time someone put a scalpel to living tissue, they hesitated, made a scratch and not an incision. John had some stones.

"Good. Now, retractors."

Slowly and carefully, she took him through the procedure until they were ready to open the abdomen.

"What do you have to worry about now," Zoey said, "before you enter?"

"Not sticking the bowel."

She smiled behind her mask. "Yeah, that would be a really good idea. What kind of things should you be thinking about to avoid that?"

As John did a pretty decent job of naming all the possible pitfalls of poking a hole in someone's belly, Zoey became aware of Declan pressed against her side. Somehow they'd ended up a lot closer than where they'd started. Nothing unusual when working in such crowded quarters, but the way her body tingled sure was.

Declan said quietly, "That's good, Syd. Now the drill."

For just an instant, Zoey glanced to her left. Declan focused on Syd's actions, and Zoey could study her without being noticed. She was so incredibly steady, so calm. As if she'd done this, done *everything*, *seen* everything, thousands of times. Maybe she had. Dani was right. Declan wasn't the usual new attending, not even the usual ER attending. Zoey couldn't pinpoint how she was different, but she was. Syd didn't notice her looking either. Her focus was riveted to the exposed skull. Syd was a natural at neuro. Zoey envied her that sureness. Funny, she didn't envy her Emmett, though.

The thoughts flashed through her mind in a second, and she turned back to John. "Lift up on the peritoneum while I do the same, get a hemostat, and slowly spread the depths of the wound until the peritoneum opens."

Once they were inside the abdominal cavity, the rest was easy. They threaded in the catheter, flushed the saline through, and collected the effluent. Tinged with pink.

She helped John suture the catheter in place and hooked it up to a drainage bottle. As John taped the bandage in place, Zoey watched Declan and Syd finish their procedure. Declan's voice was measured and firm, and best of all, she let Syd work, interjecting instructions or comments only when Syd paused or asked a question.

When they had the intracranial pressure line in and hooked up to the monitor, the pressure spiked into the red zone. Dec pulled her gloves off and fished her cell phone out of her scrubs.

"OR extension still 3455?"

"Yes," Syd and Zoey answered at once.

"This is Declan Black in the ER," Declan said a few seconds later. "Patch me in to Dr. Hassan's room, will you?...Kos, it's Dec. His ICP's twice normal with no change in his pupillary reactivity. No blood in the epidural space. Looks like diffuse brain injury, and a hell of a lot of edema. We ought to start the protocol and get him down to CT...Right. Thanks."

Declan pocketed her phone and said to Syd, "What's your next move?"

"We have to rule out a subdural hematoma, or possibly a localized intracranial bleed that we might be able to decompress."

"Right, and what happens while you take him down to CT to look for that?"

"Oh, man," Syd said with a sound of disgust. "We need to treat his increased intracranial pressure before we do anything else. Mannitol, steroids, hyperventilation."

Declan nodded. "Good. See to that."

Syd turned to speak to one of the nurses, and Declan shifted her attention to Zoey. "Where do you think the blood's coming from?"

Zoey hadn't told Declan that the fluid coming out of the abdomen was tinged pink—barely. She hadn't realized that Declan was even watching, but she must've been. Hell, had she known Zoey was staring at her too? Wonderful. Humiliating.

"I thought the fuzziness around the spleen was just edema. It might be that, but there could be something else bleeding."

"So what do you think now?"

Zoey paused. "I think we'd better get an abdominal CT along with the head scan."

"Good plan. And Dr. Cohen?"

"Yes?" Zoey said, already running through what she needed to do first.

"You might want to change into scrubs."

"What?" Zoey looked down at herself. "Oh, crap."

Her street clothes—her nice first day at work with new residents on a new service clothes—were pretty much wrecked. The pants were a loss. Probably the shoes too. And her very summery, dressy tee had a splotch of something she really hoped was saline over her right breast.

"So much for trying to look like a regular person."

"At least you're not in your underwear like Dr. Chan."

At Zoey's startled look, Declan added, "I was in the parking lot when you arrived."

"You saw that?" Zoey exclaimed. *She saw us? And she remembered me?*

"It was quite an entrance."

Zoey could tell Declan was smiling even with the mask in place. For the briefest moment, Declan's winter dark eyes softened, and the flash of heat struck Zoey like an electric shock. She bit her lip behind her mask and looked quickly away before Declan could read what was in *her* eyes. She didn't want to think about that too much herself, but her hammering heart and the warmth spreading through her depths couldn't be ignored. Declan Black lit her up.

CHAPTER FIVE

L inda stuck her head through the curtain divide where Dec and Zoey worked on the patient. "Dr. Black, Kos is on the line for you again."

"Can you transfer it to my cell?" Dec asked, her attention on the ultrasound images.

"What's the number?"

Without turning around, Dec gave it to her, and a few seconds later her cell phone rang. She put it on speaker and set it on a shelf for Zoey to hear any instructions. "Kos, it's Dec."

Kos's baritone came through with a bit of static and the background beeps of OR monitors and muted snippets of conversation. "I'm not going to get free up here for a couple of more hours. What's happening down there?"

"We've identified him—Antonio Ricci, a medical resident. We don't have head scans yet, but it's looking like a diffuse brain injury. Pupils are fixed and cranial nerve reflexes absent. We've started protocols, but his ICP is still through the roof."

"Damn it. I really need Stevens up here in the OR, and she needs to be here. Can you handle this for me until I can get loose?"

"Sure, but there's really not much more for neuro to do right now," Dec said. "We need the head CT to confirm there's no localized area we can decompress, but I don't expect to find one. I can handle that with one of the ER or general surgery residents. If we find anything surgical, I'll let you know."

"That would be great. Send Syd up."

Dec disconnected and said to Zoey, "Let's get him ready to go down to CT for head and abdomen. After you get that going, can you find out if the family has been notified, and when they'll be here."

"Sure."

"Thanks. Oh, and tell Syd Stevens if she didn't get a call from Kos, he wants her upstairs."

"All right." Zoey hesitated. "If the family's here, do you want me to talk to them?"

Dec blew out a breath. Her gut told her what was coming, but she made it a practice never to reach a conclusion until all the facts were in and the clinical course was certain. She'd been happy to be wrong before. Still, the family needed to be prepared, and the best way to do that was in stages. None of that was easy to do, and Zoey'd probably never had to do it before. Any resident beyond the first year—and most of them—had had to call a family with grim news, but this was different. Antonio Ricci's story might not end with his last breath.

"You can give them a really vague assessment at this point. Tell them he's suffered serious head trauma, and we may not know how extensive it is for a day or more, but we are doing everything we can to minimize the damage."

"All right." Zoey pulled her mask off, and the sadness in her eyes as she stood at the foot of the bed gazing at Tony Ricci's still body made Dec wish there was a way to make what was coming easier.

She knew better.

"After we see the scans to be sure we have nothing surgical," Dec said softly, "we'll have a better idea how severe the brain injury is. If the apnea test is positive, we'll have to have a different kind of discussion with them. One step at a time. Maybe tomorrow he'll look different."

Zoey pressed her lips together and nodded.

"I can do it if you'd rather," Dec said.

"No," Zoey said immediately. "I want to. He's my patient. I should talk to his family."

"All right. Can you handle taking him down to CT by yourself?"

"Yes, no problem."

Dec tossed her paper mask in the wastebasket. Zoey was an excellent resident. She cared, but she had her emotions under control—out of the way, where they needed to be for her to function. For her to do the best job she could for the patient. She'd been shaken when she'd thought she might know this guy—a friend, maybe, or someone closer.

Not her business. Zoey had handled herself well, and that's all Dec needed to know. "Call me as soon as the CT scans are done. I want to look at them myself."

"I will."

Zoey slipped out through the curtains, and Dec stood quietly by the side of the patient's bed, studying the monitors. His ICP hadn't budged despite their institution of aggressive and early head trauma protocols. They'd do all the necessary tests, but she'd seen this before. The chances of him coming back were low and getting lower every second. She took a deep breath. The last time she'd been at the bedside of a patient like this, she hadn't been the attending neurosurgeon. She'd been a patient herself, battered, broken, and in shock. But she'd insisted. She had to be sure.

"I want to see her," Dec said.

"You're in no shape to be moving around." Angela Murtagh was still in rumpled scrubs from the emergency surgery she'd just performed, and the sympathy in her eyes belied her sharp tone. "You've got three broken ribs, among other things, and I'd prefer not to have to put a chest tube in you."

"I'm okay," Dec insisted.

"Dec, you've got facial fractures, a significant cerebral contusion, and a fractured pelvis. Oh—and the ribs I just mentioned. You're not okay."

"I need to see for myself."

"You can trust Philip. You know he'll be absolutely sure. Let your friends help you through this." Angela took her hand, and the fire left her expression, replaced by tenderness Dec didn't want or need. What she needed was a cold, clear head—not comfort she didn't deserve.

"The only help I need is for someone to push this goddamned stretcher down the hall." With superhuman effort, aided by the hefty dose of morphine they'd given her a few minutes ago, she levered herself into a semi-sitting position.

"All right, all right," Angela said quickly, pressing both palms against Dec's shoulders. "We'll get you down there, but you're not getting off the stretcher. We'll just wheel you in."

Dec leaned back and closed her eyes. Every bump and jolt of the wheels over the tile floor sent searing pain through her head, her face, her chest, her pelvis, her leg. None of it really registered. She was awake, her brain was working, and she was breathing on her own. Her arms and legs moved. She wasn't paralyzed. She couldn't ask for more than that. She'd heard the hushed voices saying she was lucky. Funny, anyone thinking she was lucky when her world had just shattered.

Honor said quietly, "Why don't you take a break, Dec. I can handle this one from here."

"I'm good. But thanks."

Dec turned and moved away from the bed. She knew he couldn't hear them, but some part of her wanted to believe that a glimmer of his consciousness remained, that that rapidly falling percentage was still enough that he might come back, that he might open his eyes, that he might be one of the very few who beat the odds. "Kos asked me to do it. I told him I would."

"Kos is a really good guy. He also was thinking about the most expedient solution and not about all the rest of it."

"The patient's the only one who matters, right?"

"We all agree there." Honor smiled faintly. "And we'd all like to think we can keep our barriers up no matter what, but I can't name a single one of us who can manage that completely. We all have feelings."

Dec would have argued, would have pointed out Honor didn't know her well enough any longer to know if she still had feelings or not. But Honor was her friend, and she was done hurting anyone who cared about her. "I'm okay. I want to do this." She added what would make the difference. "I need to do this."

Honor sighed. "All right, but when the family gets here, if you want me to—"

"Honor," Dec said quietly, "you hired me—I hope—because you believed I could do the job. I can. And besides—who better than me?"

"You always were so stubborn." Honor shook her head, but her expression indicated Dec had won.

"I kinda thought you liked that about me," Dec said.

Honor laughed quietly. "If I hadn't, we wouldn't have been best friends. I've missed you, and I'm glad you're back."

From the other side of the curtain, Zoey cleared her throat. "We're ready to take him down to CT, Dr. Black."

"Good."

Zoey parted the curtains, then stepped inside, trying to act as if she hadn't heard a thing and wasn't dying to know what exactly the two of them had been discussing. One thing was for sure—Declan Black was no ordinary new hire. Zoey'd be interested in that story under any circumstances, but having spent a few intense hours up close and personal with the undeniably attractive ER doc, she was a lot more than curious. She was intrigued.

"I'll let you know as soon as we have something," Zoey said, carefully not looking in Declan's direction. The last thing she needed was to come off as a starstruck neophyte. She might be a resident, but she was a grown woman with a brain *and* a body—even if she didn't always give a whole lot of thought as to where she put her body for the night. She always knew she wouldn't be causing any trouble with it, at least. Easy and uncomplicated. That was her.

Wow. Declan sure had her mind going down strange paths. But then, it had been a hell of a morning. She could forgive herself a little harmless fantasizing.

After Zoey and two of the trauma team secured the patient's lines and monitors, they pushed his stretcher down the hall to the elevators, the portable ventilator making a rhythmic whooshing noise in rhythm with their steps. As the elevator chugged silently down to the radiology department, she thought about the conversation she hadn't intended to overhear and hadn't quite known how to interrupt. Declan and Honor were tight. That was interesting, one of those tidbits that fueled the gossip tree but really just added something new to break the string of stress and tragedy that sometimes threatened to become overwhelming, especially in the trauma unit. She couldn't quite put all the pieces together, but whatever had happened, it sounded as if Declan had had a really hard time. The few signs of what her physical injuries had been had told her that. Thinking of Declan being hurt made her chest ache, but the undercurrent of sadness in Declan's voice struck her somewhere deeper—in an unfamiliar, intimate way. She wished she could reach out and somehow lessen that pain.

The sadness settled just beyond her consciousness as she focused on the scans that appeared on the computer monitor as the CT machine whirred around Tony Ricci. As she suspected, images of the spleen revealed a capsular tear that had caused the little bit of blood-tinged fluid they'd seen earlier. Considering how bad his head injury was, she was pretty certain they would not be operating on his abdomen anytime soon. They'd just started on the head CT when Syd came in.

"Hey," Zoey said, "what's up?"

"I thought I'd take a look at this one and let Kos know if we're going to need to do anything. We've got another patient waiting for scans—skull fractures, possible epidural tear." Syd blew out a breath. "I can't believe how many emergencies we have lined up."

"This has been pretty amazing," Zoey said, vacillating between exhaustion and exhilaration. This was what surgery was all about, but seeing all these devastating injuries wore on the soul. "I've never seen so many trauma patients all at once."

"Neither have I," Syd said, "but you know, at Franklin we didn't get the level ones very often. Certainly not a mass alert like this one."

"Oh yeah," Zoey said. "I forgot you haven't always been here."

Syd smiled. "Thanks."

Zoey laughed. "I meant it. Almost all the Franklin residents have really integrated well. And most of them are really good. It's not like all the PMC residents are superstars either. That's why not everybody ends up finishing."

"Well, all the senior people will, that's for sure." Syd's voice trailed off a little as she stared at the screen. "Boy, this guy's head is a mess."

Zoey refocused on the tomographic sections of the brain appearing on the screen. "Oh. Crap. All of those densities…those are bleeds, aren't they?"

"Yeah," Syd said, leaning closer. "It looks like diffuse intracranial injury to me, almost like an adult shaken-baby syndrome. He must've bounced around inside that car like a marble in a can."

Zoey winced. She could picture it. "They said he was restrained, but the car flipped a couple of times. He still had to have been banged around."

"No question." Syd looked away from the monitor to Zoey. "Aren't you transplant this month?"

"Oh fuck," Zoey muttered. "I haven't even checked with my attending. I didn't even think of it."

"I'm sure they all know where we are. But"—Syd waved to the screen—"this guy looks like he might be a candidate."

"I better let Declan know."

"Declan?" Syd asked, looking slightly confused.

"Oh, Dr. Black. Sorry, I've been working with her so much, and I've been listening to Honor talk to her. I just kinda think of her as Declan. The new ER attending."

"Yeah," Syd said musingly. "She was great talking me through the ICP bolt procedure. What's with that, anyways? Kos knows her, at least that's the way it sounded on the phone. And he was treating her like she's neuro staff, not ER."

"I'm not exactly sure," Zoey said noncommittally, "but I think she might have been a student or a resident here. I guess people know her."

She knew it had to be more than that, knew there was more to Declan's story from what she'd overheard from the nurses and when Honor and Declan were talking, but she didn't want to be one of the people participating in the gossip about Declan Black. In fact, an odd swell of protectiveness surged within her. Shutting down the speculation, she said, "I better call Dr. Doolin and let him know I actually *am* on his service."

Syd shrugged. "I wouldn't worry about it. Just about all the ORs are held up anyhow, so you're not missing anything just yet."

"Hope you're right. I'll catch you later."

Once Zoey and the ER staff got Tony Ricci safely back to the trauma unit, she went in search of Declan.

"Hey, Linda, have you seen Dr. Black?"

"I think she's back in the break room." Linda pushed a crash cart out of the middle of the aisle where it had somehow landed after a code and winced, one hand on her back. "We really need housekeeping down here. This place is a disaster area." She paused and regarded Zoey. "How's Tony?"

Zoey shook her head. As she hurried away, she heard Linda mutter *damn*.

Declan sat at the same table where she'd been sitting almost an hour before when Zoey had come to get her. She had another cup of coffee in front of her.

"I'm not going to get to finish this one either?" Dec asked when she saw Zoey.

Zoey laughed. "No, I think you can. It looks pretty quiet out there. The scans are done." She passed her tablet over to Dec. "You ought to be able to pull them up."

"Thanks," Dec said, "but I don't have a password or anything yet. Hell, I don't even have a locker."

"That's okay, I'm signed in. Just put in his patient number." Zoey looked at the palm of her hand and read off a string of numbers.

Dec laughed. "You wrote it down on your hand?"

"Expedience counts, right?"

"Absolutely." Chuckling, Dec entered the number, and with one hand loosely gripping her coffee, which she seemed to have forgotten, she scanned through the images with the other. When she looked up at Zoey, her face was blank and her eyes that winter dark—so dark, Zoey could almost feel the chill.

"What do you think?" Declan asked.

For an instant, Zoey didn't want to put words to what she thought. Didn't want to make it all real. But that was her job, wasn't it. "Given his presentation and his ICP, coupled with the diffuse intracerebral and deep trauma on the scans, I don't think he's going to wake up."

"No, neither do I," Declan said quietly. "If there's no change by morning, trauma will institute the brain death protocol and enter him into the transplant registry."

"Should I notify transplant now?" Zoey asked. "I'm actually assigned to that service, but we got caught right before, you know, July 1 officially started. I should report to my attending but...should I tell him about...Tony?"

Declan shook her head. "Not just yet. I find that the family handles things better if the first person to talk to them isn't the transplant surgeon."

Zoey looked relieved. "So it's still okay if I talk to them?"

"I think you should. If you're going to be on the transplant service, you're going to be the one leading the case, and this way, they'll know you. I can connect with them after you give them the initial assessment."

Zoey took a breath and took a chance. "I've actually never done anything with transplants before."

"It's a little bit of a special skill, but you'll get the hang of it. We'll meet them together when the time comes."

"Thanks." Zoey wouldn't ordinarily admit to anyone there was anything she wasn't sure about doing—not until it was absolutely necessary. All her life she'd been careful never to show anything other than confidence and certainty, even when inside she knew she was acting. Fit in with the sorority girls, most of them driving the sports cars they'd been gifted for graduation, when she'd arrived at college on the bus? No problem. Always be the first to support a sister—even if it meant never competing with them. Give up the benefits part of best-friends-with-benefits with a smile? Piece of cake—just wish the happy couple well and move on. Acting like nothing ever hurt was her specialty, but the pain of telling the family their loved one wasn't going to wake up again and then asking them for permission to give their organs away wasn't something she could hide with a casual shrug. Maybe if Declan hadn't talked things over with her, hadn't treated her like a colleague, hadn't listened to her when she'd had doubts, she would have pretended she wasn't dreading the discussion. Declan had made it easy to admit she was uneasy. Most of all, Declan hadn't judged her. Zoey finally identified the feeling that washed over her. Declan made her feel safe not to pretend.

CHAPTER SIX

D r. Black," Linda said, from the doorway of the break room, "Honor wanted me to tell you that she just talked to Dr. Ricci's mother and father. They're on their way and should be here within the hour. Do you still want to talk to them? He's upstairs in the TICU now—I can get a trauma resident—"

"Thanks, but I'm sure they're just getting him settled up there. They probably haven't had much of a chance to do more than make sure he was stable. We can handle this."

Zoey added quickly, "Just have the desk page me when they arrive."

Linda nodded. "All right then."

"What year did you say you were?" Dec asked as Zoey carried a cup of coffee to the adjoining table. The program at PMC was smaller than what she was used to, and the relationships between the residents and staff closer, a little more informal, and a little more personal. She remembered that from her own training days, but like a lot of things in the time she'd been gone, she'd forgotten what she'd loved about being here—and what she missed. Honor obviously trusted Zoey to handle complicated cases, and Zoey had the confidence to respond. Dec mentally told herself her interest was purely academic—she needed to know what she could ask, and expect, of residents who would be showing up for trauma alerts or emergency room consults. She needed to learn who to trust and who to keep an eye on among the house staff ASAP. Getting to know Zoey was just part of the job.

"Fourth year," Zoey said.

"And Syd Stevens? Her too?"

"Technically, yes, sort of." Zoey raised a shoulder. "She's actually a fifth year—well, I think maybe sixth year?—since she actually did her first year twice when she moved programs, but she switched from general surgery to neuro, I guess, yesterday."

Dec blinked. "Wait. She said she was new, but I thought she meant she transferred in from another neuro program. You mean, she's actually new-to-neuro new *and* she somehow scored a senior spot?"

"Yep."

"Things sure have changed around here," Dec said dryly.

"Did you train here?" Zoey asked.

Dec tensed. Fair question after all, and she *had* opened the door by striking up a conversation. She'd gotten comfortable with Zoey Cohen after working with her so intensely for the last few hours, and she hadn't considered where a casual comment or two might go. "I did, before your time, though."

Zoey snorted. "Sorry—that only works when you're a generation or two older. I don't think that applies."

"Ah...thanks? I guess." Dec suddenly sensed she was out of her depth, mostly because she hadn't had a carefree interaction with another woman since before... "So finish the Syd Stevens saga. That's quite a story."

If Zoey noticed the not-so-subtle change of subject, she didn't let on.

Zoey grinned. "Well, actually, it really is. Maybe you don't know, but a lot of training programs have been closing because of the federal government cutting funding that supports resident salaries and training."

"I know," Dec said. "I was part of the teaching program..." She paused for a moment. "Before."

Zoey looked at her as if expecting something more.

"In Dallas."

"Parkland?"

"Yes." Again, fair question. Innocent enough. Then why did she feel like she was slowly losing at a game of strip poker? If this conversation went on much longer, she'd be down to her briefs. What could she say? Where I used to work, before I couldn't work there anymore?

"Oh," Zoey said after a moment, the curiosity plain, but then, she'd been watching Dec with that same curious, contemplative look in her eyes quite a bit in the last couple of hours.

"And?" Dec raised her brows. "The rest of the interesting story?"

Zoey blushed. She looked younger when she did that, although Dec put her no more than ten years behind her, which would be about right considering her level of training. She certainly hadn't seemed young in the middle of the trauma alert. But then, four years of surgical training would do that to you. Thirty and almost forty weren't that many years apart in experience, not when most of those years were spent fighting death and dying.

"Right," Zoey said, pushing a hand through her long blond hair.

The move was very feminine, and appealing, and caught Dec by surprise. Even before the accident, she hadn't really noticed a woman in quite a long time. Since then, she hadn't noticed a lot of anything, certainly nothing sexual. And this wasn't sexual either. It was just an observation which she quickly put out of her mind.

"So, the Franklin training program," Zoey went on, "that's in Northeast Philadelphia—"

"I know it," Dec said.

"Oh, right. Sure you would, training here in the city," Zoey said. "So anyhow, when Franklin had to close their surgery program, Dr. Maguire got permission to expand our residency. We absorbed some of their residents. Syd and some of the others came over from there."

"How many?"

"Three in every year, first through fourth. The fifth years were almost done by then anyhow, so they finished out at Franklin."

Dec worked at not showing her surprise. Integrating that many new residents was a feat in itself, but avoiding the animosity over all that new competition? Quinn Maguire must be a magician if she did that and avoided a mutiny in her resident ranks. Then again, Quinn had won Honor's heart, the heart Dec hadn't been sure anything or anyone could ever heal. Honor was clearly happy, more than happy. Fulfilled. Magician or no, the transition had to have been chaos. "That must've made for an interesting few weeks."

Zoey laughed. "Yeah, you could say that. But now…" She shrugged. "Everybody's just part of the team, you know? But Syd did this case with Kos in the trauma unit, and she quickly got the neuro bug. I guess Kos really liked her, and he had an opening, so she switched."

"Sounds like Kos." Dec smiled. "When I…"

Zoey watched her expectantly. How did she manage to get her so relaxed she was reminiscing all of a sudden? What would be next—a confession?

Dec backtracked. "Kos always did tend to make his own rules. He doesn't get shackled to protocols if they stand in the way of getting the results he needs. Makes him a very good surgeon."

"Yeah, Syd thinks he has godlike powers."

"I wouldn't go that far." Dec laughed. "But he's the one I'd want standing over me if—"

If Kos had been there, would anything have turned out differently? The question blindsided her. She had finally stopped asking what-if and replaying every mile of the ride, looking for any way she could have changed things.

Pushing down the sick rush of anxiety, Dec stood abruptly and used the cover of getting another cup of coffee to regroup. Back still turned, she waded out of the deep waters to safer ground. She hoped.

"Good for Syd. It takes guts to make a change like that so late during training. What about you? What're your plans?"

"Right now I'm just thinking general surgery," Zoey said. "I like to operate, and there's a lot of variety still in general surg."

"True enough." Back in control, Dec turned around and leaned on the counter.

Zoey looked like she was about to say something else when her eyes widened and she jumped to her feet so fast her chair tipped over and clattered on the floor. Startled, Dec set her coffee aside and started forward. Had she missed a trauma alert?

Just as quickly, she pulled up short. A big guy in green scrubs filled the doorway, his head nearly touching the top of the frame. He had to be at least six five and two hundred and forty pounds. That didn't seem to bother Zoey.

She stormed across the room, planted both fists against his chest, and shoved him hard enough he actually gave a half an inch or so.

"You son of a bitch," Zoey shouted. "Where the fuck have you been?"

"Sorry, hey, I'm so sorry." The guy, his voice a gentle tenor, wrapped Zoey in his arms and pulled her close. The fight went out of her, and she rested her head against his chest.

"You have no idea how scared I was," she murmured.

Dec swallowed and looked away. Well, she'd been wrong, apparently, that Zoey had been looking at her with interest. As if that mattered at all. But she did feel like something of an idiot.

Another female voice, sharp and cutting, exclaimed, "You want to get yourself unwrapped from him, Cohen. Just because Emmett isn't available anymore doesn't mean everybody else is fair game."

Dec stared, astounded at the venom behind the words.

"Sadie, you are such a bitch." Zoey disentangled herself from the guy and stared at the redhead, also in scrubs, who'd squeezed in next to them.

Ignoring the redhead—at her peril, Dec thought—Zoey thumped the guy on the chest.

"We were worried about you." She glared at the redhead, then, who glared back. "And if the two of you had bothered to show up on time this morning, you'd probably know why."

Dec coughed softly. "Ah, maybe the three of you want to take this personal discussion someplace private."

Zoey backed up. "We're done now."

Jerry sighed and strode to Dec, hand outstretched. "Sorry for the commotion. I'm Jerry Katz. One of the surgery residents. I'm very sorry that I was late this morning. I am..." He grimaced. "I thought I'd set the alarm, but I didn't."

"Unbelievable." Zoey shook her head and walked over to get her coffee.

The redhead—Sadie, apparently another surgery resident from the looks of her scrubs and Zoey's comments—blushed and looked contrite.

"It's true," Sadie said. "By the time we realized we'd missed the new resident orientation, we just figured we should get here as quickly as we could."

"You don't owe me any explanations," Dec said. "I suppose you've got attendings who might be looking for you, though."

Jerry glanced at Zoey, who was studiously ignoring him. "I heard about Tony."

"Yeah. It sucks."

"Yeah. It does. Well," Jerry said, backing into the hall, "I guess I better find my service."

"Yeah, me too," Sadie said far more calmly.

A moment later the room was very quiet. Zoey glanced sideways at Dec. "Sorry about all that. I was really worried about him."

"I'm glad he's okay."

"He's my housemate," Zoey went on quickly, as if she needed to explain…something. "Well, technically, he's Dani and Syd's housemate and my…duplex-mate. Emmett, Hank, and I live together in the other half of the house."

"Right. Sounds complicated." Dec slowly got the picture. What had Sadie said? *Now that Emmett's not available anymore?* "Sounds… very friendly."

Zoey stared at her before her eyes lightened and she burst out laughing. "It sounds crazy, doesn't it? I mean, it's not really musical beds or anything like that."

Really? Who's Emmett? Not going there this century. Dec smothered a grin. "Well, thanks for clearing that up."

"Oh God. I'm making it a lot worse. Right, okay. I'm going to check on the patients in the unit, and double-check that Dr. Doolin doesn't need me right away on transplant."

"Page me when the family arrives."

The laughter left Zoey's eyes, and she nodded solemnly. "I will."

Dec watched her go and settled back with her coffee, the third cup she'd tried to drink that morning. This one was cold again too. She dumped it and tried again with a fresh cup while replaying the past few minutes in her mind. Dec wondered if Zoey would thank her after they finished talking to Antonio Ricci's mother and father. Zoey was an intriguing combination of quick humor, fierce focus, and fiery temperament. She also had a dangerous knack of lulling Dec into a zone where she said more than she meant to. No one had been able to do that since she and Honor were tight another lifetime ago. Even then, Honor had never been able to get her to say more than she was ready to. Zoey was someone unique and maybe just a little risky to get too close to.

CHAPTER SEVEN

"Got a minute?" Honor said from the doorway of the break room.

"Yeah," Dec said, happy to be rescued from the last of the coffee she never seemed to get to drink anyhow.

"I wanted to introduce you a little more formally this morning, but...plans change." Honor laughed wryly. "Which is really more the norm than anything else."

"Tell me about it," Dec said. "Who would have ever thought I'd be back here. Like this, on top of everything else?"

Honor slowed, concern welling in her eyes. "Are you sure this is what you want to be doing? It hasn't even been two years. Maybe if you give it more time—"

"My eyesight isn't going to get any better," Dec said quietly. "Believe me, I know. I'm good for basic procedures, but I'll never work under the microscope again."

Honor looked pained. "Of course I know you would be sure about that, and I'm sorry for bringing it up. I just hate to think of you doing something you don't love. With your training, maybe you could—"

"Hey, no." Dec stopped abruptly. "That came out all wrong. I like the ER. Always did, even when we were students. The thing I liked best about neurosurgery was handling the acute cases—especially the traumas."

"Then why did you end up doing all the aneurysm surgery in Dallas?"

Because Annabelle and her father wanted me to. Because it was easier just to keep the peace. Dec wouldn't blame Annabelle for her own lack of spine, especially now, so she gave Honor the part that was true. "I was good at it, and the neurosurgery chief wanted to develop our department into the regional center for surgical intervention in high-risk cases."

"I suppose none of us really know what directions our careers will take when we're students," Honor said, "or our lives, for that matter. I certainly never expected Quinn."

"I gather from what I've heard so far she may have superpowers."

Honor laughed, a light in her eyes that only could be love. "She's quite human, I assure you. But she is also amazing. Anyhow, I didn't mean to interrogate you."

"First of all, you're not. You're asking because we're friends." Dec sighed. She'd had a lot of people help her out in the last two years, but none who'd been a friend as long as Honor. But Honor didn't know all the story and never would. "I appreciate your concern. Really. But I'm good. I like the ER, and I like being here."

Honor laughed. "All right. I'll stop hovering, then."

Dec grinned. "Seeing is believing."

Honor snorted and led her into a mini conference room with stadium seating, a small stage with a podium, and a big screen behind it. A dozen or so people in scrubs, lab coats, or cover gowns filled the first few rows. Heads turned as Dec and Honor walked down the center aisle.

"Everyone, this is Declan Black, our new attending."

Everyone rose and crowded around as Honor introduced her. Dec put on a smile, shook hands, noted a few familiar faces—older by a decade—and put names to the new ones. The gathering lasted only a few minutes as everyone had more important business to attend to, for which Dec was inordinately glad.

Probably she was being unrealistic, but she really hoped she could slip into the stream of hospital life unnoticed, with no questions, explanations, or sympathy.

After the introductions, Dec escaped for a quick walk-through in trauma admitting, signed off on two patients ready to go to the ICUs, and reviewed a series of lab reports with one of the ER residents. A pang in her midsection reminded her that somewhere in the morning's rush, she'd forgotten to eat. With still a little time until the family of Tony Ricci showed up, she decided to try for breakfast and a decent cup of coffee while there was a lull in the activity. As she walked through the ER to the staff cafeteria on the second floor, she noted the new additions and new faces, but the general air of action and expectation hadn't changed. Happily, neither had hospital food. She ordered up a toasted bagel and scrambled eggs and grabbed what looked like honest-to-God real blueberries from a bowl in the cold case. She took a table by the windows that looked out over the rear of the hospital toward an expanse of grass that ended in a small cluster of trees. Something you never saw in Dallas. One of the many benefits of working at a hospital in a residential area, tucked into neighborhoods where people actually lived. Rare these days, when most medical schools or medical centers of any size occupied their own mini-complexes, generally surrounded by major highways and acres of parking lots. A group of residents occupied a table a little ways from hers, looking far younger than she remembered being at the time, but then again, she felt far older than her years now too. She looked for Zoey and didn't see her, before she caught herself. She needed to stop thinking about Zoey. Zoey was just the first person she'd talked to in two years who didn't know anything about her, that was all. But pretending she had no past didn't make it so. She looked back out the window and tried not to think about anything at all.

"Would I be disturbing you if I sat down?" a woman asked.

Dec pulled her gaze away from the window and looked up. The woman looking back was about her age, with shoulder-length brown hair streaked with blond highlights, brown eyes, a sensuous mouth pulled into a smile, and a perfectly proportioned heart-shaped face. Dec thought she should know her, but she couldn't put a name to the face. With a quick reboot of her mental faculties, Dec said, "No, go ahead. I'm—"

"Declan Black." The smile took on a slightly amused curve. "I know. We were classmates. Actually we never seemed to end up in the same place at the same time, so I'm not surprised you don't remember me." She held out her hand. "Bridget Kelly."

"Ah, you're wrong there. I remember you," Dec said, smiling

now. "Fourth table down in anatomy, right? And you were a resident here too." She thought a second. "Psychiatry. That's why we didn't cross paths very much."

Bridget's brow lifted, and she nodded, surveying Dec unapologetically from beneath thick sable lashes. "Very good memory. I'm flattered."

The look, more than the offhand comment, raised a red flag. Probably everything about the exchange was completely innocent, but then again, she wasn't so out of touch she couldn't tell when a woman was flirting with her.

"I take it you're on the staff here?" Dec said.

"Yes, never left home." Bridget laughed. "I'm really surprised to see you back here, though."

"Probably about as surprised as I am to be here," Dec said.

"Are you and your wife settled in, then?" Bridget paused, and when Dec didn't elaborate further, added, "This area has gotten a lot more popular since we were residents. Houses are harder to find."

Dec hesitated. "I've got an apartment close by. I never did much like a commute, and I don't need much space."

"Oh, that makes sense, then," Bridget said, giving a not so subtle glance at Dec's bare ring finger. "Well, I better get back to work. I'm sure I'll see you around—neurosurgery, right?"

"No," Dec said flatly. "ER."

"I misremembered, then." Bridget's brows drew down. "I really do hope to see you again."

Dec nodded. "I'm sure we'll cross paths. After all, the hospital is a very small world."

As soon as Bridget left, Dec gathered up her tray. She'd had enough unexpected conversation for the morning, and it wasn't even ten a.m. As she walked out, she noticed that Zoey had joined the group of residents while she'd been talking with Bridget. Maybe she was imagining it, but Dec thought Zoey watched her as she left.

❖

"Well, that's an interesting development," Dani said, swiping a slice of bacon off Zoey's plate.

"What," Zoey said sharply, moving the rest of her bacon out of Dani-range.

"Bridget Kelly and the hot new stud from the ER."

"What? Where?" Zoey'd seen Dec across the room when she'd gone through the cafeteria line before getting swamped by a cloud of residents, nurses, and techs moving en masse to two adjoining tables at the back. Short of craning her neck and looking really obvious, she couldn't keep Dec in her sight line.

"Not pretending you don't think she's a stud any longer?" Dani smirked.

"And I didn't say that," Zoey said. "Do you ever think of anything besides sex?"

"Not really. You?"

Zoey laughed. "Yeah, point taken."

"Anyhow, you missed Bridget zeroing in on Dr. Studly like a heat-seeking missile. To use another apt analogy."

"My imagination does not constantly conjure sexual scenarios from innocent encounters," Zoey said, getting that prickly feeling along her arms again when she envisioned—contrary to her statement—Bridget hitting on Declan.

"Uh-huh," Dani said with an eye roll. "But *hypothetically*, what do you think? Is Bridget fishing in the right waters?"

"Really?" Zoey said, her irritation swelling along with the prickle that had now spread over most of her body. "I have no idea who or what Declan Black might be interested in, but if she's got any sense, it won't be Bridget Kelly."

"Oh, I hear sour grapes."

"Don't be ridiculous. I couldn't be less interested..." At the quick light in Dani's eyes, Zoey added hastily, "In Bridget or anyone else."

"Didn't you maybe get a ride home with Bridget after the end-of-the-year residents' party, just a few weeks ago?"

"Ride home. That's all."

"No good-night kiss?"

"I'm not feeding your prurient mind with any further discussion."

Dani laughed. "Okay. I was just saying...interesting, that's all."

"What is?" Bonnie Chu, a brunette ER PA, asked as she sat a couple of people away from Zoey and Dani.

"Nothing," Zoey said emphatically with a shut-up glare at Dani.

Bonnie emptied a pack of artificial sweetener into her coffee and said, to no one in particular, "So, you hear the latest hot news item?"

Heads swiveled in her direction along with a small chorus of *No, what?*s.

Bonnie leaned toward the center of the table as if about to impart a top-secret message.

"Did you see the woman who just walked out? Short dark hair, fitness trainer body, good-looking in an andro way?"

"Oh yeah." Dani made a successful foray for another piece of bacon while Zoey was distracted by Bonnie. "Here we go."

"That's the new ER attending," one of the students said.

"Right," Bonnie said. "Declan Black. I just got the scoop on her from an ICU nurse who remembers her from when she was a resident here."

"Oh yeah?" one of the guys said dryly. "What did she do to get talked about already? Get kicked out back then or something?"

Bristling with unexpected outrage, Zoey shot up straight in her seat. "Hey—"

"Hey, Zoey," Dani said a little louder, "can I have your toast?"

"*What?*"

"Just cool it," Dani said more softly, as Bonnie went on unperturbed. "At least find out what people are saying."

"Kicked out? Oh, not from the way I heard it," Bonnie said, carefully cutting her blueberry-filled doughnut in half and then in quarters. "Sean, the ICU nurse, told me Black was like a superstar or something. Everyone expected her to join the staff. She had an offer from Kos Hassan and everything."

"Yeah," the same guy said again, "so what led to her fall from stardom?"

Bonnie took a delicate bite of her doughnut, carefully wiping white sugar from her fingertips, and picked up her coffee. "A woman."

"Ah," Zoey said, unable to stifle her indignation any longer, "is this going somewhere? Because it kinda sounds like a bunch of unfounded gossip to me."

"Hey, isn't that the definition of gossip?" Bonnie said with a smile. "Besides, it gets better."

She now had the attention of everyone at the table.

Zoey plunged on. "I don't—hey!"

Dani kicked Zoey under the table and muttered, "You can worry about the truth of that later."

Bonnie, ignoring them, went on, "So here's the really good part. Like I said, she was slated to be a new neuro attending. She was Kos Hassan's star resident. Best he'd seen in his whole career."

Zoey's stomach tightened. More of the pieces she'd been trying to assemble of her picture of Declan fell into place, but others scattered even farther apart. The image she'd been trying to form of Declan grew fuzzy and indistinct, although she understood now why Declan had supervised Syd during the neuro procedure in the ER, and why Honor didn't seem disturbed about it at all. Had encouraged her to do it. But then, why was Declan an ER attending?

"Anyhow," Bonnie continued, "the story is that at the last minute, she took a position in Dallas because her fiancée's father was on the board of the hospital."

"Ha," the same guy said. "Marriage of convenience. Or just a lucky break."

"Yeah, everyone was shocked apparently. But…" Bonnie lifted a shoulder. "You know, people do that all the time. Marry up or whatever."

Zoey shot to her feet, gripped her tray, and said, "I have a lot more important things to do than sit around listening to brainless"—she emphasized the word as she stared at Bonnie—"chatter."

Bonnie, generally unruffled by much of anything, rolled her eyes. "As if."

Zoey stuffed her tray onto the already full conveyor belt and turned around to find Dani right behind her.

"What?" Zoey snapped.

Dani held up both hands. "Hey, not the enemy. You were a little sensitive back there."

"I just don't think dragging someone's personal life into the cafeteria, when you don't even know if any of it's true, is cool."

"People talk about everybody else all the time."

"Well, maybe we shouldn't."

"Don't tell me you aren't curious. I was from the minute I saw her. Something doesn't fit. And now," Dani said, keeping in stride with Zoey as Zoey marched out of the cafeteria, "I'm even more curious."

"Not you too."

"Oh, come on. Neuro resident slated to be an attending, and now she's in the ER? And what's the story with the wife? Maybe she was a doc here too, you think?"

Zoey stopped, hands on her hips. "I don't know, Dani. That's the whole point, isn't it? We don't know anything about her. Other than, you know, she's really good. You saw her handling that mass alert this morning. And she's sensitive. And doesn't deserve to be talked about by people who just want a distraction."

Dani's brows rose. "Sensitive, is she? In addition to really good-looking too. I think we both agree on the hot factor."

"I'm going to strangle you."

Dani tilted her head, a speculative expression making her look unusually serious. "You really like her, don't you?"

"I…I've been working with her a lot this morning. She's really nice. And it just seems like maybe she's been through a lot, and it's just not right."

"Okay, okay. I'll wait until, you know, she makes her move to let her jump my bones."

Zoey laughed in spite of herself. "I'm back to wanting to strangle you again."

Dani bumped shoulders. "I gotta go and see what my young 'uns are up to. I sent them off on their own, but I don't want them to get into too much trouble before I bail them out."

"Catch you later." Zoey checked her watch.

Tony Ricci's family should be showing up soon. She really tried not to think about what Bonnie had just disclosed about Declan, but it was hard not to. If she hadn't started to get to know her, hadn't seen her work, hadn't experienced her thoughtfulness, she would be casually intrigued by the mystery of it all just like everyone else. But she did know her, maybe just a little bit, and what she'd gleaned from all Declan *hadn't* said was an underlying sadness and resignation that hurt to see. Declan had suffered physically, that was clear, and she didn't deserve to be the topic of anyone's idle conversation. And, she admitted grudgingly, neither did her wife.

While she didn't consider it her responsibility to be the caretaker of other people's relationships, she avoided hooking up with women who were already involved elsewhere, formally or not. Just too damn many complications. Declan Black was nothing if not a plethora of complications. Secretive, injured in ways that Zoey couldn't totally fathom, and unavailable.

From just about any angle Zoey viewed it, Declan Black was not someone she ought to be spending any time thinking about in a personal way. Fortunately, she was an expert at quelling unwanted emotions.

CHAPTER EIGHT

Zoey detoured to the OR and leaned in the window of the control room. A middle-aged blonde in scrubs and bright pink clogs sat before an array of TV screens, a phone to her ear as she tapped on a computer keyboard.

"I can't do anything about that, Dr. Wang. I'd love to get your facelift started too, but trauma is still in there with a lacerated bowel… Well, yes, trauma does get precedence." She gazed at Zoey and rolled her eyes. "Dr. Maguire is scrubbed in there. When last I checked, she said another hour at least…I'll call your office when we're ready for you."

When Patty put her phone down, Zoey said, "Hey, Patty, sorry to bother—is Dr. Doolin up here?"

"He was in the OR lounge a minute ago. He's waiting to start an AV shunt. Lemme check and see if they're out of seven yet." She flicked a dial on one of the closed-circuit TVs and squinted at the six-by-six black-and-white image. "Nope. Ortho is doing a washout on an open tib-fib. Then they have a partial forearm amputation to complete. I don't think Dr. Doolin will get started until this afternoon."

"Thanks. Can you page me when you call for his first patient?"

Patty made a note on a clipboard. "Will do. I'll let him know you'll get it started too."

"Appreciate it."

Weirdly happy that her case was delayed, Zoey took the stairs down to the first floor. She was free for a while longer, and now she'd be able to meet with Tony's family without any problem. As hard as that was going to be, she wanted to follow through on the case she shared with Declan. As she exited the stairwell, the service elevators across the hall opened, and Emmett McCabe, in scrubs and a green cover gown, hustled out. They fell in side by side, threading their way like a couple of linebackers through the bustle of stretchers, wheelchairs, and hospital personnel clogging the corridor.

She hadn't seen much of Emmett since Emmett and Syd got together, and now that those two were practically living together, they connected even less. She missed the sex—Emmett was very good at that—but not nearly as much as she missed knowing someone might be thinking about her, might be wanting to see her, might want *her*. Emmett hadn't been one to sleep around. Zoey probably had more casual hookups than she did, not that there were tons of those, and she liked the feeling, however transient, of coming first with someone. She hadn't gone so far as to think their friendly sex was leading to anything serious, but now that Emmett was gone, she felt the vacancy in her life. Good thing she didn't have time to worry about it.

"Didn't expect to see you out of the OR so soon," Zoey said to Emmett. "What's going on? Did I miss an alert or something?"

Emmett pulled off her surgical cap and distractedly ruffled her short hair where it had been flattened beneath the paper covering. "No, a consult in the ER. Probable acute appy."

"Just business as usual, then," Zoey said.

"What about you?"

"I'm waiting to get started on the transplant schedule. Everything's held up with the traumas. Right now I'm on my way to talk to Tony Ricci's family. They should be here any minute. He's one of the traumas from this morning."

"Yeah, I heard about that while I was in the OR." Emmett frowned. "Why are you talking to the family? Isn't he up in the TICU yet?"

"He just got up there, but I took care of him when he came in. You know, I'm gonna be following him while he's here, probably."

"But you're on..." Emmett grimaced. "Oh, crap, really?"

"Yeah," Zoey said.

"Man, are they sure yet? Has neuro seen him? Kos has been in the OR all morning. Maybe there's something he can do."

"That would be great," Zoey said, "but I don't think that will happen." They paused just outside the ER. Speculation about a patient's prognosis wasn't anything that ought to be broadcast to casual listeners, even other hospital personnel, but sometimes sharing information led to a different therapeutic approach. And sometimes sharing the details just helped lessen the burden. "We got the CT, and it's pretty ugly. Syd saw it and confirmed what we thought clinically, and Declan—Dr. Black—seems pretty sure."

"Well, it doesn't take a neurosurgeon or even a neurologist to call brain death, but Black is an ER doc, so maybe…" Emmett shrugged.

Emmett's skepticism was more hope than anything else. Zoey got it. No one wanted things to turn out the way it looked like they were going, and all she said was, "Dr. Black has had a lot of experience with these kinds of cases, where she was before. But you're right. It's early. Things could change."

"Syd saw the scans too?" Emmett said.

"Yeah. We all did."

"Damn," Emmett whispered. Her shoulders tightened, and she visibly straightened. Pulling on her armor again.

Zoey recognized the gesture. She did it herself countless times a day. Putting aside the feelings and getting on with the job.

Emmett said briskly, "I better go see this consult. I sent the first year resident down to see it first."

"You mean the first *day* resident," Zoey said with a brief laugh.

"Gotta throw them in the deep end."

"Good luck," Zoey said. "I'll see you…sometime."

Emmett paused. "Yeah. Hey, you good? I haven't—"

"All good. Just don't forget the rent is due."

Emmett laughed, hit the switch for the automatic doors, and the bright lights and noise of the ER greeted them. Emmett headed for the central station to check on the consult, and Zoey scanned the trauma bay, hoping to see Declan.

Linda spied her and motioned her over. "I was just about to call you. Mr. and Mrs. Ricci just came in. The clerk brought them down to the private family room. We cleared it so there's no one else in there. I made sure there was fresh coffee and hot water for tea. Do you need me to go with you?"

"No," Zoey said, "let me talk to them. If we need to get a chaplain or priest or rabbi or somebody down here to talk to them, I'll call you. You can take care of that, right?"

"I can. I checked Tony's chart a while ago. They're Methodist. I'll call Reverend Abercrombie, to see if she's in-house. Or if not, who's covering."

"Yeah, I think that's a good idea," Zoey said. "Thanks."

"Oh, and Zoey?"

Zoey paused. "Yeah?"

"Honor talked with personnel. They have a copy of his driver's license. He's not a designated organ donor."

"Oh. Okay. Thanks." Not all that surprising that Tony hadn't noted anything on his license. Neither had she. She'd just automatically renewed her driver's license online when it came due. She'd gotten it the first time when she'd been, what, sixteen? Who thought about dying when all you wanted was to be able to drive somewhere without your parents chaperoning? Or in her case, her aunt and uncle.

Hopefully his parents wouldn't see the absence of a donor designation as meaning he didn't want to donate. *If* they ever even needed to talk about that. She'd have to ask Declan how to handle that.

Before she could overthink what she was going to say or let her nerves make her hesitant, Zoey strode down the hall, knocked softly on the closed door with the placard that read *Family Room*, and entered. The room was just large enough for a generic office-supply-issue, straight-backed blue sofa with wooden arms, four matching chairs, a brown metal coffee credenza on wheels against one wall, and recessed ceiling lights behind plastic covers that bathed the room in a cold, flat white light. She'd never noticed before how barren and inhospitable so many of the waiting rooms seemed to be. A shiver rippled down her spine, and she quickly said, "I'm Dr. Cohen, one of the surgical house staff. I've been helping to take care of Tony since he arrived."

Mr. and Mrs. Ricci sat side by side on the sofa, their hands linked. Tony's father was a big man like Tony and, like Tony, had deep brown eyes the same shade as his skin, close-cut black hair without a hint of silver or gray, and a broad open face. They looked like each other. Tony's mother was smaller than her husband by half, almost delicately boned, her pale skin drawn tight across sharp, soaring cheekbones.

Her eyes, the same shade as her light brown hair, fixed on Zoey unwaveringly.

"They told us out front that my son has been taken upstairs to the trauma unit," she said. "When can we see him?"

Zoey pulled over another blue fabric chair, like the ones they were sitting in, and sat facing them. "He just went upstairs to the trauma unit a few moments ago. It will take another twenty minutes or so before they have him completely settled. They'll want to be sure all his monitors are hooked up, that his labs are up-to-date, and whatever else he needs in terms of medication or treatment has been started."

"We understand," Tony's father said in a deep rumbling baritone. "Can you tell us what the situation is?"

"From the reports of the first responders, Tony was a back seat passenger, and he was restrained. The car he was riding in, as you may have heard already, was involved in a multi-vehicle accident on—"

"Yes," Tony's mother said anxiously. "A terrible nine-car accident on the expressway. The news said a tractor trailer jackknifed, blocking all the lanes, and no one could stop. We saw the news on the internet, but we didn't know…"

Her voice trailed off, and the look in her eyes pleaded for Zoey to tell her anything but what she feared she might hear.

Mr. Ricci drew her closer and cleared his throat. "Tony has been living at home since he started his residency. He wanted to start paying off his student loans. He doesn't have a car."

Zoey nodded silently, sensing they needed to talk until they were ready to hear what she would tell them.

Mrs. Ricci added, "He carpools with neighbors of ours who drop him off here on their way to work at the quarry. They always start early, and he likes to—" Her voice quivered, and she took a few seconds to catch her breath. Lifting her chin, she went on, "He likes to start rounds early, he said. He's very conscientious."

"I know," Zoey said, although she didn't know him very well at all.

"What can you tell us about his condition?" Mr. Ricci asked.

Tony's parents listened expressionlessly as Zoey explained his injuries, although, as the moments passed, Tony's mother gripped his father's arm more and more desperately, as if clinging to a life raft in treacherous seas.

"If I understand what you're saying," Mr. Ricci said, his voice flat and every word uttered with effort, "he has a very serious head injury and is in a coma."

"Yes," Zoey said.

"Will he wake up?" he asked.

Mrs. Ricci stifled a sob, but her eyes never left Zoey's face, and neither did her husband's.

"I don't know," Zoey said.

"When will you know?"

"We'll know more tomorrow," Zoey said. "In the meantime, he's being treated with what we call the head trauma protocol." She explained to them that he had a breathing tube that was controlling his air flow to help regulate the amount of blood flow to his brain. She outlined his medications and described the tests they would be running throughout the night.

Mrs. Ricci said after a moment of silence, "Will you please find out when we can see him?"

"I will. I'll call right now."

When they turned to embrace one another, Zoey stepped out into the hall and let the door ease gently closed behind her. She let out a long, steadying breath.

Declan leaned against the wall across from the door. "How did it go?"

Zoey walked over to her and said quietly, "That was terrible. They're handling it pretty well right now, but I don't think they have any idea what's coming."

"It's hard. It will take a little time."

"They want to know when they can see him. I need to call the TICU."

"I just did. They're ready upstairs. Why don't you introduce me to them, and we can take them up together. Then they'll know who I am too."

"I didn't tell them very much." Zoey ran through the conversation in her mind. Had she said enough to prepare them? Could anything prepare them? "I didn't tell them anything about, you know, the organ donation."

"That's fine. Until the apnea test is completed, there's no point. If they ask about his chances, you tell them the truth. They'll ask when they're ready to hear it."

Zoey glanced at the sign. Family Room. Inside, a family was on the verge of being shattered. "I guess I'm going to have to get used to this for the next couple of months."

"You'll never get used to it," Declan said softly. For a brief moment, she cupped Zoey's arm just above her elbow. A slight touch, a bit of pressure that said she understood, that she shared her sorrow, that she was *there*. A touch more intimate than any caress Zoey'd ever experienced.

Declan stepped away. "Are you ready?"

No, not at all. Not in the least. Not for any of this, whatever it was.

"Of course." Zoey kept her voice light and sure. "I'm fine."

Because no matter what she faced—fear, pain, or loss—that was what she always said.

CHAPTER NINE

When the last transplant case finished at nine thirty, Zoey helped transport the patient to the recovery room, wrote the post-op orders, dictated the op note, and dragged her flagging body into the locker room. The early morning traumas had disrupted the regular OR schedule so much, Dr. Doolin's first case hadn't even started until two in the afternoon. As senior resident on the service, Zoey was expected to stay until everything was done, and she would have no matter what her role on the team. Many of the transplant patients required shunt placement for vascular access, and those cases almost always went to the residents as teaching cases. She never wanted to miss a case, even if all she did was hold retractors. Anything could happen in the OR, and learning to handle the unanticipated made for a better surgeon.

Now the work was almost done, and she was more than ready to leave. Only one more thing to do.

She changed into yet another pair of clean scrubs, pulled the plastic bag containing the bloody street clothes she'd worn to the hospital a light-year earlier from the bottom of her locker, and crammed it in her backpack. When she got home, she'd probably trash the lot. Served her right for giving in to her urge to dress up just a teeny bit. Every now and then she wanted to feel sexy, and scrubs just didn't do it. Not on her, at least. Declan looked pretty hot in them. And *oo-kay*. That was a weird segue. Maybe she really did need to get out more. She'd gotten pretty comfortable relying on Emmett for…too much.

After a quick check back in the recovery room to make sure all the post-op transplant patients were stable, she walked down the hall to the TICU. The unit was a different world at night. Eight beds with just enough space between them to allow two people to stand back-to-back, separated by partially drawn curtains, lined the wall across from the central station. A pair of private rooms with large windows allowing staff to easily see the patients without entering occupied each end of the unit. Monitors still beeped, IV-pump motors still churned by every bedside, and ventilators cycled oxygen through breathing tubes, but the lights were turned down low, the staff tended to talk in hushed tones, and the gaggle of attendings and house staff that surrounded the patient beds during the day was absent. Other than the intensive care unit night staff who were all busy checking patients, the only house staff at the central station was Emmett. Zoey wasn't surprised to see her. This was Emmett's first day as the chief surgical resident. That made her responsible for the surgical house staff and the job they did, even if she had no way of overseeing each of them personally. Knowing Emmett, she'd try.

"Hey," Zoey said as she dropped into a chair next to Emmett. "Are you about done?"

"Just finishing," Emmett said, racking the tablet she'd been reviewing. "You?"

"Yeah." Zoey rubbed her face. "I just wanted to check on Tony Ricci."

"I just did," Emmett said. "No change."

Zoey sighed. "I'll just take a quick look. You walking home?"

"Waiting for Syd."

"Oh, right." Zoey smiled. A couple thing. Right. "I'll see if Dani's around."

"I think she left about an hour ago."

"Okay." Zoey stood. "See you tomorrow, then."

"'Night," Emmett said.

Tony had been given one of the isolation rooms, not because there was any concern for infection or contagion, but because it afforded him and his family some degree of privacy. His chart wasn't in the rack with the others either. The staff had sequestered it in the med room so curious onlookers, who had no reason to be looking at his chart, wouldn't be able to. Zoey stood in the doorway of his room and watched the monitors. Pulse, blood pressure, cardiac rhythm, urine output, O2 sat, all within normal range. His ICP had come down too as a result of the head trauma protocols, but still not in the normal range. She walked to the bed and checked his pupils. No constriction when she flashed her light into them. No evidence of reflex movement in his extremities, even in response to mild noxious stimulation. She couldn't find a single scrap of evidence that suggested higher-level brain function.

From behind her, Declan said, "Hi, Tony, it's Dr. Black. I just wanted to stop in and see you before I left."

Zoey started to step aside, but Declan motioned her to stay.

"Hi," Declan said softly.

"Hi." Zoey hadn't expected to see her and definitely didn't expect the quick surge of heat that settled in her belly as Declan turned back to Tony.

"You're in the trauma intensive care unit, with a breathing tube in," Declan said as she repeated some of the physical exam that Zoey had just done. Resting a hand on Tony Ricci's shoulder, she added, "We're keeping you super-sedated to help things heal. I'll be back in the morning."

Declan squeezed Tony's shoulder, a small farewell gesture that tightened Zoey's throat as she followed Declan out into the hall.

"How are his numbers?" Declan asked.

"Everything is about the same as six hours ago. That's the last time he had bloods. Gases are the same. Electrolytes are fine. CO2 is down."

"That's good," Declan said.

"I didn't say anything to him when I went in there," Zoey said half to herself.

"That's okay," Declan said. "He can't hear you."

She met Declan's eyes. "But you did."

Declan raised her shoulder. "Habit. Patients who *do* have cerebral function can sometimes recall conversations from when they're in a coma. It's never as dramatic as television shows would make it, but you just get used to doing it."

"It's a good habit," Zoey said.

"I got a text from Kos a while ago," Declan said, tossing her cover gown into a hamper by the door. She'd changed back into street clothes. Zoey hadn't really noticed her body in the middle of the alert earlier. Now Bonnie's words came back to her. *Fitness trainer body, good-looking in an andro way.*

Understatement. Great looking. Hot body.

Stop. Right. There.

"Um, do you need me to do anything tonight?" Zoey asked.

"No. We're having a meeting at six tomorrow, neuro, trauma, transplant, and us—well, me, since you're on transplant already—to discuss the treatment plan."

"Okay. I'll be there."

"Are you done for the day?"

"Yeah, I was just heading out."

"I'll see you in the morning, then," Declan said, holding the stairwell door open for her. "Good work today."

Zoey smiled. "Thanks."

Zoey took the stairs on autopilot, aware of Declan turning in the opposite direction on the main floor. She'd just reached the street when a Range Rover pulled up beside her and slowed.

"Zoey, it's Declan. Do you need a ride somewhere?"

Startled from her post-call haze, Zoey turned. Declan leaned toward the open window. "Oh, it's just a ways. But thanks."

The car came to a halt. "It's ten thirty at night, Zoey. Let me give you a ride."

What could she say? "Okay, thanks."

Zoey climbed in and buckled up. Alone with Declan surrounded by semidarkness and the new-car scent, Zoey, more self-conscious than she'd been at any point during the day, folded her hands and rested them between her thighs. This was not part of the script. She knew what was expected of her within the walls of the hospital, what she should do, what she should say. Or not say. Out here, in a world she barely inhabited, those rules changed.

"Where are you?" Declan asked.

In my head, figuring out how I got here. "Sorry?" Zoey asked belatedly.

"Where do you live?"

"Oh, Morris," she said. "Between School House and Chelten."

"Zoey, it's a mile and a half at least."

"How do…oh, that's right, you went to school here." Half a second later, she flushed, infinitely grateful for the darkness. Way to admit she'd been listening to the rumor mill. At least her embarrassment wouldn't show on her face.

"I did," Declan said, seemingly unperturbed. But when did

anything seem to ruffle her? "Residency too. I see that the information highway hasn't changed."

"Ah…right, somebody mentioned it."

"I imagine," Declan said dryly. "Anyhow, I'm not that far away from you now. But you know, the neighborhood is safe and all that, until it isn't. So be careful, okay?"

Ordinarily Zoey would have complained if someone suggested she wasn't capable of taking care of herself. Or didn't know how to, more to the point. But Declan's concern only made that heat low down in her middle spread a little farther. Much more and she'd need to open the window since the AC wasn't helping much. "I always am. But thanks."

Declan glanced over at her, a bit of a smile playing at the corner of her mouth. "Sorry. Not my place."

"No," Zoey said quickly. "It's fine."

"So, you've got one of those big twin Victorians on Morris?"

"Yeah. We're only a block and a half from Quinn and Honor's place. A lot of us from the hospital live around there. That's probably why nobody thinks much about walking around at night. We always tend to run into each other, working the same hours and everything."

"Honor is still on School House?"

"Yeah," Zoey said.

"I think she'd just moved in there when we started our residency. Arly was just a toddler."

"Is it weird being back?" Zoey turned to watch Declan drive, watched her hands on the wheel, her long tapered fingers just lightly cradling the rim. She drove like she seemed to do everything, with a quiet easy confidence. Although there was no traffic, she took her time. The neighborhoods were quiet except for the occasional distant wail of a siren headed to the hospital. Moonlight and the occasional illumination from the streetlights as they passed beneath made it easy to watch Declan's face too. She didn't give much away in her expression, but the tight line of her jaw said it all.

"Sorry," Zoey said. "I'm not very good at small talk."

Declan glanced at her again, a grin unexpectedly breaking her stoic facade. "I'd say you're really good at it. And yes, it's weird to be back. I keep tripping over what was and what is, and it's a little disorienting."

"I bet the hospital hasn't changed all that much, though," Zoey said. "I wasn't a student here, but it's got that sense about it, you know, all the history? You can still feel it in the halls when you walk around at night. I like that."

"I always liked it too," Declan said, turning onto Zoey's street. "It's not like that in Dallas. Everything is new and shiny, and you don't get the echoes of all the voices that came before you when you're alone at night. You know, after midnight?"

Zoey sat forward, surprised. "Yeah, I know! A while back they were renovating the on-call rooms, which basically meant painting and putting in some upgraded bathroom fixtures, and we didn't have enough space for everyone at night. Some of us ended up sleeping wherever we could. Once or twice, I slept in empty patient rooms, and I swear, I could feel...not ghosts..." She laughed. She probably *did* sound nuts. "I'm not crazy, but I just felt time stretching back. Touching all the hundreds upon hundreds of people that walked those halls before me."

"I think you're a bit of a romantic," Declan said.

Zoey laughed again. "Me? Not at all. Couldn't be further from it."

"Really? How so?"

"Oh, well..." Zoey said, wondering when exactly she'd lost the art of conversation. She didn't usually stumble about when talking to a woman. She was usually pretty cool. She always had a good line. She didn't have a line at all with Declan. She could barely put words together, and when she did, what was coming out of her mouth? Spirits? Oh my God. "I don't think any of us can claim to be romantics. Who's got time for it?"

"Just because you don't have time, doesn't mean..." Declan trailed off, and she shook her head. "Maybe you're right. Which one of these is yours?"

"Oh, it's the third one up there on the right."

Declan pulled to the curb behind Dani's Bug.

Zoey waited for her to finish, but she already knew the moment had passed. Declan had gone somewhere, somewhere she didn't want to go, and Zoey had no idea what she'd said to send her there. Declan was such a puzzle—remote and impossible to read one minute, sensitive and intuitive the next.

"Well, thanks for the ride," Zoey finally said.

"You're welcome. Anytime."

Zoey unbuckled, climbed out, and, as she closed the door, said, "Good night, then."

"Good night, Zoey."

Zoey jogged up the walk and, once inside, turned and stared back down to the street. The Range Rover pulled away from the curb, and she watched until the red taillights winked out of sight. That was weird. Weird, and unlike any conversation she'd ever had with anyone before. She couldn't remember a conversation where every word meant so much. With a lingering sense of confusion heavily tinged with wonderment, she set off down the hall to the kitchen to hunt for scraps. On a night like this, after a day where everyone worked late, no one would have cooked. The chance of anything other than fragments of leftovers was unlikely, although if Emmett and Syd were still at the hospital, there was a chance.

Dani sat cross-legged on the counter in red-and-blue checked boxer shorts, a lavender T-shirt, and Cap'n Crunch cradled between her thighs.

Zoey stopped in the doorway of the kitchen and studied her. "I think this is where you were about sixteen hours ago. I do notice that you've changed your underwear, though."

"Ha ha," Dani said around a mouthful of cereal. She chewed for a few seconds, swallowed, and added, "I'll have you know I have showered, washed my hair, performed other necessary self-grooming chores, and changed my clothes."

"You're one shower ahead of me. But I have to have something to eat first. Is there anything?" Zoey asked hopefully.

Dani held out the cereal box.

"Oh no. Absolutely no freaking way." Zoey leaned around Dani and peered into the cabinet. Score. Peanut butter on toast would do. As she prepared it, she said, "How'd it go on general surgery today?"

"Nobody killed anybody."

Zoey grinned. "Good day, then."

"I'm sorry I left without you. I didn't know if you'd be coming home tonight or not. I thought if it got late enough, you might just crash there."

"No problem, I didn't expect you to wait. I got a ride home anyhow."

"Oh yeah? With who?"

Instantly, Zoey regretted opening that avenue. "Dr. Black was leaving at the same time and offered me a ride."

If she thought that would be the end of it, she was more tired than she realized.

"Wait a minute. Back up." Dani hopped down from the counter, made for one of the slices of toast that Zoey had just slathered with peanut butter, and almost managed to grab it before Zoey snatched it back.

"There's more bread and more peanut butter. Make your own."

Laughing, Dani put bread in the toaster and leaned on the counter. "So? Tell."

"Really, it was just a coincidence. She was driving by, and I was walking home, and she offered me a ride. She lives in the neighborhood."

"What did you talk about?"

Zoey stared. "Just, you know, regular stuff."

Dani scrunched up her face. "Regular stuff? Like, what would that be? Grocery lists? Doing the laundry? Personal grooming?"

"Shut up," Zoey said with a sigh. "We talked a little bit about, you know, about what being back at the hospital was like and what it was like there at night. Just stuff."

"You mean like person-to-person. Not doctor stuff."

"No. Just people stuff."

"Did you hit on her?"

"No," Zoey said emphatically. "No, are you crazy?"

"Why would I be crazy?" Dani put half an inch of peanut butter on her toast and took a big bite. That took a while to chew. "You're having a conversation with, you know, a really hot woman in a car, alone, and it's not about hospital stuff. Why wouldn't you hit on her?"

"Because I don't hit on every woman I have a conversation with," Zoey said. "Because I don't hit on anybody, not like that, not really. And I'm sure not going to with somebody I work with who I *just met*."

Somehow Dani had managed to finish one of the mega slices of toast and reached for the second. "Zoey, you hit on people you work with all the time. Everyone does. Who else are we going to hit on? It's not like we have the chance to meet anybody else."

"Not like her."

Dani put her toast down—an almost unheard of motion, her letting go of food. "Not like her. Wow. Okay."

"What do you mean, okay?" Zoey would someday follow through on her urge to strangle Dani, despite how much she really liked her.

"I'm going to stop bugging you about her. That's all."

"And besides," Zoey said, wanting to put an end to this once and for all, "she's married."

"No, she's not," Dani said.

"She most certainly is. I heard—"

"Zoey," Dani said quietly, not an ounce of levity in her voice, "Declan Black's wife is dead."

CHAPTER TEN

I'm in the kitchen," Honor called when she heard the front door opening. A few moments later, Quinn joined her, kissed her on the cheek, and pulled the chair over next to hers at the table.

"When did you get home?" Quinn said.

"About seven."

"Jack asleep?"

"Almost as soon as I got him in the car. Robin said the kids had a big park day."

"Thanks. Sorry I wasn't here to help."

Honor rested her head against Quinn's shoulder. "You can deal with him waking up at five tomorrow."

"Done."

"Did you just get finished in the OR?"

Quinn stretched her legs beneath the table and rolled her shoulders. "No, about an hour and a half ago, but I made rounds on all the trauma patients as well as general surgery. First day kind of thing. Emmett was still there. I saw your newbie too."

"Which one? We've got a full slate of new residents."

"Actually, I was talking about Declan Black. She was just leaving the TICU when I got there."

"Really." Honor frowned. "She was there late, then. I saw her right as I was leaving, and she said she was right behind me when I asked her."

"Well, she wasn't." Quinn scooped a hand beneath Honor's hair and clasped her nape. "She was probably checking on Tony Ricci."

"I'm sure she was. How is he?"

Quinn grimaced. "No change. He's gone, I think."

"That's just wrong for so many reasons. But then, when is it ever right?" Honor sighed. "I told Declan I would take that case, but she insisted. It's got to be hard. She hasn't even been here a day."

"She's going to see it all the time," Quinn said.

"Oh, I know, and it's not like she didn't have any experience with it well before the year she spent as an ER resident."

"That probably had to be the toughest year of her life," Quinn said. "She was lucky they let her use her neurosurgery training to meet the ER training requirements, but even so, I don't think I could go back to being a resident even for that long at this point."

Honor squeezed Quinn's hand. "As I recall, you were really terrible at much of anything except being in the OR."

Quinn grinned. "Well, as long as everything keeps working the way it's working, I don't have to worry about it."

"We'll see that everything keeps working as it should," Honor murmured. She cupped Quinn's cheek and kissed her on the mouth. "And there, that's better. A kiss on the cheek after a day like today is just not sufficient."

Quinn grinned. "Sorry. Falling down on the job."

"Oh no, you're not." Honor stroked the inside of Quinn's thigh. Quinn tensed, and Honor smiled against her mouth. "I'm just anticipating a little."

Quinn's brow raised. "Oh. In that case…"

When she started to stand, Honor clasped her forearm and pulled her back down. "Arly's not home yet."

"What?" Quinn checked her watch. "It's after eleven. She's like, what, two hours past her curfew?"

"She is, yes. *But* she texted like she's supposed to and said she was with Janie and Eduardo. They were at Janie's, and she asked if she could stay a little later. Janie's dad is driving her home."

"Oh," Quinn said. "I guess that's okay, then." She paused, her eyes narrowing. "Eduardo, huh? Do you know him?"

Honor smiled. "Not personally. He's a year ahead of her. His mother teaches physics at the high school."

"So he's, what, fifteen, maybe even fifteen and a half? That's not so good."

"Well, it's pretty common for kids who are close in age but not necessarily in the same class to socialize."

"Uh-huh. Maybe. But an older guy? No. Not a good idea."

Honor laughed. "You might be a tad overly suspicious, but we can ask her about him when she gets home."

"Which is going to be when?"

Honor tilted her head. "I think right about now. A car just stopped in front of the house."

Quinn turned and looked out the window as headlights swept across the darkness outside and faded. "What, you've got bat ears now?"

"No, a teenager."

The front door opened and closed and footsteps approached.

"So, are you going to take the lead on this one?" Quinn asked.

"I don't think we have to draw up battle plans," Honor said, rising to put the kettle on. "Tea, hot chocolate, or decaf?"

"Hot chocolate," Quinn said.

"Why don't we just let her tell us about her night."

"Good plan."

"Oh, hi," Arly said as she zoomed into the kitchen in her usual summer attire of shorts, tank top, and sneakers. "You guys are still awake."

"Well," Quinn said, "since we were waiting up for you, yeah."

"Oh. Right." Arly crossed directly to the cabinet by the sink, pulled down a cup, and pulled out the box with packets of hot chocolate. "Three?"

"Yes," Honor said as she sat back down at the end of the table.

Arly took out two more cups. "How come you're up, really? I texted, and I'm back on time."

"We like knowing you're home," Quinn said.

Arly passed around the cups of hot chocolate. "Are we going to have a family meeting or something?"

Quinn glanced at Honor, who said mildly, "Do we need one?"

"No, not really."

"Not really sounds sort of like yes to me," Quinn said.

"How about you call it, Arly," Honor said. "Do we need one?"

Arly brushed a lock of hair exactly the same color as Honor's out of her eyes. The line of small black sutures that ran across her forehead just above her eyebrow stood out like a delicate tattoo. Fortunately temporary. "I don't know what about."

"Good enough." Honor sipped her chocolate and tapped the multicolored, braided leather bracelet on Arly's left wrist. "That's new, isn't it? Pretty."

"Yeah, Janie gave it to me."

"Ah."

Arly rolled her eyes. "No, not *ah*. Just…well, maybe a little *ah*."

"So?" Quinn said when nothing else followed.

"It's not such a big deal, not really."

"Okay," Honor said. "How was your night with Janie and Eduardo? Anything special going on?"

"Not really, we were just gaming a little bit earlier, and then we started talking, and it got kind of…heavy. Then it got late, and I didn't really want to leave because…well, you know, the conversation and all."

"We know Janie," Honor went on, "because you two have been pretty tight for the last year or so, but not Eduardo. What's he like?"

"Smart, popular. Nice. Not pushy."

Quinn said, "Not pushy. You mean not pushy for sex?"

Honor closed her eyes for a second.

"What?" Quinn said.

Arly grinned. "I bet you were a stud when you were younger, right?"

Quinn's grin eclipsed Arly's. "What do you mean, when I was younger?"

Honor held up a hand. "All right. We've established that we are all cool about sex talk, so is that where we're going here?"

"We were talking about, you know, sex." Arly got up, rinsed her mug, and leaned back against the counter.

"Got that part figured out," Quinn said, ignoring the little kernel of unease in her belly. Arly was an amazing kid—smart, responsible, sensitive. A great martial artist. Okay, that probably didn't make any difference right now. But all the other things did. Quinn trusted her totally, and so did Honor. Maybe she should say that.

"Arl," Quinn said after a second, "you know, if you're not ready to talk about whatever's going on, you don't have to. Whatever it is, you're not going to do something wrong or dumb."

"Really?" Arly looked from Quinn to Honor.

"Really," Honor said. "Quinn's right. We trust you. But we also want you to know that we are ready to talk if and when you want to."

"Okay. That's cool." She pushed away from the counter. "I'm going to bed, then. I have to be at the pool at eight tomorrow. I switched with Gino, so I've got the early shift, and the pollywog lessons are scheduled for eight thirty."

"We'll probably be gone when you get up," Honor said. "Don't forget to check in on Jack when your shift is over. Make sure Robin doesn't need a hand."

"I will." Arly paused in the door. "So you're both cool with me dating girls or guys, right?"

Dating. The first time Arly had actually brought up dating. Quinn passed the ball to Honor with a look.

"As long as you follow a few rules." Honor held up a finger. "We know when you're planning to go out with someone, *and* we know who they are. We know where you're going, and if your plans change, you text us an update. You do not ride with anyone unless we approve. No drugs or alcohol goes without saying. And if you even start thinking about sex, we need to discuss it."

Arly huffed. "Is there a rule book I could carry with me for reference?"

"There can be," Quinn said. "Pocket-sized work for you?"

"I was kidding, Quinn," Arly said, but she was grinning again.

"And," Honor added, "you do not date anyone who does not treat you properly. And you know what I mean by that."

"Properly. Wow." Arly rolled her eyes. "That sounds like...very motherly."

"That would be because I am."

"Yeah, I know. Okay. I got it. 'Night."

"'Night," Honor called. As Arly's footsteps retreated, she glanced at Quinn. "I think that's what she wanted to tell us."

"We kinda knew that, right?" Quinn said. "She's always said she liked boys and girls pretty much the same."

"You're right." Honor looked in the direction Arly had disappeared, as if she could still see her through the walls. As if she wanted to always keep her in sight. She sighed. "She's okay, don't you think?"

"I think she's just fine." Quinn squeezed Honor's hand. "She's the best kid I've ever met."

"I love you, you know," Honor said.

"I love you too. Try not to worry about her." Quinn rose and pulled Honor to her feet. "So, about that kiss."

Honor threaded her arm around Quinn's waist. "There are more."

"You get the hot chocolate. I'll get the lights."

❖

Declan Black's wife is dead.

"What?" Zoey said sharply. The words bounced around in her head like a wild bird trapped in a cage. Ricocheting so quickly she could barely make sense of them. No way would Dani say that if she wasn't sure, but still she resisted. "How do you know?"

"It's on the internet," Dani said quietly.

"What? Like Twitter or something? People are talking about her private life on the *internet*? Oh my God. That's horrible."

"No," Dani said shaking her head emphatically. "Not there. No one's talking. I googled her."

The white noise in Zoey's head quieted. "Why?"

"Because I was curious. She's interesting. You said so yourself. And something didn't fit, so I just looked her up."

"And what, found some, I don't know, gossip? Isn't it bad enough people are already talking about her in the *cafeteria*?"

"Not gossip either," Dani said patiently. "I found some articles about her wife. Well, about both of them, really. Did you know that her wife is an heiress? Was an heiress."

"No. How would I know that? I just met her." Had she really just met Declan that morning? They'd handled traumas together, shared the wrenching experience of telling a family their son might never wake up, and even found they had similar feelings about being on call, alone, late at night. And she hadn't stopped thinking about her for more than a minute or two when she hadn't been with her. Declan had walked into her life in a way no one else she'd ever met had done. Not the time to think about any of that now. "I did hear they were some kind of power couple."

"Oh, for sure. Very high society," Dani continued. "Her father is some Texas oil billionaire guy who practically owns half the medical system in Texas. Big chunks of various hospitals. That solves one mystery."

"What do you mean?" Zoey asked, still stuck on readjusting her view of Declan. No wonder she was so remote and reserved. She was probably still in mourning.

"As to the question of why Black didn't stay on here…" Dani gave her a perplexed look. "Her father-in-law practically owned a hospital—a prestigious one. Who wouldn't take a job offer when it came wrapped up with a billion-dollar bow."

"We don't know that," Zoey muttered. "Her wife was a doctor?"

"No, chief financial officer of one of the family businesses. But she was a superstar at Wharton, and I guess they met somehow and got married when Dr. Black was a chief resident." Dani shrugged. "Anyhow, when Annabelle Jeffries died, it was big news."

Zoey frowned. "Annabelle Jeff—oh, you mean Declan's wife."

"Yeah," Dani said. "I saw a headline about their wedding. Maybe she wanted to keep the famous family name."

"Can we not speculate for a little while," Zoey said, temper rising out of nowhere. Talking about Declan like this left her vaguely uncomfortable, even though the information was out there for the world to see. And how sucky was that. "How did it happen?"

"Car accident."

"Of course," Zoey murmured, picturing the scar on Declan's face and the lingering shadow of a limp.

"Yeah," Dani said. "Their car went off the road after some hospital benefit dinner thing where Annabelle got some kind of award for something."

"Oh, that's terrible," Zoey said.

"Apparently Annabelle Jeffries died two days after the accident. Lots of funeral coverage, but I didn't read those. I found a couple of brief follow-up articles that said Dr. Black was discharged to rehab about six weeks later."

"That makes sense," Zoey said. And the whole horrible story

somehow led to Declan being here, although she still couldn't see the whole picture. She didn't want to hear any more of it this way, though. "Well, I hope people give her a little privacy. I have to be in earlier than usual, so I'm going to go to bed."

"I didn't mean to bum you out," Dani said.

"No, you didn't." Zoey put some lightness into her voice. Time to retreat behind the mask. When she was sad or disappointed, she'd learned not to show it. She was both now.

"So, Zoey…" Dani said as Zoey turned to head upstairs.

"Yeah," Zoey asked.

"Mind if I sleep over here tonight? Because, you know, Emmett and Syd are practically living at our place now. I'm totally glad they got together and all that, but the couple thing, it's starting to wear on me."

Zoey shrugged. "Hank's been staying with his girlfriend a lot, so I'm the only one over here most nights."

"So you don't mind?"

"No, we've got four bedrooms, and even if Hank comes home, you can have the spare. There are clean sheets in the closet. I'll show you."

"Well, we could save messing up the clean sheets. I could sleep with you."

Zoey would've laughed, but Dani sounded completely serious. Maybe even a couple of days ago, she might have considered it. She hadn't slept with anyone since she'd stopped sleeping with Emmett. She liked Dani, and Dani was super cute with a small tight body, completely different than Declan's tall, lean…oh, for fuck's sake. She ought to say yes to Dani and get her mind off impossibilities that she really had no reason or business imagining.

"You know what," Zoey said after a minute's more consideration, "I would rather have a friend than anything else right now."

"That's a nice way to say no," Dani said.

"But I mean it. You know you're hot, so I shouldn't need to tell you. I'm just not there right now."

"Hey," Dani said, sliding an arm around her waist. "You don't need a reason. I'm good with it."

"Thanks," Zoey said as they headed down the hall.

Dani hugged her and let go. "But you know, if you change your mind, I'm available."

Laughing, Zoey led the way upstairs.

❖

Declan found a parking place half a block from the single-family Victorian that had been divided into apartments. She had the top floor, her own entrance at the back by way of an outside staircase, a small rear porch, and a sense of déjà vu that had plagued her since the moment she'd arrived ten days before. She'd had an apartment very much like this one when she'd been a student and later a resident. She'd loved the place. Tall ceilings, big windows, trees in the yard, and a good morning run to the hospital. A small park two blocks away where she'd stop and sit on her way home at night. In the summer, on the rare occasions when it was still light when she left the hospital, she'd stop there and watch the ducks in the pond. In the winter, the pond would be frozen, and the locals would shovel it and kids would skate.

Then in her third year of residency, she'd met Annabelle. Annabelle hadn't liked it. Too small, too long a commute, too…shabby. They'd moved into a high-rise apartment building farther away than Declan really wanted to be, but close to Lincoln Drive and a faster drive for Annabelle to Wharton.

Declan flicked on the kitchen light and the memories faded. She hadn't really done much since she'd arrived. She'd furnished the place with the bare minimum and stocked the refrigerator pretty much the same way. She checked and found half of the cheesesteak she'd ordered out the night before, nuked it, and sat at the two-person table beneath the window to eat it. She hadn't had anything like that in a long time. An honest-to-God Philadelphia cheesesteak and not the fake things that everyone made everywhere else in the country that didn't resemble anything like the real thing. When she'd finished, she opened a bottle of Dogfish Head pale ale and carried it into the bedroom, turning out lights as she went. She'd left the window open that morning, and a bit of a breeze had moved some of the evening heat out of the room. She sat on the side of the bed and sipped the beer. One day down. The day she'd been anticipating and dreading just a little bit.

She hadn't been sure how she would feel being back. Turned out she'd felt a bit like she still belonged, even after so much had changed. Especially for her. She'd left a neurosurgeon and returned an ER doc. Still seeing the same patients with injuries she'd treated thousands of times before. But she was a different doctor now.

She thought about Tony Ricci and his parents. God, so much pain yet to come.

And not a thing she could do to stop it.

She stripped off her clothes on the way to the shower and didn't bother turning on the light in the bathroom, leaving the door open wide enough to let in the moonlight from the adjoining bedroom. She'd discovered she liked the darkness. Something soothing about flickering shadows that softened the hard edges of objects, much the way the shadows in her mind danced around the memories, never obscuring them, but somehow making them a little bit easier to tolerate day by day. Eventually she'd be able to look at them like distant photographs in an album from a different era. Like the ghosts she and Zoey had talked about, walking the halls where they'd struggled in the age-old battle between life and death, patients and caregivers alike. She ought to have been surprised that Zoey felt them too, but she wasn't.

Zoey had a lot more going on beneath the surface than she let show much of the time. But every now and then, she'd slip and let something show. Those parts she thought she was hiding made her even more intriguing. She was confident and wasn't worried about admitting when she wasn't. She cared but never let her caring interfere with her doing what needed to be done. Someone like her could be trusted. The ones who were experts at hiding their true selves, who drew you along, unsuspectingly at first, until you finally understood who they really were, were the dangerous ones.

Zoey was nothing like Annabelle. But then, very few women were.

Declan stretched out naked, pulled the sheet up to her waist, and folded her arms behind her head. She watched the moonlight dance across the ceiling and thought about what had been and what would never be again.

Chapter Eleven

When Zoey woke the next morning, the house was quiet. She peeked in the spare bedroom and smiled. Dani lay on top of the covers, her arms and legs spread like a sleeping snow angel, minus the snow. She admired Dani's ability to play hard, sleep hard, work hard, and never appear to be fazed by much of anything. That most likely wasn't really true. Wisecracks or a quick laugh or a who-cares-anyhow attitude hid a lot of troubles and insecurities. Especially if you never let down your guard and never let anyone see beneath the smile.

Of one thing she was certain. Dani's friendship, once given, was unshakable. Another time, an earlier time, she would've given serious consideration to the benefits that sometimes went with a friendship like that. She'd enjoyed what she'd had with Emmett, but looking back now, what they'd shared hadn't been enough for either of them. Sex was great. All on its own with someone you trusted and desired and, hopefully, liked too? Totally fine. And just that *had* been fine for a long time. Then Emmett had chosen something more, something she had with Syd that she hadn't had with Zoey. At the time, Zoey hadn't thought about it very much and couldn't seem to help thinking about it now.

Emmett had wanted it all. Why hadn't she? Why hadn't she even considered more? Sure, she hadn't grown up witnessing much in the way of passionate love and couldn't really say she'd ever experienced it herself, but she recognized it when she saw it. So did Dani—and maybe that was why Dani was sleeping alone in the spare bedroom. But why was *she* suddenly asking questions she'd never asked before and couldn't freaking answer? Emmett had changed everyone's game, damn her.

That's all it was. Emmett had thrown everyone off-kilter.

She jumped in the shower and put random, unanswerable, and annoying musings about life and love aside. There'd be time to think about that in another few years, when she was done with her residency and could have a life of her own. Wasn't that what they all did? Put life on hold, back-burnered their personal needs, until they were done training. At least if they were smart they did. She'd seen the residents in marriages and committed relationships struggle to meet the family responsibilities at home and the professional responsibilities of the hospital while competing to make the best impression with the people who'd decide their future, to get the best cases, to learn as much as they possibly could in the short period of time they had before suddenly finding themselves standing alone in a room with a dying patient and no one to turn to while everyone looked to them for a decision. Just the picture of that was enough to make celibacy look good. Okay, maybe not celibacy, but singledom. No, now was not the time for anything more than now and then and casual.

With her head clearer, she dressed in scrubs. Enough with trashing her date night clothes, which she really didn't have much of a chance to wear anyhow. Since she hadn't been on an actual date-date since before she could recall, even *having* a nice outfit was overkill. Still, no reason to throw good clothes in the garbage.

She didn't see any sign that Hank had been home, even to shower and change, when she got down to the kitchen. Maybe he really would be moving in with his girlfriend soon. That would leave the house far more empty than it was now, to say nothing about the rent. Then again, Dani could move over, especially if Emmett kept sleeping with Syd. Which was as likely as the sun rising in the morning. Dani would be a great roomie, and Jerry was welcome too. Just Jerry, though. No way was she sharing the house with Sadie.

She'd last about two minutes before strangling her.

Of course, everything could change in a few days—relationships tended to be mercurial when no one had time or energy to put into them.

She quickly downed a cup of instant coffee, disgusting but effective, stuck a Pop-Tart in the toaster, and ate it as she walked to work. Five fifteen in the morning, already hot and a little bit hazy. July in full bloom. The heat wasn't all that much of an issue since she rarely left the hospital before evening, and the long hours of daylight were welcome on the walk home.

When she reached the hospital, she pulled up the list of patients on the transplant service on her tablet, started on the top floor, and quickly did a walk-through, checking with the nurses to make sure there were no critical problems. The junior residents would collect all the vital statistics they'd need to review before the day began. She made a point to make sure the pre-op patients were ready to go. At a quarter to six she started for the TICU, steadfastly ignoring the tickle of eagerness rapidly growing into a flicker of heat inside. Nothing but anticipation for the upcoming meeting and the packed day ahead. Absolutely nothing to do with seeing Declan Black again. So what if the ride home had been niggling at the back of her mind the entire time she was making rounds. Just leftover snippets of conversation, a glimpse of Declan's face in the moonlight, that rare flash of a smile, so enigmatic and so much more compelling for its rareness. Those were just tidbits that her unconscious mind sorted through in the interstices between the moments when she was focused on her patients. Involuntary, automatic, meaningless.

When she rounded the corner, the stairwell door opened, and Declan walked out.

Declan smiled. "Good morning."

And that flicker of heat ignited into a torch.

Zoey took a deep breath. Put on her professional face. "Good morning."

Declan wore scrubs, as she did, but Declan's were the signature ER navy blue whereas hers were generic OR green. A stethoscope draped around Declan's neck, her phone left a telltale bulge in her shirt pocket, and the trauma beeper hung on her waistband. She looked exactly like every other staff member who spent the day in the ER or OR but somehow managed to make the oh-so-familiar and ordinary outfit subtly, undeniably, flame-inducingly sexy. Her dark hair was tousled and slightly damp. She'd probably just come from the shower. Along with that thought came a very brief, completely unexpected vision of what Declan would look like in the shower, and Zoey desperately averted her eyes.

All right, all that BS she was feeding herself about friends-with-benefits not doing it for her? She needed to rethink that fast, because she needed sex if she was imagining random women naked in the shower. Celibacy was doing serious damage to her brain.

"Zoey?" Declan's smile morphed into an amused lift at one corner. Along with the faintly quirked brow, she'd gone from a ten to stratospheric on the sexy scale.

Zoey jerked to attention. Wonderful, now she looked like a space cadet. First she talked about spirits wandering the halls at night and now this. "Sorry, I was just running my list in my head."

"Oh. Right." Declan smiled again.

Zoey desperately wished she wouldn't do that. Had she smiled that many times in the entire day yesterday? She didn't think so, because she was sure she wouldn't have forgotten.

"I haven't seen Tony yet," Zoey said, planting her feet firmly on solid, nonimaginary, totally nonsexy ground.

"I was by an hour or so ago," Declan said, her smile disappearing and that distant expression returning to her eyes. Not cold, just remote— as if she'd retreated somewhere.

Zoey wondered where she went, and why.

"He's the same," Declan said.

Zoey sighed. "That sucks." She hesitated, struggling to put words to her feelings.

"What?" Declan asked.

"I'm on the transplant service now," Zoey said.

Declan nodded.

"When I was a med student, I wanted to be a family doctor—that was my plan when I arrived that first day." She paused. What was she doing? As if Declan would care.

"So what changed your mind?" Declan's gaze held Zoey's. Intent, interested. A look that said, *I'm listening.*

"I got bored."

Declan laughed. "Why am I not surprised."

"I never felt like I was *doing* anything," Zoey went on, "or maybe not doing enough. Then the first day of my third year I started my surgery rotation, and bam, I knew. This was for me."

"I know what you mean. When it's in the blood, you just know. Anybody in your family in medicine?"

Zoey snorted. "Uh, no. They were…are…not ambitious that way."

"Doesn't mean you don't have the blood," Declan said.

"Seems that way. How about you?"

Declan hesitated.

Zoey mentally kicked herself. *Did it again. She's gone.* Damn it.

"I've got a cousin in DC who's a trauma surgeon, and my mother is a hand surgeon."

"Wow. You run true."

Declan laughed, and Zoey's worry vanished.

"So what are you worried about?" Declan asked.

"Worried. I'm not worried," Zoey said quickly.

"Zoey," Declan murmured softly.

Zoey's stomach clenched. How could the sound of her name strike her so hard, stir her up so much she trembled? What could Declan see that no one else ever had? She had to choose quickly—run or risk. Truth or dare.

Declan waited, watching, letting her choose.

"Yesterday I spent eight hours straight doing routine transplant cases. AV-shunts, one kidney transplant. The rest of the time I was running around checking on patients."

"Uh-huh."

"I loved it."

Declan smiled. "In the blood."

"But…"

"Tony?"

Zoey nodded. "I want him to wake up."

"So does everyone else. Including Tom Doolin." Declan sighed. "We're always torn between the enjoyment and satisfaction of tackling a tough problem, a crisis, and empathy for the patient who is enduring it. Maybe that's why we try so hard to take good care of them all the rest of the time. I don't know. But I do know that when a person dies and wills their organs to help or possibly save a dozen other people, no one is glad, but everyone is grateful."

"I don't ever want to be glad," Zoey said softly. "But I want to be there to do the surgeries when it's time."

"It's a tough specialty, but you'll be good at it."

"You think?"

Declan nodded. "You were a natural with Tony's family yesterday. And you've got good hands."

"Thanks." Zoey could feel herself blushing. What a weirdo, thrilled by a compliment only a few people would understand.

"And Zoey?"

"Yes?"

"If it's all right for me to call you Zoey, you should call me Dec. Up to you."

"Zoey is fine," Zoey said, her heart pounding. "Dec."

"Good. Let's check Tony again before the meeting."

Zoey nodded. Stolen moments that fed the needs she ignored as much as possible might be all she had, but none she'd ever experienced had touched her as deeply as these few minutes with Dec.

Kos Hassan arrived in the TICU just as Dec and Zoey finished reviewing Tony Ricci's status with Quinn Maguire. Dec heard Kos's distinctive baritone in the hall outside the unit before he'd even gotten through the door. She hadn't seen him since they'd shared a drink after a neurosurg meeting in Chicago almost eight years earlier. Even then, their interactions had been strained. Kos had been more baffled than angry when she'd decided to leave PMC and give up the coveted staff position he'd offered her for Dallas. She'd tried to convince him the choice had been hers. But maybe she hadn't been very convincing even at the beginning. By the time she'd seen him again, she hadn't been too sure herself. She'd let down her friend and mentor, and she regretted it now. If she could go back and undo that and so many other things, she would. But she could only be certain never to repeat the same mistake, starting with putting the one thing she was good at first—her job. And avoiding what she'd proved to be so ill-equipped for. Annabelle had convinced her of that.

"Dec," Kos boomed when he saw her, tossing a heavy arm across her shoulders. "Finally got you here!" His broad, handsome features grew solemn. "I'm damn sorry about Annabelle."

"Thanks," Dec said stiffly. Zoey, who'd been standing with Quinn a few feet away, pointedly looked elsewhere. Dec avoided her gaze. If

Zoey hadn't heard about Annabelle yet, she undoubtedly would soon, the hospital grapevine being the most efficient on earth, but for some reason she couldn't explain, she'd hoped it would take longer than this. A fresh start for her was impossible, here or anywhere. She carried the past with her in the scars that ran much deeper than the one on her face. And even if others forgot her past, she never would. But still, those moments spent talking with Zoey—in the car, reminiscing in the quiet moonlight, in the hall just now, carefully navigating the often unspoken guilt shrouding personal reward at the cost of the patient's pain—had taken her out of herself. Had given her the freest moments she could remember in years. Selfishly, she had dared hope for more.

Quinn broke the awkward silence. "Tom should be here any minute. There's coffee in the conference room."

"How about food?" Kos asked.

"Rumor has it."

"Come on, Cohen. Show me the patient."

Kos and Zoey headed for Tony's room, and Dec let out a long breath. "Well, that wasn't too bad."

"Kos doesn't seem the type to hold a grudge," Quinn said as they walked to the conference room.

"No, and I wouldn't blame him if he was still angry."

Quinn held the door, and Dec stepped inside. The room was just barely big enough for an oval fake wood table, half a dozen chairs, and the coffee caddy in the corner. A tray of bagels and doughnuts filled most of the center of the table. Dec poured herself coffee.

"Honor insisted I get privileges in Neurosurg too," Dec said. "I wasn't sure Kos would be happy about that."

"If Honor said do it, she'd already made sure Kos was on board."

"I just don't want...favors." Dec snorted. "That sounds ridiculous, considering everyone I know has been doing me favors for two years. I wouldn't be here otherwise."

"Pretty hard on yourself," Quinn said mildly.

"Yeah, I sound that way, don't I." Dec shook her head. "Sorry."

"Work help?"

"It does. I feel useful, at least."

Quinn looked at the still closed door. "Probably not my place, but do you think maybe talking to someone—"

"Been there. Even took medications for a while. I'm okay. Officially not clinically depressed. Just a little battered and bruised, psychologically speaking."

"That's the official word for it?" Quinn grinned. "Sounds like you'll survive."

"I already have," Dec said, not bothering to state the obvious.

"I'm around anytime you want company." Quinn met her gaze.

"Thanks."

The door opened and a short, boyish-looking redhead radiating exuberance bounced into the room. "Sorry I'm late. My twins are both teething, and my wife threatened to leave me if I left the house before they were both fed."

He held out a hand to Dec. "Tom Doolin. I'm the transplant guy. You must be Black."

"Dec Black," Dec said, returning the handshake.

Doolin looked from Quinn to Dec. "Where do we stand?"

"We're just waiting for Kos," Dec said just as the door opened again and Kos and Zoey entered.

"Well, Zoey?" Doolin asked immediately.

For a second, Zoey sought Dec's gaze. So quickly, Dec doubted anyone else could see it, or the pain in her eyes that she just as quickly hid.

"Tony Ricci isn't showing any signs of brain activity. Dr. Hassan recommends we start the brain death protocol now."

Doolin glanced at Quinn. "Your team will handle that?"

"Yes," Quinn said. "Officially the trauma service is in charge of his care, since you can't be involved other than to communicate with the family through the registry coordinator."

"Good. We'll notify the transplant registry. Zoey?" Doolin said.

"On it," Zoey said briskly.

"What about the family?" Doolin asked. "I'm in the OR this morning. Zoey—you know them, right?"

"Yes," she said.

"Why don't you let them know what's happening and remind them that the trauma service is in charge now. Once brain death is confirmed, we're not in conflict communicating with them. Quinn—make sure your residents know to keep a close eye on his vitals. We're going to want his heart and lungs."

"They're aware," Quinn said.

Dec added, "I spoke with the family yesterday. Why don't I call them now, let them know there's no change, and tell them the plan is to run more tests. Then when Zoey meets with them, they'll be a little more prepared."

"Good. Great." Doolin grabbed a bagel. "If we can get the consent, we can notify the recipient teams and schedule the harvest for this afternoon. Zoey—you're on this until we know."

"Right," Zoey said as Kos and Doolin walked out together.

Quinn said, "I'll let the staff know what we're doing."

An instant later Dec and Zoey were alone.

"You need help with anything?" Dec asked.

"No, I'm good," Zoey said. "Besides, to ask for help is a sign of weakness, right?"

"That's BS, you know."

"Maybe, but plenty of people still believe it."

"I don't."

Zoey smiled. "Then I'll know who to call."

Unexpectedly pleased, Dec said, "You don't have to wait till you need help for that."

Zoey didn't ask what she meant, and Dec was glad. She wasn't sure herself, but she didn't regret the offer.

CHAPTER TWELVE

Dec found an empty conference room where she'd have some privacy to call the Riccis with an update. She doubted either of them would be asleep despite the earliness of the hour. Once she had them both on speakerphone she said, "Tony's status is unchanged overnight, but the trauma service will be running many different forms of assessment this morning, so we'll have more information then."

"Can we see him first?" his father asked.

"Of course. You can see him now, Mr. Ricci," Dec said. "All you need to do is go up to the trauma intensive care unit and let the nurses know that you and your wife are there. You'll be able to see him right away."

"And these tests," Mr. Ricci repeated, "they'll be able to tell us when he might wake up, correct?"

Dec said, "They'll give us an answer to many of your questions. It will be easier to explain those things after the tests are completed when you're here in person."

A long silence followed, and then Mr. Ricci cleared his throat and said, "We'll be there within the hour."

"It may be several hours before any of the test results come in, but Dr. Cohen will be available to speak with you this morning, after you've seen Tony."

"That's fine, fine," Mr. Ricci said distantly. "Thank you."

"You're welcome," Dec said softly. She disconnected, pocketed her phone, and rubbed her face with both hands. The first steps had been taken in what would prove to be a difficult process, and hers had been the easiest part of the job. Zoey would have the much harder task when she sat down with the Riccis and finally said what they did not want to hear, that Tony was not expected to wake up.

Zoey could handle it, but the first time was going to be the hardest. Dec had done her fair share of head trauma cases despite having specialized in aneurysm microsurgery, and far too often the patients were young and otherwise healthy, and perfect donors. The message never got any easier to give.

And she knew, no matter how well-prepared or how informed a family member might be, the message was nearly impossible to absorb.

With a sigh, she headed for the ER break room for another cup of coffee before shift change. Blessedly, the room was empty and the coffee reasonably fresh, and she sat in her usual spot at the table to drink it. As usually happened, footsteps approached almost immediately, and she mentally adjusted her expectations. At the very least, she'd have company, and considering that she'd be spending more time with the ER staff than anyone else she was likely to meet, she needed to be minimally conversant. On the other hand, someone might need a consult or a patient might need to be seen right away, in which case she would not be finishing her coffee. A third possibility quickly formed and jolted her pulse like a shot of adrenaline. Zoey might be looking for her.

Dec tensed, watching the door with a wholly unwarranted and foreign burst of anticipation.

A teenager popped into the room and skidded to a halt.

"Oh, sorry," she said, "I was just going to wait in here for my mo—uh, Dr. Blake."

Not Zoey. Absolutely no reason it should be and even less reason for her reaction.

Dec took a second look at the newcomer and smiled. The eyes were unmistakable, as was the red-blond hair. The nose was a little narrower, and the mouth just a little bit wider, but there was no doubt who she was. "You're Arly Blake, right? I'm Declan Black, one of the ER docs."

"Arly Maguire-Blake," she said, coming forward with her hand outstretched. "Hi."

"Hi."

"Is it okay if I wait in here?" She pointed to a fine row of tiny black sutures marching just above her left eyebrow. "I'm supposed to come in this morning to get them out."

"Sure. I think your mom is in a meeting. I can take them out for you, if you want."

"You don't mind?"

"No. Not at all."

"That would be cool. Thanks." Arly added, "You're my mom's friend from medical school, right? I heard her say you were coming."

Dec nodded. "That's right. I just moved back up here from Dallas."

"Sorry, I don't remember you."

Dec laughed. "I wouldn't have expected you to. You weren't very old when I left."

"You knew my other mom then too, right? Terry?"

"I did," Dec said. "We played handball together pretty often. She beat me most of the time too."

Arly grinned. "I don't think I ever heard that."

"What about you?" Dec asked, surprised at how natural it seemed talking about the past and, for the first time, recalling a part of it that wasn't painful. "What's your sport?"

"I'm pretty decent at soccer, but"—Arly's eyes brightened—"martial arts are my thing."

"That's pretty tough sometimes, I hear, especially if you compete."

"Yeah, but that's what makes it fun." Arly shrugged. "I don't think I'd like it so much if it was easy."

Dec stood. "How did you get the laceration on your forehead?"

"Breaking boards during my black belt test," Arly said offhandedly as she walked with Dec to the door. "A piece flew up and hit me in the face. I was fine. They could've just put a bandage on it, and I could've finished, but Quinn wouldn't let me."

"I can see why. You can't really take a chance doing something that physical if your vision isn't quite right."

"Quinn doesn't take chances," Arly said matter-of-factly. "Especially not where any of us are concerned."

And there it was. Arly Maguire-Blake. Honor's new family. Dec didn't envy her that. Honor had always been about family, and even when she'd been a med student had talked about having children as soon as she could find a space in her training to manage it. Hell, she'd been with Terry since they were teenagers, which at the time—and even now—Dec found remarkable. Remarkable but not enviable that anyone could form a bond that deep. She'd never really thought much about children. She'd only vaguely given any thought to love or, even more remotely, marriage. She'd always been far more focused on her professional goals, a lot like her parents had been. She hadn't been conceived until her mother was in her late thirties, after she'd finished her training. One and done, her mother'd often said, as if referring to an obligation she'd had to fulfill. Her father, prosecutor then judge, was rarely more available then her surgeon mother, and both parents valued achievement more than anything else.

So family hadn't been a priority for her—at least not at twenty-seven.

And Annabelle—well, Annabelle hadn't been about children. Annabelle had been about success. That was enough for her—everything for her, really—and, after a while, that was enough for Dec too.

She pointed to an empty cubicle. "Hop up there, and I'll get a suture removal tray. I'll be right back. You sure your mom will be okay with me doing this?"

"Oh yeah. Emmett put them in, and she said I could call her to have them removed, but that seems kind of dumb when you're right here. You don't need to be a surgeon for sutures, right?"

Dec smiled wryly. "Nope. ER docs can handle this kind of thing just fine."

❖

"Hey," Honor said, slipping inside the curtained-off cubicle. "Andre told me you were here."

Dec paused, the last few sutures still remaining. "We ran into each other in the break room, so I thought I'd take care of this."

"That's great. Thanks." Honor came closer and looked over Dec's shoulder. "That looks good. Shouldn't be much of a scar after a while."

"So," Arly said directing her words to Dec, "you'll tell Quinn I'm ready to start competing again?"

"Oh, I'm getting out of the way of that one." Dec laughed. "Let's just ask the ER chief. Honor?"

Honor laughed. "Nice try, both of you. I think we'll let the surgeon, who also happens to be one of your sensei, take a look at it and decide for us. What do you think?"

Arly snorted. "I think she's going to make me wait at least two more weeks. Let's see—that should be the point at which the wound is strong enough to handle getting hit again. Just in case."

Somehow, she managed to sound a lot like Quinn Maguire, and Dec laughed. "Very good."

Arly grinned back. "Yeah, I get plenty of practice at that." She swung her legs over the side of the stretcher and sat up. "Can I see?"

Quinn handed her the vanity mirror they kept on the shelf in every exam room for just that purpose. "Here you go."

Arly brushed back her hair from her forehead and studied herself with a solemn expression. "The orientation is good. It's just gonna look like a wrinkle at some point, you know, when I'm as old as you two."

"Oh, now," Honor said with mock affront.

Arly jumped down. "Okay, I need to get to the pool."

"Whoa," Dec said. "Are you planning on getting that wet today?"

"Well, I'm a lifeguard, so I'd say it's in my job description."

"In that case, let me put a couple Steri-Strips on it. Leave them on until they fall off."

Arly leaned back against the stretcher and waited while Dec applied the Steri-Strips.

"Thanks," she said and shot out through the curtain.

Dec smiled. "She's quite a kid."

"You're right about that." Love shone in Honor's eyes.

"And you've got another one, what is he, three?"

"Almost."

"She asked me how long we've been friends," Dec said. "And if I knew Terry. I said I did."

"She knows all about her," Honor said. "So does Quinn."

"I figured that. Knowing you." Dec hesitated. "I don't know what your life is now, but I can tell you're happy. I'm glad."

Honor smiled. "You knew me with Terry, and without her. Terry was the love of my life. The life I had before she died. Now I have another life, one that took a fair amount of time for me to get ready for, but I changed, and so did my life. Now Quinn and Arly and Jack are my life."

"I'd say you're lucky, but I don't believe that," Dec said. "I'd say you're one of the strongest women I've ever met, and one with a tremendous capacity for compassion and love. So I'd say you're not lucky—you have the life you deserve."

"Why do I think you're saying you don't believe that you deserve the same thing?"

Dec couldn't say anything to that without explaining more than she cared to. More than she wanted to examine in her own mind and certainly more than she wanted to share with an old friend. "I'm not saying anything about me."

"Good, because no matter what we think or feel at any point in life, we all change."

"No argument." Dec pulled the curtain aside, and they stepped out into the hall together.

Honor followed her out. "How did the meeting go this morning about Tony?"

"Kos took a look at him, confirmed what we already knew. Quinn is instituting the protocols, and we contacted the donor registry."

Honor sighed. "Oh, his poor family. I can't imagine…"

"Yeah."

"God, I am sorry, Declan."

Dec shook her head. "It's okay, it's fine."

"Well then," Honor said briskly, "let me know how things work out. In the meantime, we've got some stragglers left over from the night shift who ought to be ready to go home."

Dec nodded, more than ready to leave the personal behind. "I'm on it."

Zoey ordered eggs and oatmeal in the cafeteria and grabbed a coffee. She spied Dani and her team just finishing morning report and headed in that direction. As she approached, the residents and students rose and scattered. When Dani saw her coming, she settled back and waved her over.

"Hey," Dani said as Zoey sat down opposite her. "How did things go in the TICU?"

"No change," Zoey said.

"I'm guessing that's not good." Dani quirked a brow. "You look like you've just come off a killer twenty-four-hour call, which I happen to know is not true."

"Feels like that too. I just finished talking to Tony Ricci's parents." Dani sucked in a breath. "Oh, man. I'm sorry. How was it?"

"They heard me, but I don't think my words were actually hitting home just yet. I don't think anything will totally convince them that he's not going to wake up until they can see him a few more times."

"What about the tests?"

"They'll be done early afternoon, but honestly, I'm not sure that will be enough."

"Yeah," Dani said, "I get that. How hard must it be to accept that someone you can see lying there just...isn't there? So what happens next?"

"I told them that just as a matter of protocol we would notify the donor registry of his possible donor status. That nothing was final or certain until they agreed." Zoey ate automatically, tasting little but so used to fueling whenever she could, it didn't matter. She ate when there was food because there might not be another time for hours.

"How did they take *that*?"

"Pretty much the same as when I said we weren't holding out a lot of hope for him to wake up. Words with no meaning for them just yet."

Dani squeezed her forearm, her characteristic irreverence missing. "How are you doing?"

"I'm okay," Zoey said, and she wasn't pretending. She'd done what needed to be done, what her job was to do, and what she *wanted* to do, for all the people that might benefit from Tony's organs. And for his parents too, who needed not just time but also guidance to accept what had happened.

"Tough way to start a new service," Dani muttered.

"Oh, you know, it's better in a way," Zoey said, spooning up the last of her oatmeal with the last bite of eggs. "I was just saying to Dec this morning that I—"

"Dec?" Dani's eyes sparked, and that tone was back in her voice again. That *oh, this is news* tone that Zoey found both incredibly aggravating and incredibly endearing. Sort of.

"Don't go there," Zoey said promptly, trying to sound patient rather than defensive. "We were just talking about the case, and I happened to mention that I feel about transplant surgery the same way I did about surgery, back when I was a student."

"Yeah, we'll get to the part about surgery in a minute," Dani said, "but I want to talk about the Dec part. When did she become Dec?"

"Well, you know, we always talk about the attendings by their first names."

"Yeah, we talk about them that way, but is it Dec just, you know, between us, or is it Dec between you and her? Because it sounded really familiar, and it rolled off your tongue pretty easily."

"It's no big deal. We've been working really closely together," Zoey said, "so she said that if she was going to call me Zoey, then I should call her Dec."

"Aha," Dani said, leaning forward, one finger pointing at Zoey. "You know what that means, don't you?"

"That she's friendly and considerate?"

Dani rolled her eyes. "Oh, come on. It's a power thing. She's leveling the field. She's putting you both on the same level, which isn't really all that necessary because she's not in a position of power relative to you. She can't get you fired or give you a bad recommendation. She's not a surgeon."

"I think that's putting way too much weight on things," Zoey said, standing and gathering her tray. "Besides, she is a surgeon. Technically, she's on the neurosurgery staff."

"Technicality is more like it." Dani joined her on her way out of the cafeteria. "Besides, the name thing is personal. I think you are ignoring the obvious."

"Dani," Zoey said, "you see sex and seduction everywhere."

"Well, yeah," Dani said with a *whatever* look, "that's because it is."

"Well, not this time," Zoey said.

"How can you be so sure?" Dani said.

"Because Declan is not available." And before Dani could protest, Zoey added firmly, "And neither am I."

CHAPTER THIRTEEN

Honor held up one finger as Quinn appeared in her open office door. "Are you sure you don't need Annie to stop by?"

"I'm fine, Honor, really. I saw Annie and got a gold star," Linda said. "I didn't have a good night—didn't sleep much—and if you thought my feet were swollen yesterday, today makes that sound like an understatement."

"Let me talk to Robin," Honor said.

Linda laughed. "And what, the two of you can hatch a plan to supervise me? I love you for the thought, but I'm really okay."

"All right." Honor surrendered, almost. "But I'm going to call you later just to check."

"And I'm going back to sleep. I love you, good-bye."

"How's Linda?" Quinn asked when Honor set her phone down on her desk.

"She says she's just a little tired, but even that worries me. Because that's not Linda. She never admits to anything, no matter how uncomfortable she is. But Robin is home with her, and I intend to check in at regular intervals."

"Good. That will probably make Robin feel better too. Should we make other arrangements for Jack? I've got cases until the middle of the afternoon, but I might be able to rearrange my office hours this afternoon." Quinn grimaced. "How long did Phyllis say she'd be gone?"

"The cruise is two weeks, but then there's the stopover with the *girls* in Miami."

"Maybe we should tell her no more vacations until Jack is in high school."

"Fine, you can do that. In the meantime, I'll call you if I can't get him." Honor shook her head. "This is one of those moments when I'm glad you've never been pregnant. Worrying about Linda is bad enough."

Quinn's brows rose. "Might I say that this is one of the *many* moments that I'm glad I've never been pregnant." She came all the way into the room and closed the door. "And may I also say that I love our children, but you being pregnant had to be one of the most terrifying times of my life."

Laughing, Honor came around the desk, threaded her arms around Quinn's neck, and kissed her. "It really wasn't all that bad, and you know, as things go these days, I'm still not too old for a repeat."

"If you're feeling an empty nest," Quinn said carefully, "there are also such things as adoptions."

Honor studied her face. "Are you serious about that?"

"I'm open to anything that you need. I'm completely happy with our family, but I like kids, and we have a lot to offer, I think." Quinn paused. "Were you serious about wanting to carry another one?"

Honor circled Quinn's waist and leaned back. "I was a couple of years older than everyone else when I started med school, and I put off a lot of things that I wanted for a long time. I can't say that being pregnant is one of my most favorite things in the world, but if we have another, I'd like to try it again."

Quinn kissed her. "I wouldn't even consider it for a second unless we got the okay of about fifteen OBs and twice as many midwives."

"I'm not sure we have that many at our disposal."

"We'll hire some."

Honor pressed closer and kissed her again. "We can talk about it."

"Anytime."

"And what are you doing down here? Did you just show up to tease me in your scrubs? Because you know how much I like that look."

"I'll remember that." Quinn grinned. "But I was just waiting for a repeat hemoglobin on my next patient and had a minute. I'd much rather spend that with you. Am I interrupting?"

"I've got just about a minute myself. With Linda out, we're already behind." She shrugged. "You just missed Arly, by the way. She came by to get her sutures out."

"Oh, that's right—she has to be at the pool early this morning. Everything look okay?"

"Yes, the incision looks great. Dec took her sutures out and Steri-Stripped her." Honor grinned. "Arly also tried to talk Dec into signing off on her resuming martial arts competition."

"Did she now." Quinn laughed. "The kid is resourceful. What did Dec say?"

"She's not gullible. She wisely said it was up to you and me." Honor smoothed a hand down Quinn's chest. "I, of course, being just as wise, reminded her that you are the surgeon, and you've already said two weeks."

"Good call." Quinn sobered. "How did she seem to you?"

"Dec?"

"Yeah."

"Fine. Why?"

"I don't know her the way you do," Quinn said, "but we talked a few minutes this morning, and I just got the sense that she's struggling. It's a hell of an adjustment, what she's going through."

"It's only been two years," Honor said. "And her whole life has changed. She's always been driven, always been focused on work even when we were students, but she's also always been compassionate and caring. She still strikes me as being that."

"I'm not saying she's not a steady doc," Quinn said quickly. "She is. I can tell just from interacting with her a few times. I can relate to a little bit of what she's going through, from a career point of view. The other…" Quinn shook her head. "I really don't even want to think about that."

"I do know what she's going through there," Honor said quietly. "Two years for some people might not be enough time."

Quinn cupped Honor's jaw and brushed her thumb across her cheekbone. "I'm sorry, baby. I know you know."

Honor shook her head. "I'm okay. I only meant I know what she's going through, and I remember how it feels, but I'm not there anymore. You don't have to worry about that."

"I always worry about anything that might hurt you," Quinn murmured.

"I know, and that's one of the biggest reasons that I don't hurt."

Honor covered Quinn's hand and laced her fingers through Quinn's. "Dec strikes me as being far more serious than I remember, and I'm glad the two of you talked. She could probably use a friend. She didn't have many."

"I know what that's like, when the only thing that matters is getting to the next rung up the ladder—the best residency, the best fellowship, the best clinical appointment. Everything else gets put on hold."

"We've all been there." Honor laughed. "Although I had a head start on both you and Dec—at least until Dec met Annabelle. Then her focus seemed to shift from her career path. I was surprised."

"I understand that," Quinn said. "You pretty much changed the direction of my life overnight. What was her wife like?"

"Annabelle?" Honor hesitated. "Well, I didn't know her that well."

Quinn raised a brow. "But?"

"I can't say I warmed up to her a lot. She was beautiful, intelligent, socially adept. She could charm an entire room in an instant. She just struck me as being…a little cold."

"Ha. Well, I'm sure Dec wouldn't have changed her entire career path unless it's what she wanted."

"Yes," Honor murmured, wondering who had wanted it more, Dec or Annabelle. Not her business and certainly not what mattered now.

❖

Dec spent the morning seeing back-to-back patients, mostly minor injuries and routine medical problems until a trauma alert for a single-victim, one-car accident—the texting driver missed a curve, went off the road into a drainage ditch, and ended up overturning. Fortunately, the driver had been restrained and, other than multiple extremity fractures and a possible punctured lung, had sustained no other major injuries. Unlike Tony Ricci, they would survive. After discussing the disposition of the patient with the ER resident, she finally managed to break away long enough to make it to the cafeteria before they closed the lunch line. If she hurried.

Her phone rang just as she got to the door, and she checked the caller ID: *Zoey Cohen.*

Lunch would have to wait.

"Zoey, it's Dec."

"I just talked to Tony's family again. Are you in the ER? I can come down there."

"I'm about to grab lunch in the cafeteria. You want to meet me here and tell me?"

"Yes, I'll be right there."

Dec waited to go in until Zoey arrived, an unfamiliar swell of anticipation momentarily catching her off guard. She attributed the unexpected sensation to her ongoing concerns over Tony Ricci's case and pushed the feeling aside. Zoey came around the corner at a fast walk, the faint tightness around her mouth betraying her tension. Her hair was tangled as if she'd just run her fingers through it, and shadows that hadn't been there earlier in the morning haunted her eyes now.

She'd had a hard morning, as Dec expected she would, but she still wished she could make it a little easier.

"Buy you lunch?" Dec asked.

Zoey laughed, just a spark of her usual humor showing. "There's an invitation I can't pass up."

Dec smiled. "I realize it's not the greatest choice of menus, but for today it's what's on order."

Zoey sighed. "Honestly, I'm not very hungry."

Dec shook her head and slipped a hand beneath Zoey's elbow, gently steering her through the door and up to the cafeteria line. "Doesn't matter. You have to eat. Come on."

She and Zoey grabbed trays and went through the line, both of them taking the special of the day, which was meatloaf and mashed potatoes with a vegetable medley.

"Very good," Dec commented as they moved down the line, "that covers all the essential food groups. But you need dessert."

"I do?" Zoey asked.

"Yes. I recommend the apple pie."

Zoey tilted her head and frowned. "I'm a berry person myself."

"A reasonable second choice."

Zoey laughed again, this time a little of the light returning to her eyes. "But seeing as they haven't any, I'll take the apple."

Dec put a piece on each of their trays, and they badged their way past the cashier. Most of the tables were unoccupied, and Dec led the way to an empty one off to the side of the room. When they sat down, she said, "Did the trauma team run the protocol tests?"

"Yes, nothing unexpected. He has no brain stem function."

"It didn't go well with his parents when you spoke with them?"

"You could tell?"

"I suppose there's no way it *could* have gone well, no matter what, but you look like you put in some hard time," Dec said. "You want to tell me about it?"

"They are devastated, of course," Zoey said, her tone sharp and brisk, entirely professional.

"I don't know if it will make them feel any better," Dec said, "but he arrived that way. He never had a chance."

"I know. And they might be able to accept that at some point, but they can't right now. They won't give permission to donate his organs."

Dec nodded. "I'm not really surprised."

"Is it always like this?" Zoey asked.

Dec put down her fork and leaned back, studying Zoey's face. Strained, but composed. She was all right, just the normal signs of a tough case.

"Delivering the news? It's always like this. It will never be easy," Dec said. "Hearing the news? Depends on the family. Some never accept it, and we end up with these patients in long-term care facilities with a family that devotes all their emotional time and energy to hoping they'll wake up again. Then there are the families who accept it because they know their loved ones are gone, and they want to believe there's some purpose in their loss. Some redemption for their suffering. Right now, Tony Ricci's parents could be either of those."

Zoey let out a breath. "I feel really bad for them."

"Course you do. How about you? How are you?"

Zoey looked surprised. "Me? I'm fine."

"I know you're fine," Dec said emphatically, "but how do you feel?"

"Sad."

"Yeah. That's okay, you know."

"So what do we do?"

"We give them a little bit of time, and then we'll talk to them again," Dec said. "The trauma service will keep his body as healthy as possible."

"Are you going to see them?"

"I will, with you, unless Tom prefers to do it. At this point it's probably best that they only talk to the doctors they know." Dec hesitated. "Sometimes it helps if a family can talk to the families of other donors."

Zoey grimaced. "I should have thought of that. I'll talk to the transplant coordinator tomorrow. Thanks."

"You're welcome." Some of the odd pressure in Dec's chest eased. "Eat your pie, Dr. Cohen."

"Thank you, Dr. Black, I will."

This time, when she laughed, the smile reached Zoey's eyes.

CHAPTER FOURTEEN

D r. Black," the first year ER resident called as Dec rounded the corner on her way upstairs to check on Tony Ricci. "Do you have a minute?"

"Sure." Dec turned around and walked back to Julian Graham, who looked like a stereotypical surfer dude with his shaggy mop of sun-kissed blond hair, broad shoulders, and cheerful, carefree expression. Dec had made a point of reviewing all the resident profiles during the few free minutes she'd had since starting in the ER and appreciated that looks could be deceiving. Julian *did* seem to have an upbeat, even temperament, and he also had the highest board scores of any of the new residents by a wide margin. Who knew—maybe he was a surfer dude too, although being from Chicago, she rather doubted it.

"What do you have?" Dec asked, the question one that she repeated dozens of times every day. How well the resident answered was a good litmus as to how much their assessments could be trusted, and ultimately, how quickly they could be given more independence.

"A two-year-old healthy toddler who managed to climb out of her crib, open a childproof baby gate, and go downstairs all by herself. She missed the last stair, fell and smacked her head, and has a three-centimeter laceration on her forehead. The laceration runs just below and parallel to her hairline and extends down into the muscle."

Julian nailed the presentation as far as the injuries were concerned, which was the easiest part of the evaluation. Now Dec wanted to see how deep his assessment had gone.

"Where were her parents?"

"Dad at work, Mom at the gym. Their usual babysitter was watching her." Julian shrugged. "Mom usually goes to the gym during nap time a few times a week. Both parents are here—the Turkovs." He looked at his tablet. "Mother, Bonnie. Father, Armen. The toddler's name is Angie."

"Has the baby had any other ER visits?"

Julian shook his head. "Nope. And she doesn't have any other bruises or scars. And other than not being happy about being here, she seems like a solid kid. Not super fearful or withdrawn."

"Okay then. You're comfortable this was an accident as described?" Dec would check for herself, but she didn't get any red flags indicating they were looking at child abuse.

"Yes," Julian said.

"Let's go see her, then."

The toddler curled up on the lap of a thirty-year-old woman with a short, dark brown bob wearing pink and black spandex workout tights and a fuchsia tank top. Her luminous chocolate eyes widened with anxiety when Dec walked in.

Dec introduced herself, pulled on gloves, and peeked under the gauze Julian had taped over the laceration, which was just as he'd described it. Straightening, she said, "That will need a few sutures, but it's very close to her hairline and will likely be invisible in a year or two."

"The other doctor said you could do that right here?" the mother said.

"That's right. You are welcome to stay," Dec said, "but she's not going to like this, and she's probably going to cry quite a bit. We'll have to immobilize her—wrap her up, like in a cocoon—to do it, and toddlers can get pretty vociferous when they're restrained. I promise you, the discomfort will be minimal."

Bonnie Turkov glanced at her husband, a solid, weathered-looking guy with salt-and-pepper hair, a tan work shirt with a utility company logo over the chest pocket, and a faint flicker of panic in his eyes that he probably thought no one could see.

"I think we should stay," he said in a gravelly baritone, and his wife nodded.

"That's fine. There's a stool over there, Ms. Turkov, if you'd like to sit down."

"I'm fine, thank you. Can I hold her hand?"

Dec nodded to the resident, who got the baby board from behind the door and laid it on the stretcher. "I'm afraid you won't be able to do that, because her hands can't be free. Otherwise we won't be able to work. The sooner we do this, the sooner you can take her home."

She held out her hands and waited until the toddler's mother was ready to hand her over.

"Are you sure it wouldn't be better to do this in the operating room with her asleep?" Bonnie asked for the fourth time.

Dec shook her head. "Putting children under anesthesia is a challenging procedure, and far more than we need to subject her to. Once the local anesthetic is injected, she won't feel anything at all. And the injection itself is on the magnitude of a bee sting for a mere few seconds. That I can tell you from experience. She's not going to be traumatized by it. This is the kind of thing that children forget very quickly."

"All right," Bonnie said, relinquishing her hold on her daughter and reaching for her husband's hand.

Dec said to Julian, "Sheet first, over the baby board."

"Right." He didn't move, his expression saying he had no idea what he was supposed to do.

Dec mentally shrugged. Well, he'd done extremely well so far, but first years always had holes in their knowledge base. From the top, then.

"Put the baby board down and lay an unopened sheet across it—the other way. That's good."

"Okay, sweetie," Dec said to Angie, "let's lay you down here."

As quickly as she could, she settled the toddler on her back on top of the sheet and, in the few seconds she had before the baby realized what was happening, pulled the sheet over her, tucking it around her arms and underneath her, and then folded the other end back the other way, pinning her arms to her sides.

Angie struggled once and set to screaming, right on cue.

"You get the leg straps," Dec said as she Velcroed the torso straps over Angie's chest. For the parents' benefit she added, "She's not going to be able to move, and in about thirty seconds, she'll stop crying."

Julian immobilized her legs, and they were set. Angie couldn't wiggle, kick, or grab. She gave it a try a time or two, red-faced and sweaty from the exertion, and then her cries settled down to a whimper, and she closed her eyes. In a few more seconds, she was asleep.

Standing between the bed and the parents, Dec nodded to Julian. "Let's see the bottle."

He held up the 1 percent lidocaine with epinephrine bottle so she could see the label and confirm what they'd be injecting, watched him as he drew it up, and nodded for him to go ahead. "Inject it very, very slowly, and you may not even wake her up."

His hand shook a little bit, but he knew what he was supposed to do and got it done carefully and thoroughly. Angie, exhausted from the stress and excitement, slept through the whole thing.

"Is she all right?" Bonnie Turkov asked.

"She's fine," Dec said. "Go ahead with the first layer, Dr. Graham."

"Armen?" Bonnie Turkov said. "Armen, are you all right?"

Dec looked over her shoulder. Armen Turkov's face shaded to gray beneath his tan. "Sit down on the floor, Mr. Turkov."

Turning back, Dec wiped the damp hair back from Angie's forehead. "Let's get this done now."

After irrigating the incision, Julian inserted several dissolvable sutures beneath the surface to keep the tension off the wound edges and put in a row of fine fast-dissolving sutures. With a child this age, suture removal would be as traumatic or more so than putting them in in the first place, and the slight bit of inflammation that might arise from the body's efforts to dissolve the sutures was an excellent trade-off to more injury.

"There you go," Dec said, lifting the child and passing her over to her mother. Angie, calm and smiling now, had completely forgotten the entire event. "Antibiotic ointment three times a day," Dec said, "and those sutures should fall out in five to ten days. After that, keep sunscreen on it. Any problems, you can bring her back here or have your pediatrician check her."

"Thank you so much," her mother said.

Mr. Turkov got his legs under him and pushed upward, still pale.

"Are you feeling all right?" Dec said.

"Yeah, fine. Sorry about that."

Dec smiled. "Not a problem. Dr. Graham will finish up the discharge instructions, if you'll just—"

"Sorry to interrupt," Honor said from the doorway, "but can I see you for a minute, Dec?"

"Of course. Julian, go ahead and finish up. Good job."

"Thank you." Julian beamed.

Dec slipped out of the cubicle. The tension in Honor's voice and the strain around her eyes signaled something seriously amiss. Honor rarely looked ruffled, even in the midst of a mass trauma alert. "Problem?"

Honor nodded. "Annie Colfax, Linda's midwife, just called. Linda's blood pressure has spiked, she's tachycardic, and her edema is worse."

Dec grimaced. "Right. Preeclampsia?"

"It sounds that way. I've alerted her OB, Hollis Monroe. Hollis is doing a C-section right now, but Annie's coming in with Linda. Annie's an experienced high-risk pregnancy midwife, and if she thinks it's necessary, it is."

"What do you need me to do?" Dec asked.

"I know you're off at second shift, but I might need you to take my first-year lecture at four. First, though, can you see her with me?"

"Of course, to both. If you need me to do anything else, let me know."

"Thanks, I will." Honor started for the ER entrance. "I want to monitor her status myself until Hollis gets down here." She paused. "Hell, Linda's wife is watching all our kids. She's going to want to be here."

"Do you have an emergency backup sitter?" Dec asked.

"Usually Phyllis, my mother-in-law—Terry's mom, Arly and Jack's grandmother—fills in, but she's on a cruise ship. Arly can watch the kids until Quinn or I can get free, but who knows when that will be."

"I remember Phyllis," Dec said. "How about we see to Linda first and then figure out what to do about the other kids. We'll work something out."

The ambulance arrived a minute later, and Dec and Honor met it outside.

A redhead with heather eyes in casual mint-green pants and a short-sleeved, violet-print shirt emerged from the back along with the paramedic, a slender freckle-faced guy with close-cropped, wiry black hair, who guided Linda's stretcher down to the ground.

"Hey, Annie," Honor said briefly as she hurried to Linda's side. Linda reached out and Honor took her hand, leaning over the moving stretcher as Annie and the paramedic steered the stretcher through the entrance and toward an open bay. "How are you doing?"

Linda, her face beaded with sweat, one hand resting on her abdomen, said weakly, "I've had better days. Honor, can you call Robin? She's trying to get hold of a sitter…"

"Don't worry about Robin or the kids. We'll get them covered. Your only job right now is to work on staying calm. We will handle things. I promise you."

When they entered the treatment area, Honor released Linda's hand and backed up a step, keeping eye contact. A bevy of ER staff descended, the team working in fluid synchrony as they had hundreds of times before, inserting IVs, attaching monitors, and drawing blood for lab tests.

Annie grasped Honor's elbow, drew her a few feet farther away from the bed, and said in a low voice, "I just saw her yesterday, and her pressure was normal. When I talked to her at noon today, she complained of more edema and a little abdominal discomfort. That was new, and I was worried, so I stopped by for a quick check. The clinical picture is pretty clear for preeclampsia."

Honor frowned, watching the monitors. "She's what, thirty-four weeks now?"

"Almost," Annie said. "If she progresses, Hollis might decide to section her. The baby may have a little respiratory distress, but we ought to be able to safely deliver if we have to. Not ideal, but given the circumstances, it'll be Hollis's call."

As Honor and Annie talked in the background, Dec listened to Linda's heart and lungs, noting a faint crackle of edema. Linda's lungs were fluid overloaded, suggesting her kidneys might not be working as well as they should. Everything together suggested her clinical picture was deteriorating. She said to the PA, "Let's call the lab and get those electrolytes run stat."

"On it."

Dec said to Annie, who was setting up for a fetal ultrasound, "Are we starting mag sulfate along with the antihypertensives?"

"Yes," Annie said, "and steroids."

"Good enough," Dec said and relayed the orders to the nurses.

Honor slipped up to Linda and squeezed her shoulder. "I'm going to call Robin. Hollis will be in to see you as soon as she's done with the C-section. Shouldn't be long. We'll get you admitted to the OB floor as quickly as we can."

"Honor," Linda said, her breathing the faintest bit labored, "we ought to hold off on a section. The baby's not quite far enough along."

"Don't worry about that—you've got the best OB team going. Annie and Hollis will do what's best for both of you."

Linda closed her eyes. "God, this sucks."

Laughing softly, Honor stroked her cheek. "That's my girl. I'll be right back."

"Tell Robin I love her," Linda said.

"I will." Honor moved a few feet down the hall and called Robin.

"How is she?" Robin said as soon as she picked up the phone.

"She's doing fine right now," Honor said. "Annie's being cautious, and she made the right call. Linda's blood pressure is higher than we want to see it, and the increased swelling is worrisome. We'll be treating both right away."

"You think she has preeclampsia."

"We have to assume that," Honor said. No point in being evasive. Of course Robin would know everything about a high risk pregnancy. She'd been through three pregnancies herself, and they would've talked about all the risks this time, knowing Linda.

"I'm trying to find a backup sitter," Robin said. "Can I talk to her?"

"I'm going to call Arly," Honor said. "She should be finishing up at the rec center soon. She can come and watch the kids until Quinn or I can get free."

"If I can't find anyone else, I'd really appreciate it," Robin said. "It's making me crazy being here and not with her."

"Of course. Don't worry. I won't leave until we're sure that she's stable, but Annie's here to oversee treatment, and Hollis will be seeing her soon."

"What about the baby?"

"The baby is doing well too. Linda should be moved up to OB any minute. I'll call you if there's any other news," Honor said.

"Thanks, Honor."

Honor caught Arly just as Arly was about to start her last lesson.

"Hi, Mom," Arly answered.

"Hi, honey," Honor said. "Linda's here at the hospital and is going to need to be admitted. Can you watch the kids until we can get home to give you a hand?"

"Sure. I have the tadpoles now, and once they're finished, I can leave," Arly said. "Is Linda okay?"

"For now, and we started treatment, so…we'll know more in a few hours."

"Okay."

"Robin's making some calls for a backup sitter. If she finds one, you can just take Jack home."

"No problem. We'll all have SpaghettiOs for dinner."

"Jack's had SpaghettiOs three nights in a row."

"So? Who doesn't love SpaghettiOs." Arly laughed. "I think they're completely gross, but the kids will be happy."

"All right, I love you. Call me if there's any problem."

"I will."

Just as she started back to the cubicle, the overhead system blared. *Trauma alert, trauma admitting. Trauma alert, trauma admitting.*

Honor made an about-face and sprinted toward the trauma bay.

"What is it?" she called to the PA who'd taken the call.

"GSW to the chest," he answered, joining her on her way toward the entrance. "Major blood loss, in cardiac arrest. They're doing CPR in the van."

"Let's get set up for chest tubes, and get the surgeons down here," Honor said to the resident who'd joined them.

"On it," she said.

The outer doors slid open, and Honor grabbed the front end of the stretcher as an EMT pushed the other end and a second ran alongside, performing chest compressions.

For the moment, the life in the balance took precedence over everything else, and Honor went to work.

CHAPTER FIFTEEN

Dec arrived just as Honor and the staff transferred the man with the gunshot wound onto the treatment table. From what she could see of his slim body and smooth face beneath the tape around the ET tube, he appeared to be in his late teens or early twenties. She said to the EMT, "I'll take over the compressions. Do we know how this happened?"

"His grandmother heard a shot and found him on the front porch. She kept saying it was his girlfriend when we got there. No shooter on the scene. Police are on it."

"Good." Dec had never experienced it personally, but she'd heard of plenty of instances where a shooter arrived in the ER to finish whatever altercation had prompted the assault.

The EMTs stepped away, and Dec took up the count while Honor supervised the resident inserting the chest tube on the right side. The bullet wound was adjacent to the young man's nipple, suggesting a deflated lung at the very least and the possibility, considering how much blood soaked the gurney, of a major vascular injury.

Emmett McCabe arrived a few seconds later, moved up next to Honor, and scanned the patient. "Anything coming out of the chest tube?"

"No," Honor muttered. "I think he's lost most of his blood volume already."

The ER resident working next to Honor said, "I can't get a decent line anywhere."

Dec, mentally keeping count and watching the blood pressure

readouts, said, "Cut down on the femoral. Don't worry about being neat. Just get something big in there. He's got no blood volume."

"Right." The ER resident turned away to grab the cutdown tray.

"We need to open his chest," Dec said. "I can't get enough compression with him being so low in blood. Emmett, you want to get on that?"

"Yeah," Emmett said without the slightest hint of uncertainty.

"Do it." Dec had never worked with McCabe before, but Quinn Maguire wouldn't have made her the chief surgery resident if she wasn't practically ready to be an attending. Technically she was still being supervised, and right now that hardly mattered. If they didn't get some kind of blood flow to this kid's brain, he'd be joining Tony Ricci as a possible organ donor. But unlike Tony, he'd arrived with a chance, and to lose him now would be an unacceptable failure.

Dec edged up a little toward the shoulder to give Emmett room to get in on the left side, where she quickly doused the torso with Betadine straight from the bottle, pulled on gloves, and said to Raymond Chang, the ER tech, "You've done this before. Can you assist?"

"You got it." Chang, a former Navy corpsman, pushed a stainless steel instrument stand up close to her right arm and ripped open a sterile instrument pack. With the alacrity born of hundreds of repetitions, he popped open a scalpel from its sterile pack and dropped it onto the tray. Emmett picked it up, walked her fingers down the ribs to the fifth space, and made a wide incision from the midline of his chest toward his armpit. Chang handed her the rib spreaders without being asked.

"Thanks," she muttered, inserted the blades, and ratcheted open the ribs to expose the lung and, in the midline, the heart. The lung inflated and deflated as the ventilator attached to the endotracheal tube rhythmically delivered oxygen, but when she moved a portion of it out of the way with her hand, the problem was clear. The heart lay pale and flaccid, beating slowly and completely ineffectively.

"The heart's empty. We've got to get more volume into him. Where the hell's the blood?"

Honor called, "Let's get another cut down in the other leg. Slide the intravenous tubes directly into the veins, and dump the Ringer's wide open. Come on everybody, move."

"Do whatever you can, Emmett," Dec said as she stopped the

external compressions. "I'll see if I can get a central line, but with him this dry, I doubt it."

Emmett cradled the heart in both hands and gently squeezed. As she began direct cardiac compressions, Dec attempted to insert a third catheter in the subclavian vein.

"I've got a line here," the PA said from across the table. She made a nick in a major branch into the femoral vein and slid in an intravenous tube that she'd snipped at an angle to facilitate its passage. When she opened the line from the hanging bag of electrolyte solution, the fluid poured in.

"Where's the blood?" Honor called. "Omala, squeeze the bag and hang another."

A nurse said, "Marcy's on her way down with it now."

Honor said. "Armand, do you have a line yet?"

"I got it," he said a little breathlessly and started another liter of fluid running into the right femoral vein.

"What's the pressure?" Emmett said, unwaveringly focused on the heart in her hands.

"You got sixty palp," Dec said. That was barely enough pressure to perfuse the brain, but with a hundred percent oxygen being delivered by the ventilator in a kid this young, it would be enough. Had to be enough.

"We need the blood," Emmett muttered.

"We've got more blood coming out of this chest tube now," Honor said. "Something major's been hit. We need another surgeon down here now."

As if she'd been conjured, Quinn ducked into the cubicle and said, "Where are we?"

Honor gave her a brief glance. "Gunshot wound, right side. I think there's a hilar injury. We're getting blood out of the chest tube as fast as we put it in everywhere else."

"Let's open him up, then," Quinn said.

"Get another chest set over here," Honor said and sidled back to let Quinn step in opposite Emmett.

"You okay over there?" Quinn asked as she pulled on gloves.

"Yeah," Emmett said. "The heart looks okay, but we're way behind on volume."

"Probably coming out this side as fast you put it in," Quinn said. "Somebody hand me a scalpel."

Dec reached for the one Emmett had used and passed it across to her. "Here you go."

"Thanks." With a swift unwavering motion, she opened the chest with an incision similar to Emmett's, pulled the rib spreader off the tray, and had it in and open in less than a second. With her hand deep inside the chest and a look of calm determination in her eyes, she said, "Got a hole in the right pulmonary. Give me a second. Emmett, how's the heart look?"

"It's starting to fill."

"Well, I'll just have to hold on to this until we get upstairs," Quinn said. "Let's everybody get ready to move. Where's the blood?"

Honor said, "Hanging it now in all the lines."

"Call the OR—tell them we're gonna need to go on bypass."

In an instant, the wheels were in motion. Emmett, the nurse anesthetist, and two of the ER staff pushed the bed out of the unit toward the elevator while Quinn kept her hand in the chest, squeezing off the bleeding vessel.

In just as many seconds, Dec and Honor stood alone in the aftermath, the floor littered with cast-off IV bags, sterile packaging, and bloodied drapes.

Dec grinned. "Just like old times."

Honor blew a strand of hair away from the corner of her mouth, surveyed the chaos, and shook her head. "We were younger back then."

"Yeah, but we're better now."

Honor tugged down her mask and met Dec's eyes. "We are, aren't we."

"Have to hope so." Dec pulled off her cover gown and trashed her mask and gloves, her body still buzzing with the adrenaline high. "That's gonna be a save. No way that surgical team is going to lose him."

Funny, how she'd already begun thinking of herself as separate from the surgeons, a feat that hadn't really happened the entire time she was working in the ER as a resident. Mostly for that fifteen months, she hadn't felt like she'd belonged anywhere. Of course, she hadn't wanted to feel much of anything. Now she not only had a burgeoning sense of belonging, she'd actually had conversations with people that weren't about her recovery. The moments in the car with Zoey came back to her again and, along with the conversation, the image of Zoey studying her as she drove. Zoey probably hadn't realized Dec had been aware of the scrutiny. She'd wondered then what Zoey had seen. Her instinct had been to shutter any signals she might be sending, but now, she wasn't quite sure why. Zoey's attention was exhilarating, in a way she'd long forgotten.

And that she needed to forget about right now.

"I'll take care of the charting," Dec said.

"You don't have to, but I appreciate it. I want to—"

A nurse hurried around the corner and exclaimed, "Dr. Blake! Annie Colfax is on the line. She says it's an emergency, and she needs to speak to you."

"God," Honor breathed, already running. "Linda."

Dec hurried after Honor, checking the admission board out of habit as she passed. The digital board indicated all the patients were being seen. Nothing urgent needed to be done. Honor put her phone away and turned to Dec, her eyes a sea of worry. "Linda had a seizure."

A fist tightened in Dec's chest. "Serious?"

"She responded quickly, but they're having trouble controlling her blood pressure. I need to get up there."

"Go," Dec said. "Everything down here is under control. The next shift is here already. There's plenty of coverage."

"Damn," Honor said. "Robin's not here yet. She's got her kids and mine. Arly won't be able to get over there for another hour—"

"Look," Dec said, "I was about to go off shift anyhow. I'll go over there and wait until the sitter or Arly shows up."

"Dec, you don't have to—"

"Honor, I'm free, and it's right on my way, for crying out loud. Robin knows me. It's not that big a deal. I won't be able to do your lecture—"

"Forget about that," Honor said, already on her way to the stairwell, Dec keeping pace. "I'll get someone else or cancel. Quinn's going to be in the OR for a while, and I don't know how late I'll be, but as soon as Arly is done at the pool, she's headed that way. She can relieve you."

"I'm not worried about that. Just go."

Honor squeezed Dec's hand. "Thanks."

Dec reversed course, stopped the charge nurse, and told him she was leaving. "I don't have anyone to sign out."

"Right," he said. "See you tomorrow."

She nodded and hurried out to her SUV. On the drive in that morning, she'd decided to start running to work, but thankfully now she had her vehicle. She hadn't thought to ask Honor if Robin and Linda still lived in the same place, but chances were that they did, and that's where she went. Six minutes later she pulled up in front of a single-family, jaunty blue clapboard house with white gingerbread trim set back from the street behind a short white picket fence and a small grassy front yard. The wide front porch held a trio of chairs around a small table and a scattering of kids' toys. She hadn't even made it up the flagstone walkway before the front door opened and Robin stepped out. Linda's wife looked much the same as she had the last time Dec had seen her, her short red-brown hair without a touch of gray and her muscular body still fit in jeans and a black polo. Today the open, easygoing expression Dec remembered was clouded with worry.

"Dec?" Robin said. "What are you doing here?"

Dec held out her hand, and Robin automatically took it. "Robin, I came over to watch your kids."

Robin blinked. "What? You?"

Dec grinned. "I assure you, my babysitting skills are…well… really nonexistent, since I never did it before, but I think I've got the basics down. I'll just be here temporarily until your sitter or Arly shows up."

"What's happened?" Robin held a towheaded toddler in her arms, who regarded Dec with a wide-eyed stare somewhere between curiosity and suspicion. He looked an awful lot like Honor.

"Linda's been moved up to the OB floor, and she's stable for the moment, but she had a small seizure just a few minutes ago."

Robin visibly staggered before she caught herself, her jaw tightened, and her chin lifted. She took a deep breath. "Annie's with her?"

"Annie and Honor. Hollis will be there as soon as she can."

"She's going to need a C-section?"

"It's possible."

Robin closed her eyes. "I need to be with her now."

"Go. I've got this." Dec held out her arms. "Who's this one?"

Robin jostled the toddler and said, "This is Jack. Jack, say hi to Dec. Dec's going to stay with you for a little while."

A young girl around ten appeared by Robin. She had Robin's red hair and matching dimples. "What's up, Mom? Is it Mama?"

"This is Dec Black," Robin said, dropping a hand to the girl's shoulder. "Mama is going to be at the hospital for a while. Maybe until the baby is born, so I need to go over there to be with her. Dec is going to stay here with all of you. She's an old friend of ours from before you were born."

The girl studied Dec. "I'm Kim."

"Nice to meet you, Kim. You can show me the ropes, okay?"

Kim notably straightened and nodded. "Sure, I can do that. It'll be time for supper soon."

"That works for me." Dec glanced at Robin. "What about pizza?"

Kim looked at Robin too. "Mom?"

"Show Dec where the menus are. You can order whatever you want."

Dec held out her arms. "What do you say, Jack? Pizza?"

"SpaghettiOs," he exclaimed.

Dec raised her brows and glanced at Kim. "We got any?"

She grinned. "We've always got SpaghettiOs."

Robin hurried down the stairs, calling back, "I owe you, Dec."

"Don't speed," Dec called after her. "And I'll collect, don't worry."

Robin pulled away, fast, but not recklessly. Kim moved up next to Dec and watched the Subaru disappear around the corner.

"Is she going to be all right?" Kim asked.

Dec didn't need to ask who she meant, and she knew just what Kim wanted to hear. She'd wanted to hear the same words, even knowing they might be lies. Looking back, she was grateful for the truth, and she gave Kim the only answer she could—the only one that wouldn't, ultimately, be cruel. "The best of the best are there taking care of her.

Every single person I'd want to be there if it was someone I loved is there."

Kim gave her a long look, and Dec knew that Kim knew Dec hadn't really answered the question. After a minute, she nodded. "We should go inside."

Wordlessly, Dec followed.

CHAPTER SIXTEEN

As soon as Dec got inside the house, Jack squirmed and demanded, "Down."

"Here you go." Dec watched him zoom down the hall and glanced at Kim. "Who else do we have?"

"Just my little brother Mike," Kim said, leading Dec into what must be the family room, as evidenced by the comfortable-looking overstuffed sofas on either side of a wide multicolored striped rug and the big, widescreen TV against one wall. At the moment, a plethora of kids' toys populated the space between the sofas, and a young boy who looked around six or seven crouched over Transformers of various sizes and shapes in differing degrees of annihilation, accompanied by verbal sounds of combat in a noisy war of the worlds. Jack immediately plopped down by Mike, grabbed a rocket ship, and joined the fray.

Dec asked Kim, "So what do you do while"—she tilted her head toward the combat zone—"interstellar war's going on?"

"Usually I command the rebel troops." Kim's smile faded. "But I don't feel like playing today."

Dec figured she knew why. Her brother wasn't quite old enough to grasp the severity of what was going on, but Kim was. "What time do you usually have dinner?"

"Pretty soon," she said.

"You think everybody's hungry?"

"Pizza, right?"

"That's what I heard."

Kim grinned. "I'm pretty sure everybody's hungry right now."

"Okay. Where do you order from? Pete's?"

Kim's smile, which had been a little tentative, widened. "Yeah. You know Pete's?"

"Sure I do. I just got back to town, but I lived almost around the corner from here for a long time when I was a resident at the hospital."

"That's how you know my moms, right?"

Dec nodded. "Yep. I left, I guess, not that long after you were born. What are you now, eleven, twelve?"

Kim straightened, her eyes bright. "Almost eleven."

"Well, you fooled me. Come on, you know what to order for this crew. Why don't you do it."

"Okay," she said enthusiastically.

A long oak table with eight chairs around it centered the kitchen, while a row of windows above the sink gave a view of a backyard with a picnic table and swing set. Sun bathed the yard even at almost five in the afternoon, one of the gifts of a July evening. Dec leaned in the doorway to keep an eye on the boys while Kim brought her the menu.

"What do you usually get?"

Kim filled her in on the various pizza tastes, which varied for each kid. Dec rubbed her chin. "Um, well I don't think we can get one for everyone, but what about if we do halves on two?" When Kim looked dubious, she added quickly, "No, I guess we better make that three, huh?"

"There's always leftovers."

Dec grinned. "And leftover pizza is the best."

They sorted out the order, and Kim made the call. After she recited the order, she held out the phone, her expression suddenly uncertain and maybe a little scared, and said, "Um…are you going to do the credit card part? One of my moms usually does that."

"Oh, right!" Dec laughed, took the phone, and gave them the number. She handed the phone back to Kim and said gently, "Thanks for doing that."

"My mom's gonna be okay, right?" Kim said in a low, tremulous voice.

"I bet you know Annie Colfax, right?" Dec said.

"Sure. She's my mama's midwife. She comes by to check on her sometimes."

"Well, Annie's there with her right now. So is Honor."

"Honor's there?"

"Yep."

Kim looked relieved. "Okay, but—what about the baby? Her too?"

"Her, huh? That's cool."

"Lucy," Kim said, her face alight. "I'm sorta glad I'm getting a sister. I already have brothers."

"Annie, Honor, and Hollis will be looking after your new sister too—*if* she gets born soon. Okay?"

"Okay," Kim said, finally looking relieved. "Can you call my mom soon and ask her if Mama is all right?"

"Let's wait a while, and maybe she'll call us, okay?"

"Okay."

The doorbell sounded, and Dec said, "That was fast. You want to get it? I'll come help you carry it."

"I got it." Kim took off at a run.

Dec checked that the boys were still engrossed in the battle to save the universe—or maybe destroy it—and followed her.

A second later, Kim gave a little cry of surprise, and Dec hurried down the hall. She jerked to a stop when Zoey stepped inside.

"Hi," Zoey said, sounding as surprised as Dec felt.

Well, surprise at Zoey's unexpected appearance might not be exactly all she felt. She was…excited. No, not excited. Just caught off guard. That was it. That was safer.

Zoey'd shed her scrubs for shorts and a sleeveless tank. Maybe she ran, or maybe she swam, but she did something to maintain the tight, toned body that was very much on display. She looked…great. Realizing she hadn't said anything, and Zoey was watching her with a puzzled, almost uncertain expression, Dec said quickly, "Hi. It's good to see…I mean, hello."

Zoey smiled, the doubtful look morphing into amusement. "When I finished in the OR, I found a message on my phone from Robin asking me if I could sit with these monsters…I mean…angels."

Kim giggled.

"So," Zoey said, grinning at Kim, "I came over as soon as I was off call, but I see that my job has already been taken."

Dec held up both hands. "Hey, I'm just subbing. It's all yours."

Zoey rested her hand on Kim's shoulder. "I used to babysit this troop a lot when I was an intern. I still fill in every now and then when they can't get their regular sitters."

"I'm surprised you had time," Dec said as they all walked back to the family room together.

"Well, student loans—not a lot of choice. I was happy to get some extra money."

Dec would have said she knew what Zoey meant, but that wasn't strictly true. She didn't have any student loans, and she knew how crippling they could be. "It's tough handling that on top of everything else you need to do."

Zoey shrugged. "I try not to think about it too much. I just want to get through my training."

"Good plan." Dec hesitated. She wanted to ask where Zoey'd grown up and where she'd gone to school, but now seemed the wrong time to get personal. If there was even a right time. "Anyhow, it's good to see you."

Zoey glanced at her. "Did you need rescuing?"

Dec arched a brow. "Actually, I had things very well under control. I just meant I'm glad to see you."

Zoey flushed.

The unexpected and altogether sexy response incited an unanticipated tingle in Dec's midsection. "We ordered pizza."

"Then I'm doubly glad I'm here," Zoey said, and this time there was no missing the flirtatious lilt to her tone.

"Oh?"

Zoey's playful expression softened, and she said quietly, "I'm very glad to see you too."

And damn it if *Dec* didn't blush. She hadn't blushed at something a woman said to her in, well, possibly forever. She'd had a lot of responses to women in the distant past, but none that made her feel foolishly happy. Maybe it was just that *happy* hadn't been in her emotional repertoire for quite a long time. Or maybe it was the way Zoey had said it. A little shy, and a little seductive. The combination was devastating.

And now was so not the time or place to be thinking about Zoey, seduction, or the growing pressure in the pit of her stomach. Yet another sensation she hadn't experienced in a very long time.

Thankfully, when they reached the family room, Zoey stopped abruptly, surveyed the kids and the battlefield, and announced ominously, "Make way for the supreme commander."

The boys exclaimed, "Zoey!" as she plopped down with them. This time Kim joined in, and for half an hour a raucous siege ensued—at least that's what Dec *thought* was happening amidst the frequent demolition of rows of ground troops and rocket ships. When the doorbell rang, she got up to answer the door.

Arly showed up along with the pizza delivery girl.

"Hey, Dr. Black," she said.

"Dec is fine," she said and took the pizzas from the delivery girl. After handing her a tip, she motioned Arly inside. "Your timing is excellent."

"I didn't know you were going to be here," Arly said.

"Robin needed to leave, so I came to fill in until you arrived."

"Sorry it took me a little longer than I thought to get here. Is everything okay?"

"Your mom and Annie were with Linda when I left. Linda's up on the OB floor, and they're monitoring her. It's better if Robin is there instead of here worrying."

Arly seemed satisfied with that and said, "Great, pizza. I'm starving."

When they reached the kitchen, Zoey, who sat at the table with Jack on her lap, called, "Hi, Arly."

Jack smiled and echoed, "Arly!"

"Hi, Sprite," Arly said. "Boy, everybody's here."

"Well," Zoey said with a wink, "I heard there was pizza."

"I can take him if you want," Arly said as Kim and her brother crowded around the table, all eyes on the pizza boxes.

"No, we're good," Zoey said, nuzzling Jack's neck. "Aren't we, Jack-o?"

"Jack-o," he declared.

Arly grinned. "He's going to be putting *O*s on the end of everything now—considering his favorite food."

"Sorry." Zoey laughed, looking not the least bit apologetic.

Dec enjoyed watching Zoey with Jack. She was a natural with kids. Maybe she had a lot of siblings. Dec didn't know, and suddenly, she wanted to. She wanted to know a lot of things about Zoey that she didn't know yet. Where she grew up, how big her family was, did she always want to be a doctor.

Zoey caught her looking and raised a brow. Dec smiled a little and shook her head. She could hardly start asking her about her favorite color, or favorite kind of food, or favorite book to reread. Or if she was dating anyone. Especially not the last one.

Zoey studied her a few more seconds, as if trying to interpret the silent communication. Finally, she looked away, leaving Dec faintly unmoored. Unsettled, she occupied herself helping the kids get their pizza. When the meal wound down and the kids along with it, Zoey and Arly, obviously practiced at handling the younger ones, herded them off to get cleaned up and bedded down, while Dec and Kim straightened up the kitchen.

Just as Arly and Zoey came downstairs, the doorbell rang.

Arly said, "I bet that's Quinn. I'll get it."

A minute later, Quinn walked into the kitchen looking a little tired, but more relaxed than the last time Dec had seen her. "Hey, Dec, Zoey, thanks for answering the call. Is that pizza?"

"No problem, Chief. It's always great to see the kids," Zoey said brightly. "And yes, there's pizza. Cheese, pepperoni, or veggie?"

"Veggie." Quinn pulled out a chair at the table, motioned for Kim to come closer, and gently clasped her shoulders. "I saw your mama just before I left the hospital. She was asleep, but your mom was with her. There's lots of super people taking care of her."

"Is the baby coming?" Kim asked in a whisper.

"Maybe. Honor is staying with your moms for a while, so we'll be sure to know right away."

"Are you going to stay with us tonight?"

Quinn grinned. "I can do that."

Dec said, "I can handle it, Quinn. I'm switching to second shift tomorrow, so I don't have an early day, and I'd wager you have surgery in the morning."

Zoey chimed in, "And I'm short call tomorrow, so I'm good too. I can stay until everybody's asleep…or whatever."

Quinn glanced between the two of them. "So you're all good, then?"

"Yep," said Dec as nonchalantly as she could manage.

"Great!" Zoey turned to Kim. "You good with it?"

"Can we watch *Frozen*?"

"You bet," Dec said as Zoey nodded.

Quinn said, "All right then. Arls? Jack asleep?"

"He ought to be by now," she said. "I'll get him."

A minute later, she came back with Jack slumped over one shoulder, his eyes closed and his face unbelievably peaceful. Dec caught the expression on Quinn's face, her strong, always in command expression softening. She cupped a hand around the back of Arly's neck as the teen came up to her, and dropped a brief kiss on top of her head. "Thanks for getting over here so fast."

Arly rolled her eyes, but she didn't move away. "No problem."

Grinning, Quinn said, "Let's get you guys home."

Zoey walked them to the door and came back a few minutes later. She met Dec's gaze over Kim's head. "Well, now I guess it's movie time."

"I like movies," Dec said.

"Do you?" Zoey said softly.

There it was again—that almost shy and subtly seductive tone, as if Dec had just told her a secret. The tone that made Dec *want* to tell her secrets. Almost. The chill that rippled down her spine warned her that was a dangerous idea.

"Can we have popcorn?" Kim asked.

"Big yes." Zoey, her gaze still searching Dec's gaze, held out her hand. "Come on, let's make a double batch. I bet Dec eats more than her share."

"Hey," Dec said, pretending affront while internally easing away from the hold of Zoey's attention.

Zoey shot her a grin, a mischievous grin that did nothing to quell the turmoil in Dec's midsection. Dec watched her walk into the kitchen, realized she was watching her ass, and averted her gaze. Not as if Zoey would actually know, but somehow, she thought she ought to wait. For something. Something, or sometime, safer.

CHAPTER SEVENTEEN

Zoey came quietly down the stairs after getting Kim settled. They'd turned the room lights off for the movie, but the adjacent kitchen lights gave enough illumination for her to see Dec's face as she lounged in the corner of the sofa, the half-empty second bowl of popcorn by her left hand, and her feet propped on a round leather footstool. She still wore her scrubs and tennis shoes, an outfit Zoey had seen her in a dozen times, but somehow here, in the semi-dark, she looked…sexy. And they weren't at the hospital, and they were alone for the first time. Zoey's pulse skittered, and she blessed the dark. She was pretty sure the heat that rose all the way from her core to her neck would show otherwise.

"She okay?" Dec asked when Zoey sat down.

"She's a smart kid." Zoey grabbed a handful of popcorn. "She's worried, and scared too, I imagine, but I sat with her a minute and reminded her that her other mom was there along with everybody else who knew just what to do."

"You're really good with them. All the kids." Dec reached for more popcorn at the same time Zoey did, and their fingers brushed.

Zoey pulled her hand back, jolted by the tingling in her fingers. Static electricity? Had to be it. Except…they were sitting down, and the shock was distinctly pleasant and seemed to join forces with the heat already spreading through her entire body. Another minute, and she'd need ice water to cool off—or an entire ice bath. Couldn't be a hot flash, but it sure felt like what women described. To distract herself from cataloging all the ways her body was behaving like not-her-own, she said quickly, "I grew up with younger cousins—not that much younger in years, but it felt that way. I did a lot of babysitting, so I sort of had to fill in as a second mom."

"Did you live with your aunt and uncle?"

Dec's question was casual, innocent, just the kind of thing someone would ask in a friendly exchange, but warning sirens blared, and Zoey's shields flew up with a resounding clang. She didn't talk about her family. The entire time she'd lived in the sorority, she'd somehow managed to be vague enough about her background that no one ever really guessed that she didn't really belong there. Oh, she'd pledged along with all the others and passed whatever unwritten social and personal tests were needed to get invited to join, and she had the attitude and the grades to fit in. Even though she didn't have the same social interests in guys as her sorority sisters, she'd been low-key enough about it that if anyone was actually bothered by her choices, it never came up. For some of her sorority sisters, her interest in women was even a plus. The curious among them were some of her most enjoyable lovers. But for all of that, they didn't know her, and she never wanted them to.

Even Emmett didn't know her—not beyond what she'd accomplished as a resident and had to offer as a casual, convenient lover. That had been fine too. After all, Emmett was gone now, and Zoey had survived her leaving just fine. What if she'd invested more—revealed more? How would she feel now?

Dec had asked a really simple question that encapsulated just about everything Zoey'd kept secret. If she answered, she'd be exposed, defenseless, something she swore she would never be again.

"Something I said?" Dec murmured.

Zoey shifted a little, turning to look directly at Dec. "No. Well, maybe."

"We could start with something simpler. What's your favorite color?"

Zoey tilted her head, a little confused by the quick turn in the conversation. Had her discomfort been so obvious? What did *that* look like to Dec? Disinterest? Worse, boredom? God, she hoped not. When had she gotten so hopeless at connecting with a woman she found hot? Not just hot—not *just* anything. Dec was so many layers of not-simple that she could imagine exploring her forever. And wow, was she blowing it tonight. She seemed incapable of holding a conversation. She laughed, mostly at herself. "Purple?"

And that sounded like a question. Could she come off any less together?

Dec seemed to give it some thought before she nodded. "I can see that. Purple suits you—a complex color, deep in the color palette, rich and full."

Zoey should have said something clever or sexy or suggestive, but the words disappeared as the fluttering in her midsection broke out into an entire flock of butterflies. Did butterflies even come in flocks? Hordes? Armies? Something that robbed her of breath and speech while setting a torch to her blood.

"I would've guessed some shade of green," Dec said musingly. "You wear that a lot."

Zoey's heart beat a little faster. Dec recognized what she wore? Like, when had Dec ever had time to notice what she was wearing? And why hadn't *she* bothered to get dressed up for work more often? Who cared if she only had her street clothes on for five minutes if Dec saw her in them? "Green? You mean scrubs?"

Dec laughed. A real honest to God laugh that was low and a little throaty and outrageously sexy. Zoey's stomach tightened. This had to be the weirdest conversation she'd ever had with anyone, and she prayed it didn't end. At least not before she managed to relay that she was very, very interested and not the least bit bored.

"Well, scrubs too," Dec said, "but in terms of that outfit, I think I might prefer the blue."

"Same palette."

"True." Dec's eyes narrowed as if she was considering something. "Favorite movie? I mean, other than *Frozen*?"

"You're gonna laugh."

"I can't promise I won't, especially if it's another Disney movie," Dec said.

"What?" Zoey said, feigning shock. "You don't like Disney?"

"I should've clarified. As long as it's not another animated movie. I like to watch actual people."

"Oh, come on, tell me that you never watched cartoons as a kid."

Dec's expression flattened for just an instant. "Actually, I never watched TV. My parents didn't believe in it. They didn't much believe in anything that wasn't directly educational. I think I told you my mother is a doctor. My dad's a judge. They believed in work. In professional things."

"No sibs?" Zoey asked, incredibly curious and incredibly aware she was asking for exactly the same things Dec had asked of her. Maybe Dec wouldn't notice. Because as much as people talked about Dec and pretended that they knew things about her, they were wrong. They didn't mention her dry sense of humor laced with a little bit of irony, or the easy way she drew you in and made you *want* to tell her things you'd never told another soul, or the incredible depth of her compassion when she spoke to a patient or their families. People talked about her high-profile marriage. They talked about what she'd been like as a resident, and they talked about who she'd be dating next. But none of those things were really about Dec. They were just about the image of her. Zoey understood images all too well and how little they might reflect the person beneath the facade.

She wanted to know the woman inside the image.

Unlike her, Dec answered.

"No sibs," Dec said, "but like you, cousins. Also professionals, but I have to say, most of them seem to have a little better balanced life than my parents."

"I don't have any sibs either," Zoey said, and just that tiny revelation made her breathless. Hurriedly, she added, "What's your favorite color?"

"Depends," Dec said. "I'm pretty partial to purple right now."

Zoey blushed. A little, tiny compliment like that and she broke out into a whole-body fever. She needed to get a grip.

"Are you going to tell me about your cousins and how you ended up living with your aunt and uncle?" Dec said softly, knowing she was pushing just a little, but needing to. Every time they got close to the personal, Zoey's mask of a bright, carefree persona emerged. A persona that was really all about putting distance between them.

"My mother…" Zoey took a raggedy breath, and a sea of sadness washed through her eyes.

Zoey's pain pulled at Dec's heart in a way she'd never experienced before. In a way that made her want to reach out and brush the unhappiness away. "You don't have to tell me, Zoey. It's just that I want to know who you are. I don't know if I can explain it any more than that."

"I know what you mean," Zoey said softly. "It's just that I don't talk about it very much to anyone. It might take a little practice."

Dec grimaced. "Believe me, I know what you're saying. I don't…"

She rubbed her eyes. "I'm not even sure I know how anymore."

"Well, there's no hurry, right?" Zoey said, the brightness back in her voice but the pain still so very clear.

Dec grabbed for the tenuous thread of connection they'd had just moments before, moving before she even knew what she planned to do. She just didn't want Zoey to disappear behind the mask. She leaned over the bowl of popcorn, distantly aware that she was probably going to spill it all over the place, slipped her hand behind Zoey's neck, and kissed her.

Zoey's mind blanked, but her body, instantly alive, registered every sensation. Warm silk brushing across her mouth, barely a whisper of heat, growing, growing, firm and supple, calling her name. Zoey's breath caught in her throat, full and hot. The palm cupping her nape seared her flesh, melting her from deep within, molten. Zoey gasped—for air, for solid ground in a world atilt—and found only swirling clouds of pleasure.

Dec groaned, a low, almost pained sound deep in her chest, and her other hand came to Zoey's jaw, holding her face in a gentle vise, tender and unyielding. Zoey's lips parted of their own will, opening with the same sure certainty that flowers opened to the sun, innate, intrinsic, essential. Dec's tongue swept in, salty and sweet, a gentle probing that grew more insistent, deeper, the demand sweeping through her until Zoey grew dizzy. If she'd been standing, she surely would have fallen. Out of desperation born of hunger, she gripped Dec's shirt in her fists, clinging for balance, finding unyielding muscles, tight and strong. Not enough. More. She needed to feel more—more of the faint quivering in Dec's chest, more of the taste of her, more of the wild ache growing inside her, filling her up, threatening to spill over. She tugged, dragging Dec closer until Dec leaned over her, her chest pressed to Zoey's, one thigh over Zoey's. Dec's hands gripped hers and their fingers intertwined. The kiss fused them, molded them with the fiery insistence of a welder's torch.

Zoey's head fell back against the sofa, her body boneless but craving Dec's weight on top of her, Dec's hands…Dec's mouth…on her everywhere. She jerked, the pressure deep inside so exquisite she wanted to scream. Dec's hand swept under the hem of her shirt, touched her bare abdomen, and Zoey arched with a sharp cry.

Dec pulled back. "I'm sorry."

"No," Zoey gasped. "No. Touch me. Please."

Dec made that pained sound again, and her mouth was on Zoey's throat, kissing the pulse that beat there like a caged bird breaking free, then the angle of her jaw, her mouth again, her ear. "You taste so good. God, you *feel* so good. Zoey."

The ache in her voice struck Zoey's heart, a piercing blade of pleasure so sweet she could die on it. She drove her fingers into Dec's hair, guiding her head downward to the base of her throat, needing her mouth, the tug of her lips, needing, needing. *Oh my God.*

"Dec. Dec, I can't…"

Shuddering, Dec stilled and slowly drew back. She cupped Zoey's jaw again, brushed her thumb against the corner of her mouth. "I know. I didn't mean…God, Zoey. I just…"

Zoey pressed her fingers to Dec's mouth. "I think I wanted you to kiss me since almost the moment I saw you. So if you're trying to apologize, don't."

"I can't think straight right now," Dec said, her voice hoarse. "Maybe I should go. Can you stay?"

"Of course." A cold hand settled around Zoey's heart. "Don't be sorry. I'm not."

Dec shook her head, her eyes dark and unreadable again. "Not for the kiss, never for that."

"Good." Zoey forced a smile, tried to sound in control when her whole being resonated with one message…*more, again, again.*

"You're covered in popcorn," Dec said, her fingers lightly tracing the length of Zoey's neck before she finally drew away until their bodies no longer touched.

Zoey looked down at herself. Kernels of popcorn littered the sofa between them, and a few stuck to her leg. She laughed shakily. "Good thing we finished most of it."

She brushed the stray bits back into the bowl, struggling to find normality, balance, when her body was on fire and her brain short-circuited. What just happened? And God, when could it happen again? Dec was a tornado, a whirlwind of heat blasting through her, searing her nerve endings, igniting her the way no one ever had. Even now, she shuddered inside.

"When will I see you again?" Zoey asked before she could censor herself.

"I'll see you tomorrow at the hospital," Dec said, standing abruptly.

Zoey looked up at her. *Don't be sorry*, she wanted to say, but she wasn't sure that's what she was seeing written on Dec's face. Shadows of something…pain? But why? Regret? God, she hoped not that. *It was just a kiss.* The words wouldn't come. She couldn't voice the lie—for her, anyway.

Zoey straightened, forced a calm she didn't feel. "I was planning to go in early to see Tony and talk to his parents again."

"What time?" Dec said.

"Seven."

Dec nodded perfunctorily, her posture rigid and her voice tight. "I'll be there."

She turned to walk away, paused, looked back. "Good night, Zoey."

Zoey swallowed the want beating in her throat. "Good night, Dec."

❖

Dec couldn't remember driving back to her apartment. Her mind didn't start functioning again until she'd fit the key in the lock and stepped into her dark, silent, empty apartment. Zoey was all she could think about, all she could smell or taste. She hadn't meant to kiss her, she hadn't been thinking about it before that instant, but she'd been thinking about *her*. Constantly. When Zoey hadn't answered what she'd thought was a simple question about her childhood, she should have realized Zoey's silence was some kind of self-protection. She had no business kissing her, no invitation to do it, no sign that Zoey had wanted it. But Zoey had looked so damn sad for an instant before she'd hidden it again. Dec had just wanted to bring the light back to her eyes. She hadn't been thinking—she'd just acted.

And Zoey had kissed her back. Zoey had gripped her shirt and pulled her in. Zoey had radiated heat and passion. She didn't have to castigate herself for taking advantage, pressing herself where she wasn't wanted, she was pretty sure of that, but she had no right, no business assuaging her pain or her loneliness or her guilt with someone like Zoey, who had no idea who she was or what she'd done.

❖

Zoey carefully picked up every errant bit of popcorn, took the bowl into the kitchen, dumped the remnants, and washed it out. Methodically, mechanically. As her arousal quieted, and her head started working again, she tried to make sense of what had just happened. But then, what kind of sense did she have to make out of a kiss? Dec had kissed her. A kiss could mean so many things, though. Who knew what a kiss meant for Dec. Loneliness? Biology? Chemistry? Nothing at all to do with Zoey?

And what about her? What the hell had she done, or better question, why had she opened up the way she had—body and soul—for Dec, like a drowning person struggling for air, a starving person falling on food, a prisoner breathing the first hint of freedom? Wild, insatiable, and God, she wanted her again. She wanted Dec's mouth and her hands everywhere, all over her, inside her. She was losing her freaking mind. And all she knew about Dec was that she liked the color blue and her perfect wife was dead, and maybe that was the answer to all of it. Dec was alive and so was her body, but maybe her heart wasn't. The idea left a cold empty feeling at the very core of Zoey's being. All her life she'd been second, and she'd learned to pretend it didn't matter. But it did.

CHAPTER EIGHTEEN

The family room was still dark when the ringing woke Zoey. She rolled over on the sofa, groaning faintly at the stiffness in her lower back from the awkward position in which she'd fallen asleep. Groping on the floor, she found her phone and held it up to her face. The ringing sounded again, but her phone was silent.

Doorbell.

Zoey shot upright, a jolt of adrenaline punching her heart rate into overdrive. Dec. Dec had come back. She jumped up, running her hands through her hair, then over her face, knowing it was hopeless. She'd have bed hair and creases on her face and, God forbid, drool. Rubbing at her mouth, she hurried through the house while trying to straighten her clothes with the other hand. Skidding up to the front door, she pulled it open with her heart thudding in her chest. And stared at the beaming, gray-haired woman in a sunny yellow shirt covered in big white daisies who waited with a bag of groceries in her arms.

"Mabel?" Zoey said in confusion.

Mabel Bellevue said cheerily, "Hi, Zoey. I'm so sorry I wasn't here last night. My bridge club ran late, and I didn't get Robin's message until this morning. I really should learn to check my phone, but I'm terribly bad at it."

"Um, that's okay, that's fine…" Still a little befuddled, Zoey stepped back. She was awake, but the anticipation of seeing Dec was so firmly fixed in her mind, she was having trouble pulling away from it, or dampening the disappointment that she absolutely knew was ridiculous. Of course Dec would never come back. She wouldn't have left if she hadn't wanted to get away, and Dec wasn't the sort of person to waffle. Nothing about her suggested waffling. She hadn't waffled an instant before kissing her.

Thinking about the kiss was not helping.

"The kids are still asleep," Zoey said quietly as they walked through to the family room and into the kitchen. She turned on a light, wincing a little at the brightness, and stared longingly at the coffee pot. "Did Robin call you with any news?"

"Four thirty. She knows I'm always up early," Mabel confided, bustling around the kitchen after she set her food on the counter.

"How's Linda?"

"All Robin said was they didn't know yet if they'd need to do the C-section." Mabel bypassed the coffee maker and picked up a kettle. "You look a little sleepy still. I'll put water on for tea."

Zoey winced inwardly. Tea was not her wake-up beverage of choice. "You know, that would be wonderful, but I really need to get home to shower and change my clothes. I'll get...something there."

"Well, if you're sure," Mabel said.

"Are you going to be able to stay later today?" Zoey asked. "I have no idea when I'll be free again, so I won't be able to fill in."

"Oh," Mabel said with a shooing motion of her hands, "I'm planning to be here as long as they need me. I told Harold I might be staying overnight, possibly for a couple of days. Told Robin too. Robin and Linda are going to need help if they bring the baby home."

"That's wonderful. Well, I'm going to get home because I've got to be back at the hospital soon. You know."

"Of course, of course. That's most important. You go now." Mabel pulled a box of muffins from the bag. "I'll just start getting things ready for when the children wake up."

The muffins almost made Zoey reconsider accepting the offer of tea, but she really needed to get going if she wanted to be on time to meet Dec at seven. She needed time to get some distance from the slightly unreal evening they'd shared.

She glanced at the sofa on her way through the family room. Not even twelve hours ago, she'd been sitting there with Declan Black, eating popcorn, watching a movie, and then somehow talking—or almost talking—about her childhood and her mother, and how unreal was that? She could almost believe that was all a dream. She hadn't dreamed the kiss, though, and if she had, she never would've done as good a job as the real thing. She hadn't even gotten to the point of daydreaming about kissing Dec, although she'd been looking forward to seeing her every time they were apart, and she'd absolutely noticed how hot she was from the very first day. But given everything she'd heard—about Dec and her wife and what had happened to them—she hadn't let herself imagine that Dec would be interested in anything personal. But Dec had kissed her first. A kiss to outdo every other kiss she'd ever experienced, and she liked to think she was a pretty experienced kisser. Definitely enough to know there were kisses, and then there were kisses. There were quick kisses, fast and hard and clumsy, the prelude to buttons flying and scrubs being kicked halfway across the room, and those were okay, because the finish line was all that mattered, not the getting there. Then there were the tentative kisses, the maybe this was something that might go somewhere kiss, but that very often never did. Dec's kiss was nothing like either of those. Dec's kiss had been about *kissing*, about exploring, about discovering, about claiming, about hunger. God, so hungry. She wasn't the only one who'd been hungry, either. Dec's body had vibrated with it, burned with it.

And as Zoey strode the few blocks home, the cool predawn air wasn't anywhere nearly cool enough to offset the heat that flushed her whole body at the memory. She had to stop reliving it. She was torturing herself. Thank God she had a little bit of time before she had to turn around and head back to the hospital, because if she didn't do something about the constant pounding in the pit of her stomach, she really would scream.

She went through the front door and headed directly for the stairs. Dani met her halfway down.

"Oh hey," Dani said, her face still a little fuzzy from sleep. "I was about to text you. I didn't think you were on call last night."

"I wasn't," Zoey said, pausing on the stair below Dani. "I was at Robin and Linda's. Linda got admitted late yesterday. Preeclampsia. They needed an emergency sitter."

"Oh wow, that sucks," Dani said. "Have you heard anything this morning yet?"

"Secondhand message from Robin," Zoey said. "It sounds like status quo, but they're still considering a section."

"So you stayed the whole night?" Dani said. "You're a saint."

"I didn't mind," Zoey said, and the heat of the damn kiss ignited on her lips again. And then Dec's hand… She shook herself. Literally.

"What?"

"Nothing," Zoey said quickly.

"Something." Dani leaned back against the wall, her arms crossed over her chest and her feet blocking the stair below. "Give. What happened?"

"Dec was there too."

"Where? Robin and Linda's?"

"Yeah, apparently Honor had asked her to stop over. So we both showed up."

"Ha. How was that? Awkward?"

Zoey looked away.

"What?" Dani said insistently.

"She kissed me."

Dani's eyebrows shot up, her eyes widened, and her mouth literally fell open. "You're kidding."

"Would I kid about that?"

"Holy hell, wow. What did you do?"

"What do you mean, what did I do? I kissed her back. Wouldn't you?"

"Well, hell yeah, I would've stripped naked and lain down in the OR lounge." She grimaced. "Maybe not in there—the floor is disgusting. But naked somewhere."

Zoey laughed. "Why do I believe you."

"Because it's the truth?" Dani sobered. "I take it you didn't?"

"No, it was…It got a little awkward. I'm not sure why exactly, but Dec left."

"Oh."

Zoey smiled, hoping the pain behind it didn't show. "Well, it was a kiss. No tragedy occurred." She straightened and edged around Dani. "I gotta get a shower."

"We'll talk more later, yeah?" Dani said.

Zoey didn't look back as she climbed the stairs. "I don't think there's anything more to really talk about. She kissed me, and then she left. End of story."

Easy to say. Exactly the kind of thing she'd said after every disappointment her whole life. This time she couldn't even pretend to herself she meant it. The only thing she wanted—well, not the *only* thing—but the thing that rampaged over every other thought in her head just this moment was the desire to kiss her again.

She hurried through her room to the adjacent bathroom, stripping off her clothes as she went. Standing under the water, trying to relax while it ran through her hair, beat on her shoulders, and streamed down her torso and belly, she let her mind go blank. But as the conscious thoughts disappeared, the sensations in her body became all the more intense. And with each beat of her heart, each pulse of her blood, each twist of tension deep in her pelvis, the memory of the kiss grew stronger. The wanting, the needing, the heat and urgency built inside her until she braced herself with one arm against the wall and slid her free hand down her belly and between her thighs. When her fingers found her clit, she moaned softly, stroking the ache that rapidly built to torrents of pleasure spreading into her depths and down her thighs. Shuddering, she squeezed her eyes shut and gasped as the orgasm rose from within her and finally, mercifully, broke over her in a tidal wave of release.

Dec woke restless and thoroughly unrested. She had an hour at least before she needed to be at the hospital. Before she'd see Zoey again. Before she'd have to act like that kiss hadn't shaken her to the core. She'd not anticipated it, not prepared herself for anything like it. She'd prepared herself for what she thought the future would hold in the two years since Annabelle's death. The first six months had been easy, when she hadn't had to think about the future at all. She'd only needed to think about conquering each day, beating back the pain, in her body and her soul, learning to function again, even while knowing she would never be the same. Her only goal had been to find something worthwhile, something to make her feel there was a reason for her to get up in the morning, that there was any value in her being alive. She'd been taught from the time she could walk that goals were their own reward. That the only thing that mattered was raising the bar each and every day and surpassing even that, until one's worth was apparent in the gold stars, the perfect grades, the best scores no matter what the test might be.

After the accident, she'd resurrected those goals and thought achieving them would be all she'd ever want. She'd make a place in medicine again, and she'd prove her worth. Sex hadn't even been on the horizon. Surely not while she was recovering, and not after that in the grueling months while she qualified for the emergency medicine boards, spending many more hours in the ER than required, to blank her mind, to fill the endless time, and to do penance. Living without something she didn't miss had never been a hardship.

Until last night. Last night had breached a dam, and the needs and urges she hadn't even been aware she still had came roaring back. Tasting Zoey, absorbing her heat, reveling in the responsiveness of her body and the urgency of her passion had revived a part of her she had been happy, she'd thought, to leave dead and buried. Now her flesh burned. With the memory, with the reawakened need.

Somehow, when she saw Zoey that morning, she'd need to hide it. Struggling alone was her modus operandi. What she'd learned to do. What she'd grown comfortable with doing. Hiding to avoid sympathy, and yes, maybe hiding to avoid repeating the mistakes she'd so blindly embraced. Right now, though, she needed to find her equilibrium. She needed to run.

As she went through the mechanics of getting ready for the day, showering, reminding herself to eat something, she struggled for a reality check. Zoey was bright and beautiful and filled with passion, and no doubt had many opportunities to share her desire. And why shouldn't she? For her, the kiss had probably been no more than exactly what it was. A kiss.

Dec pulled on running shorts, a tight support tank that left her midriff bare, and her running shoes. She needed to wear herself out physically before she tormented herself any further. Six fifteen in the morning. She had time for three miles and a quick shower before she had to meet Zoey. Time enough, she hoped, to forget the night before.

"You waited for me," Zoey said, surprised, when she came downstairs fifteen minutes later.

"You walking to work?" Dani said.

"Yeah."

"So, I thought maybe you'd want to talk."

Zoey blew out a breath. "Does that equal answer questions?"

Dani tossed her a protein bar. "Your favorite, blueberry."

"You really are angling to move in, aren't you?"

Dani smiled sweetly, and her smile really was sweet, reminding Zoey why everyone liked Dani, even when she was driving them to distraction.

"Syd mentioned to me that she and Emmett wanted to live together," Dani said nonchalantly.

Zoey said, "Oh, well, that makes sense."

"How do you feel about it?" Dani said as they walked out the door.

"About what?"

"Emmett and Syd."

"Oh." Zoey shrugged. "I don't feel any way at all. I mean, I'm not surprised. They're made for each other. If I was them, I'd want to do exactly what they're doing."

"Oh," Dani said, her usual half-provocative, half-curious tone absent. "I kinda thought you were more serious about Emmett than that. I'm glad you're not bummed out."

Zoey paused, thinking back to how she'd felt with Emmett. "You know, I really wasn't really serious. I like Emmett—she's great. And, well, you know, the sex…"

Dani snorted. "Trust me—I can figure that part out, considering how much time Syd and Emmett spend in their bedroom."

"Yes, well," Zoey said hurriedly, "Emmett always was there, you know? So I counted on her, but well…" She couldn't very well say that one kiss from Dec struck someplace deeper than anything she'd ever felt with anyone. She couldn't say that looking into Dec's eyes, searching for what lay beneath the shadows, called to her, touched her, more than anything she'd ever expected. She for sure didn't want to say that Dec made her want to talk about her past. Talk about stripping naked—Dani had no idea how close she had come to the truth. She didn't even want to say the words out loud to herself. "So, anyhow, I'm totally fine with you moving in. I'm sure Hank will be too, if he ever comes home."

"Oh, he's back, and he didn't even seem surprised to see me. I think he's still asleep. He came in around seven and crashed after mumbling something about never understanding women."

Zoey laughed. "Well, then I guess we're three again."

Dani nodded. "Yeah, I guess we are." She stopped abruptly and muttered, "Whoa."

"What?" Zoey asked.

In a hushed voice, Dani said. "Look."

Zoey looked where Dani pointed and stumbled to a stop as abruptly as Dani had.

Dec had just rounded the corner ahead of them, running in the road, *really* running in long, fluid, apparently effortless strides. The only slight imperfection in her form was an almost minuscule tilt of her hips to the left which probably no one else would've noticed, but Zoey took in every detail as if examining her through a laser scope. Her black tank ended just below her breasts, leaving a long stretch of toned abdomen bare. Her shorts rode just above her hipbones and cut high on her thighs, every ounce of her smooth, strong, and sleek. Dec's image, bright and sharp, seared Zoey's retinas. "She looks…good."

"Good?" Dani sputtered out a laugh. "She's so hot I can feel the heat from here."

"Shut up."

"You might want to breathe soon," Dani said, "or you might faint."

"Shut up."

"Does she kiss as good as she looks?"

"Better," Zoey said before she could catch herself.

"Oh," Dani said on a long, exaggerated, and completely fabricated moan. "I'm so sad I might never know."

"Shut up."

Dec had disappeared into the hospital by the time Zoey and Dani arrived. By then Zoey had conjured up a heroic level of willpower and blotted every last fragment of Dec's image from her mind. If her blood still hummed a little, and her insides still tingled a little, she chose to ignore it.

Dani headed off to the cafeteria, and Zoey hurried to the locker room to change into scrubs and dump her backpack in her locker. She pulled off the jeans she'd worn on the walk over and grabbed a clean pair of scrub pants from the rack inside the door along with a stack of shirts and pants for the rest of the week. She hadn't even noticed the shower running in the adjacent bathroom until the water abruptly shut off, and the silence registered. She thought she was alone in the locker room and then turned at the sound of a movement behind her.

Dec stood a few feet away, her hair wet, her shoulders still beaded with water, and a towel wrapped from torso to thigh. Just a towel.

"'Morning," Dec said.

"'Morning," Zoey said, praying to God she sounded normal when she felt anything but. Up close and nearly naked, Dec was gorgeous.

"Good run?" Zoey said, appalled to hear a tiny squeak in her voice.

"It helped," Dec said, turning to open her locker.

When it looked like she might actually shed her towel, Zoey abruptly spun around and peered into hers as if the mysteries of the universe were written on the inside of the door.

"Help what?" Zoey studiously rearranged the stack of scrubs on the top shelf of her locker.

"Run off some nervous energy."

Zoey laughed abruptly. "I know what you mean."

"Oh? Were you running too?"

Zoey's face flushed as she remembered the interlude in the shower. "Not exactly."

"I'm decent, Zoey," Dec said softly. "You can come out of your locker."

Embarrassed—no, make that mortified—that Dec knew she was intentionally not looking in her direction, Zoey straightened, chin up, and turned to face her. Dec was indeed decent in scrub pants and a white tank top. Her shoulders and arms were bare—and nicely muscled—and the remaining moisture clinging to her skin molded the thin tank to her breasts. Zoey's throat tightened. This was torture.

"I'm going to go check on Tony," Zoey said, determined to be cool.

"I know." Dec pulled a scrub shirt over her tank. "I'll come with you."

"Great." Zoey kept her eyes focused just past Dec's shoulder.

"Do we need to talk?" Dec said softly.

"No." Zoey wasn't about to pretend she didn't know what they were actually talking about. "Everything's fine."

"Good," Dec murmured. "I'm glad."

Glad wasn't exactly what Zoey felt as they walked out together. She didn't have a name for the turmoil that the barest glimpse of Dec stirred inside her. And if she couldn't name it, she couldn't control it, so she had no choice but to ignore it.

CHAPTER NINETEEN

Honor rolled over as the on-call room door opened, and a sliver of light angled toward her. She sat up quickly, expecting someone to report that Linda was in trouble, but the quick adrenaline rush galvanizing her into motion ebbed almost instantly, and she settled back, her heart still pounding. Even half shadowed, she recognized the form framed in the door.

"Quinn?"

"Sorry, baby. I didn't mean to startle you." Quinn stepped inside and closed the door.

"Linda's all right?" Honor said.

"Just came from checking on her. No change." Quinn stretched out on the bed beside Honor and slid an arm behind her shoulders. "It's not quite time for you to head down to the ER. You've got a little while yet."

The OB on-call room, just a small ten-by-ten space with no windows and barely any furniture, cocooned them in warm darkness. Honor let out a long breath and rested her cheek on Quinn's shoulder, threading one arm around Quinn's waist. "God, what a night."

Quinn kissed Honor's temple. "Did you get any sleep last night, baby?"

"On and off."

"The nurses said her seizures have stopped."

Honor rested her cheek against Quinn's chest, curling against her as she so often did when they were alone in bed, connecting after long hours apart, listening to Quinn's heart beat. She'd heard it thousands of times before, relied on its steady presence, the certainty that, no matter what, she could count on Quinn's unyielding strength. "But not a lot of progress in settling everything else down, though."

"What do you think?"

"I don't think Hollis is going to wait much longer. The baby ought to do all right, and the main thing right now is making sure that the C-section doesn't end up being an emergency section."

"I agree with that," Quinn said.

"Where's Arly?"

"Home asleep still, Jack too. They're okay."

Honor sighed. "I miss being able to see them first thing in the morning, even if they're asleep."

"I know, me too."

"I take it Arly didn't need to stay too late with Kim and Mike last night," Honor said.

"She had more than enough help when I got there about nine thirty. Dec and Zoey were there too."

Honor laughed. "All three of them showed up? How did we manage that?"

"I guess you asked Dec, and Arly was already on call, and Robin contacted Zoey."

"Sounds like a party." Honor smiled and kissed Quinn's jaw.

"If you consider hanging out with three young kids and a teenager an exciting night."

"I guess it all depends on what you do after that."

Quinn chuckled. "I'm not even going to speculate on that one."

"I was speaking from memory," Honor teased.

"I believe I may recall an evening or two like that, but then we *have* to be inventive with two kids at home. Although," Quinn said musingly, "Zoey seemed awfully anxious to stay, even though she didn't really need to. Dec didn't look too keen to leave either."

"At the risk of being reprehensibly snoopy, are you saying there's something going on with them?"

Quinn shrugged. "I don't know. I just got a…feeling."

"Huh," Honor murmured. "Zoey and Dec. Zoey's nothing like Annabelle."

"Something tells me that you think that's a good thing."

"I don't really know," Honor said quietly. "Dec isn't the same woman she was twelve years ago. Who is? She wasn't so much young, then, as maybe inexperienced. She was so ultrafocused, so determined to succeed. More than that, really. Not just set on succeeding, but to outdo any expectation. Oh, not so horribly competitive that no one liked her. She more competed with herself. And then along comes Annabelle, someone who seemed to value her for exactly that."

"I'm not so sure I see how that's a bad thing," Quinn said.

"It wouldn't be," Honor said quickly, "if she valued Dec for all the other wonderful things about her too. Dec's very perceptive and has a deep well of caring. She's steady and always dependable in any kind of disaster, rather like you."

"Hmm," Quinn said. "I feel a challenge coming on."

Laughing, Honor slapped her on the stomach and slipped her hand underneath the edge of Quinn's scrub shirt. "You know better."

"I do, but I like being reminded."

Honor leaned up on an elbow, her hair fanning over Quinn's cheek. She found Quinn's gaze in the semi-darkness. "I love you."

Quinn stroked her fingers through Honor's hair and kissed her. "I happen to be very much in love with you too."

"How much time did you say we have?" Honor slid on top of Quinn and fit her thigh between Quinn's legs.

Quinn wrapped both arms around Honor's waist, one hand sliding down her butt, molding Honor even closer. "Plenty of time."

❖

Zoey stood next to Dec at the end of Tony Ricci's bed in the TICU. She felt like she'd stood there a thousand times already, and not one thing had changed. The ventilator cycled at a steady fifteen breaths per minute, the monitors flickered with red digital numbers, the EKG tracked across the screen in a steady unbroken pattern, the blood pressure tracing rose and fell apace. Everything perfectly normal. Except Tony was gone.

They moved back to the door and then stepped outside into the main trauma intensive care unit. The night shift had just finished making rounds, and the day shift nurses, PAs, a few surgery residents, and lab technicians in yellow cover gowns moved between the beds, drawing bloods, taking X-rays, checking vital signs. The business of the day had begun, and as long as Tony's vital signs didn't deteriorate, his care was the least demanding of any patient in the unit.

"There's not much time left, is there," Zoey said very quietly. He couldn't hear them, but she couldn't bring herself to discuss the situation at his bedside. That somehow seemed disrespectful. He was still theirs to care for. Dec seemed to understand, and they stepped a little farther away.

"No," Dec said. "Before long, his organs will start to deteriorate, his heart rate will become erratic, and the rest of his body will fail."

"What should we do?" Zoey said. "I don't know the right way to tell them that."

"Sometimes you won't know what to say until you're sitting with them. Every instance is different, because every case is different." Dec glanced at her watch. "What time do you expect them?"

"Anytime now."

And as if summoned, Mr. and Mrs. Ricci pressed the buzzer outside the closed doors to the intensive care unit.

Zoey let them in and said, "When you're done, we'll be in the conference room just down the hall. You know, the one where we met before. We can talk there."

Before Zoey had finished, Mrs. Ricci had already moved to Tony's bedside and taken his hand.

Mr. Ricci looked after his wife. "We won't be long. We can come back after we speak with you."

Dec and Zoey waited in silence in the conference room. Zoey spent the time checking labs on her other patients, hiding in her tablet so she wouldn't have to look at Dec. She was afraid if she did, she'd give something away. Like how much she wanted to say *something* about the night before. *Last night was incredible and I'd really really like to kiss you again* was not only wildly inappropriate given the circumstances, but no way was she going to put herself in the position of hearing Dec say it was just a kiss and there wouldn't be a repeat.

Sooner than Zoey expected, Tony Ricci's parents appeared in the doorway, and the kiss—and the swirl of conflicting emotions attached to it—disappeared. Dec rose and gestured them in, closing the door behind them. She pulled one of the generic blue waiting area chairs closer to Mrs. Ricci, who sat next to her husband across from Zoey in the small cluster. Dec gave her a faint nod, barely perceptible, but enough to let Zoey know she had the lead in this.

"Mr. and Mrs. Ricci," Zoey began gently, "Tony's condition hasn't changed. He doesn't show any signs of awareness. He's not just in a coma. His brain has stopped functioning."

"But that could change, right?" Mrs. Ricci said. Her husband's gaze had gone distant, as if he was no longer looking at Zoey or anything else in the room.

"No, I'm afraid it won't change." Zoey had said much the same thing before, but today she had to be sure the message was clear and unambiguous. The Riccis deserved that from her. "Tony is never going to wake up. If the machines were not keeping his heart and lungs functioning, everything would stop in a matter of minutes."

Mrs. Ricci caught her breath and closed her eyes.

"So what you're saying," Mr. Ricci said, enunciating each word very carefully, "is that Tony is already dead."

"I'm afraid that's true, in the sense that his brain is dead, and his body is just being kept alive by all the machines."

"And if we turn off the breathing machine and stop the medications?" he said.

"Then his heart will stop beating, and he will stop breathing very soon," Zoey said.

"Are you saying that's what we should do?" he said.

"I can't tell you what you should do," Zoey said, "but there are several options. We could stop all life support, and he would be gone in a matter of minutes. If we continue the life support, his body will eventually shut down—in a day or a couple of days—and the result will be the same. The last thing is, with your permission, we could transplant many of his organs into other people, to help keep other people alive."

Mrs. Ricci shuddered. "I don't know, that seems…like a desecration almost."

Zoey said, "Would you like to talk to some people whose loved ones have been donors, to ask them about the experience? To hear how they felt?"

Mrs. Ricci glanced at her husband. "I don't know if I would feel comfortable talking to strangers about something like this."

Dec took a breath, one Zoey doubted the Riccis noticed, but she did. She seemed to notice every little thing Dec did. When Dec saw her look over, she straightened, as if preparing for something. Zoey eased back just a little, letting Dec know she would wait.

Dec said, "Mrs. Ricci, may I tell you something?"

Mrs. Ricci shifted her gaze from Zoey to Dec. "Of course."

"Two years ago," Dec said, her voice low and steady, "my wife and I were in a car accident."

Mrs. Ricci's gaze flickered in the direction of the scar that crossed Dec's forehead, and then back to her eyes. Zoey had to order herself to keep her expression neutral, despite the sudden racing of her heart.

"I don't remember much about the crash, or much of anything right after the accident," Dec said, "but when I finally became aware of what was happening, I was in the emergency room. I worked at that hospital, and I knew the people there. They knew us—my wife and I."

Mrs. Ricci watched Dec's face, her whole body unmoving, as if mesmerized by the soft, warm depth of Dec's voice. Beside her, her husband reached for her hand, and their fingers automatically entwined. For the barest moment, Zoey recognized the movement, the way she had reached for Dec and found her hand the night before, and then she too fell back into the sound of Dec's voice.

"They told me she—her name was Annabelle—they told me that Annabelle had been severely injured in the accident, and even though they'd done everything they could, they were unable to save her."

Zoey's chest tightened. Up until this moment, she had wanted to know everything about Dec, about why she'd left PMC so unexpectedly when she'd had such a golden future awaiting her, and about the woman who could entice her away from here, and about what had happened to Dec after they'd left, and why she had returned a different person. But now, all she wanted was to somehow reverse time, even if it meant that the kiss they'd shared would never happen, that the fascinating woman who was Dec would never have walked into her life, and she would never know the longing that she felt every time she looked at her. If reversing time would erase the pain, would eradicate what must have been an agonizing time for Dec, she would do it. Even if *she* remembered everything that had transpired between them, even if she was forced to live with the loss, she would gladly trade Dec's pain for her own.

But she couldn't do any of those things. All she could do was listen.

"They assured me," Dec went on, "that Annabelle had not survived the accident. That despite everything that was done at the scene, she was gone when she arrived in the ER. Like Tony. Even by the time she arrived at the emergency room, it was too late. Like Tony."

Mrs. Ricci caught her breath, but still her eyes held Dec's. Not searching, but strangely calm. As if the truth was the solace she had sought.

"I needed to be sure," Dec said so softly, Zoey wasn't sure she meant to speak.

"Yes," Mrs. Ricci murmured.

"I had to see her, and when I did, I knew. Annabelle wasn't there."

"You *do* know," Mrs. Ricci whispered.

"Yes," Dec said. "I knew. All the monitors, all the measurements, they said that her body was still functioning, but what made her *her*—what makes all of us who we are—was gone."

"Did they ask you…what you're asking us?" Mrs. Ricci said.

"They would have," Dec said, "given a little time, but I knew they were holding back because they were my friends, and they were hurting for me. Annabelle had never stipulated, but I believe if Annabelle could have made the decision, that she would have wanted to do whatever she could with what remained of her presence. So I said yes."

"Did it help you?"

"Not then, not really." Dec's expression never changed.

Zoey recognized that look. Dec appeared as calm and steady and controlled as ever—the expression Zoey understood now kept Dec's pain contained. Dec didn't want sympathy. Perhaps she didn't want absolution. Zoey wasn't sure where that thought came from, but it felt right.

"A day or so after the procedures were done, when I was ready, I asked about the recipients. They won't tell you who they are, but they will tell you some things. I know that Annabelle's kidneys went to a young woman who'd been born with a disease that destroyed her kidneys when she was barely twenty, and to a father of four. And her heart"—Dec swallowed then, the first outward sign of the enormous pain that must still remain for her—"went to a mother with a two-year-old child. And I know about the rest of the recipients, and I know it was the right decision."

Tears streaked down Mrs. Ricci's face.

"I can't tell you what is the right thing to do," Dec said, "but we'll need to know today. Tony can't stay on the life support much longer." When Mrs. Ricci fell silent, Dec said softly, "Would you and your husband like some time to talk things over?"

For the first time, Mr. Ricci cleared his throat and said, "I believe we both know what Tony would want."

Mrs. Ricci closed her eyes for a moment, then turned to her husband, clear-eyed, and nodded. "We do."

"Will it be today?" Mr. Ricci said.

"Yes," Dec said, "once you sign the consent forms, Dr. Cohen will notify the transplant team, and all the medical centers who will be receiving donations will prepare the recipients for surgery."

"We shouldn't wait, then," Mrs. Ricci said with surprising strength and determination. "All those people shouldn't have to wait any longer. Tony would not want them to suffer any longer."

Zoey's throat tightened. She'd experienced great tragedies and great triumphs so far in her career, but she wasn't certain she'd ever witnessed such bravery on the part of so many, in such different ways. She stood. "I'll have the paperwork ready for you in just a moment."

Mr. Ricci said, "We'd like to stay with Tony until it's time."

Zoey nodded. "The intensive care staff will need some time right before he's transported to prepare, and you may have to step out then."

"We understand."

Dec rose as Zoey said, "I'll be right back."

Zoey stepped outside with Dec and closed the door.

Dec said, "You'd better let Tom Doolin know, so he can put the OR on standby and notify the registry to contact the recipient hospitals."

"All right." Zoey wanted to say so much more and feared it was not her place. Not her place to offer sympathy, certainly. Everything she'd learned and guessed about Dec so far had said sympathy wasn't what she wanted. She wished she knew what Dec did want. "Dec... thank you."

Dec nodded curtly and turned away. "I need to get down to the ER."

"Dec," Zoey said, unable to help herself.

Dec glanced over her shoulder. "Zoey?"

"I'm sorry."

Dec regarded her for a few seconds that felt like an eternity. "I appreciate it, but you don't need to be."

An instant later Dec pushed through the stairwell doors and disappeared. Zoey imagined she could hear her footsteps descending, but she knew that was her imagination. She was usually so very good about separating reality from dreams. She'd taught herself the difference when she was very young, and she couldn't afford to forget those lessons now. Especially not now, when so much of her longed so very much to dream.

CHAPTER TWENTY

The stairwell, dim and quiet for a few blessed moments, gave Dec the chance to find her balance before she had to step back into the present from the past. She hadn't meant to talk about Annabelle when she'd walked into the conference room. In fact, she hadn't been thinking about the Riccis in the few moments that she'd sat in silence with Zoey. She'd almost smiled as Zoey dove into her tablet, much as she'd climbed into her locker a little bit earlier. Zoey wouldn't look at her, although she *had*—she'd looked at her long enough in the locker room for Dec to see the appreciation in her eyes, the flicker of desire that passed across her features before she'd quickly turned away. She could think of only one reason for Zoey's sudden, and not altogether unenjoyable, behavior. Zoey had been thinking about the night before, just as Dec had been thinking about it, and knowing that had brought heat to Dec's skin along with a stirring of pleasure. Even if she wasn't ready to do anything about it, even if she was determined *not* to do anything about it, she still liked knowing she was not alone in her attraction. She liked knowing that Zoey was no more immune to the passion that had flared between them than she was.

And as they sat in the silent conference room, she'd felt the effortless connection again. The pull, the urge to reach out, to touch Zoey, with her words if not her body, was as instinctual as it was undeniable. She'd held back and kept her silence, because Zoey's body language signaled she wasn't ready. At least that's how Dec read it when Zoey purposefully looked away. Still, she enjoyed watching her, found the little crease between her brows, and the way her lips pursed as she concentrated, appealing. The movement of her fingers over the tablet, swift and sure and delicate, mesmerized her. Sitting there, watching, she'd imagined those fingers on her skin…and remembered.

Zoey had gripped her hands when they'd kissed, and just that touch had awakened a need she'd thought long extinguished. When their fingers had linked, a satisfying sense of possession had coursed through her. Zoey had tugged her closer, Zoey had said *Touch me.* Zoey had wanted as she had wanted. As much as she hungered for that resurgence of desire again, she hungered more for Zoey. She'd had her hands on Zoey's skin, had stroked the sleek softness and subtle strength of her, had reveled in the tightening of Zoey's body at her caress. And she wanted her again.

At the sound of footsteps outside the conference room, she'd let the night before fade and focused on what the Riccis would need. The shift as she set her life aside came naturally, repeated dozens of times a day. That was the work she chose. She'd been content to let Zoey take the lead with the Riccis, trusting her to find the right words, and Zoey had. Compassionately, yes, but truthfully. Delivering the message that had to be delivered, using the words that had to be said. But finally, they'd reached the point where she was the only one in the room who could answer Mrs. Ricci's unspoken questions.

How will I know the best thing to do? How will I honor my son?

And then Dec had answered because she was the only one who could.

She hadn't intended for Zoey to hear that story. Hadn't planned on sharing it with anyone here, in this world to which she had returned. But she couldn't be true to the only oath that mattered to her—to do all she could to heal the sick, and that included their families—if she didn't speak out. She'd have to decide later how much more to tell Zoey.

Zoey was very good at hiding her deepest feelings. Dec had figured that out from watching her, from talking with her, from touching her, and as she'd told her story to Tony Ricci's parents, she'd seen Zoey's emotions flicker like a candle's flame, flaring to life and just as quickly extinguished. Dec hadn't needed to see more. Zoey hurt for her, and that was the last thing she wanted. She didn't deserve to share her pain with anyone, especially not Zoey. She couldn't bear to have anything but truth between them, even if it meant there could be nothing more between them.

And right now what she needed was a little time and a little distance to figure out what she could live with—and without. Thankfully, the ER provided a strange kind of sanctuary that gave her both. She wasn't scheduled to work until the second shift, but she didn't care. She was there, the work was there, and she needed to occupy her mind.

And the boss was headed her way.

"Morning," Dec said as Honor strode down the hall.

"Hi," Honor said. "I was about to call you and thank you for last night."

"You're welcome. It was no trouble."

Honor laughed, but she had shadows beneath her eyes that weren't there the day before, and Dec suspected she hadn't gotten much sleep. Honor was like that. Linda was her friend, and Honor would do anything for her. Dec had earned that friendship once, and she hoped to again.

"Actually, it was kind of fun," Dec said. "Kim was a major help, and Arly is great with them. She looks just like you, by the way."

"I've heard that." Honor shook her head, a smile lightening the tension in her face. "But you know, she acts a lot more like Quinn."

Dec laughed, the first flicker of humor she'd actually felt since she'd lain down the night before and tried to sleep, mostly unsuccessfully. "I kinda got that too. It's a pretty spectacular combination."

Honor rolled her eyes. "That still remains to be seen." But her voice was filled with love.

"How's Linda?" Dec asked as they walked to the central station.

Honor filled her in and then asked, "What are you doing here? You have second shift, don't you?"

"I was at a meeting with the Riccis."

"Ah, God. How are they doing?"

"They're holding up. They're going to sign for organ recovery. Zoey did a really great job explaining the situation to them."

Honor noted the first name, but then, it wasn't all that uncommon when discussing residents to refer to them that way. Dec had worked with quite a few of the ER and surgery residents so far, though, and she and Zoey had clearly forged a unique relationship. Maybe it was just a good professional match, but then Quinn had very good instincts, and she'd seen something more between them. While she might have been out of close touch with Dec for years, Dec had once been as close a friend as Linda. She could still read Dec's face, and right now, Dec was hiding something. "I'm not surprised. Zoey has always had natural rapport with patients. With everyone, really."

"Yes, I imagine she has," Dec said. Honor was watching her intently, and she knew the look. Honor was probing—she had a great natural sense for recognizing when something was troubling someone, at least she always had with Dec. Maybe if she and Annabelle had stayed here, where Dec couldn't have hidden her misgivings for so long, things might have turned out differently. She could add that to her long list of errors.

"I'm glad the Riccis have decided on organ recovery," Honor went on, granting Dec a reprieve she suspected would only be temporary. "I think in the long run that will help them heal."

"I think so too." Dec looked away. "I hope it will."

Honor squeezed Dec's forearm. "Have I mentioned that I'm glad you're back?"

"You have. And if I neglected to say, I'm glad to be here too."

As they separated to get to work, Dec admitted the truth of what she'd said and admitted too she was glad for more reasons than she'd anticipated. One of those reasons was Zoey Cohen, and she couldn't quite bring herself to be sorry.

❖

Zoey walked the Riccis back to Tony's bedside after they signed the consent. She'd already called Dr. Doolin and alerted the transplant coordinator, who would notify the regional center to match the recipients and mobilize the other transplant teams. After hurrying to make quick rounds with her junior residents on the in-house patients, she caught up with Tom Doolin in the OR lounge.

"Good job with that," Tom said.

"Thanks, but—" Zoey cut herself off. What she'd heard in that room went far beyond private. Dec had revealed a part of herself that Zoey was positive, although she couldn't exactly say why, Dec had never wanted to share. "It wasn't all me."

"Either way, you've got a feeling for this kind of work," her chief said. "So if you're interested, you should think about a fellowship. Now's the right time."

Zoey didn't hesitate. Some things you just knew. The rightness of them clicked—the person you met you knew would be a friend, like the moment she'd met Dani, or the career decision she'd made the first time she'd been in an emergency room. She'd been ten, but she'd understood that was a place not just of strength and healing, but the power to make a difference. In the first moments that she'd stood next to Dec over a grievously injured human being and fought with her to save that life, the connection had been right. That certainty had grown with every moment that they'd shared.

This was another of those moments. "I'm definitely interested."

"Good." He got to his feet and stretched his lanky frame. "Come talk to me soon."

"I will." As soon as she said it, Zoey wanted to tell Dec and see what she thought of the plan. The idea startled her. She ought to be worried. But if she knew that, then she probably didn't need to worry. She already knew what she was doing—and what she wouldn't do.

"We have a recipient lined up for the liver," Tom said. "You'll be with me on that, so call me as soon as we get an ETA for the recipient teams."

"Okay," Zoey said, rapidly running through what she knew about liver transplants.

"It's going to be a long night," Tom said as he walked away. He sounded happy about it.

Dec worked without a break all morning until the steady stream of patients dwindled down to just a few at midday. Her phone rang around noon. Zoey.

"Hi," she said.

"Hi," Zoey said. "I just wanted to let you know we're getting ready to start around two."

"That was fast."

"Most of the recipient organs are going to places in-state, so those teams are already here or will be soon. The last team is in the air now."

"Have you had lunch?"

"Um, no?"

Dec smiled at the question in her voice. "Well, if you're not sure,

I think you probably haven't. How about I buy you lunch. You're going to be in there for a while once you get started."

"Sure. I can't go very far."

"I'd suggest pizza, but I think we had that for supper last night. How about we grab sandwiches from the cafeteria and walk over to the park. You'll be five minutes away if you have to get back."

"I'd like that," Zoey said softly.

"I'm just finishing up a chart. I'll meet you in the cafeteria in five minutes."

"Okay," Zoey said. "Bye."

Dec put her phone back in her pocket and stared at the chart she'd been about to sign off on. What the hell had she done that for? Every time she made a decision about Zoey, she broke her own rule. Maybe it was the buzz she'd gotten at seeing Zoey's name come up on the phone. Or the quick surge of heat at the sound of her voice. And maybe she was lying to herself about wanting distance between them, because all she wanted right at that moment was to see her. Maybe she was kidding herself about not heading for trouble too.

None of that stopped her from closing the chart, walking to Honor's office, and announcing, "The board is quiet. I'm going to take a lunch break."

Honor looked up. "Have a long one since you aren't actually supposed to be here yet. I'll walk with you. I was about to head up to check on Linda."

"How is she?"

"Hollis texted me she was on her way to check her. I expect she's going to make a decision one way or the other."

"Zoey called," Dec said. "The recovery's on for two."

"Oh," Honor said, studiously staring straight ahead, "that's good. The less time the family has to wait, the better, I imagine."

"Yes." Dec blew out a breath. No point pretending Honor wasn't lasered in on her and Zoey. "About Zoey…"

Honor stopped walking and stepped to the side out of the stream of people in the hallway. "What about Zoey?"

"I'm not sure exactly. Damn." Dec ran a hand through her hair. Why had she started this? But if Honor saw something, sooner or later, others would too. "I don't supervise her in any capacity."

"No, you don't."

"It's just that we both were involved in Tony Ricci's care when he came in, and his parents know us."

"I know." Honor raised a brow as if to ask, *Is there something more?*

"You're not making this easy," Dec said.

"Maybe you're making it difficult?" Honor asked lightly.

"I just didn't want anyone to get the wrong idea."

"Who would that be, Dec?" Honor's tone was gentle. "Zoey is an adult. So are you."

"Well, most everybody in the hospital is interested in what everyone else does," Dec said, knowing she sounded grumpy. She felt grumpy.

"That's certainly true. This is a small city unto itself. Maybe even an entire universe. Most people outside these walls don't really understand what goes on in here. And those of us who work here spend the vast majority of our lives here. Still, other than the inevitable gossip about just about anything, what has you concerned?"

"I'm not concerned," Dec said quickly.

Honor just watched her, waiting.

"Okay, that's bullshit. I don't care about gossip about me. I care that people talk about Zoey."

"That's probably up to Zoey to be concerned about—don't you think so?"

Dec gritted her teeth. She hadn't intended to start this conversation any more than she'd intended to discuss Annabelle with the Riccis in front of Zoey. When had she lost control of what she talked about? "Yes, of course."

"I can't pretend to know how you feel right now," Honor said. "But I know what it's like to be torn between what was and what might be. I'm your friend, but I can't know how you feel after losing Annabelle, or if you're in a place to move on, but I can tell you that when that time is right, you'll know."

"It's not what you think," Dec said.

"Then what is it, Dec?" Honor asked in that soft but direct way she had of hitting a problem head-on, a steel fist encased in velvet.

"I don't want..." Dec couldn't lie to Honor. Hell, she wasn't even able to lie to herself. She wanted Zoey. She wouldn't have kissed her if she hadn't wanted her, and she wouldn't be thinking about her every second that her mind wasn't occupied if she didn't want her. "I don't want to want to move on."

"That's not the same as not being ready," Honor pointed out. "Why is that?"

"It's not about Annabelle—it's about me."

"Then," Honor said, "you're the only one who can answer the question of what's right and what isn't. But you're a good person and an honest one, and I trust that you'll be honest with Zoey. She deserves that."

"I know."

"Give it time, Dec. Sometimes the answers are there, and it just takes a moment to see them." Honor hooked her arm through Dec's. "Come on. Looks like someone is waiting for you."

Zoey leaned against the wall by the cafeteria doors, trying to look casual. Dec didn't bother to ask how Honor knew Zoey was waiting for her. Maybe Honor could hear the way her heart skipped a beat before racing away.

CHAPTER TWENTY-ONE

S orry I got held up," Dec said as she approached Zoey.
Zoey put her phone away. "No problem."

"Still got time to get out of here for a bit?" The second before Zoey answered managed to seem endless. Dec just *needed* this time with her. For herself. She should have been wary, she should have been smarter, she should have been anywhere else but standing there— waiting breathlessly.

"Everything's pretty much on hold for the next couple hours until the other teams show up," Zoey said. "The juniors are covering all the floors. They'll page me if they need me."

"Let's go, then," Dec said quickly, leading the way into the cafeteria. "Cheesesteaks from the grill, or we can grab a quick sandwich?"

"The last time I checked the sandwiches, they had peanut butter and jelly or ham and cheese." Zoey made a face. "Neither is my favorite. I had enough peanut butter and jelly when I was a kid to last a lifetime."

Dec laughed. "I'm with you."

"Somehow, you don't strike me as the peanut butter and jelly type," Zoey said.

"Neither do you."

She lifted a shoulder. "When kids are making their own sandwiches, that's pretty much the go-to thing."

"Good point." Dec had a feeling Zoey had been in charge of making a lot of sandwiches when she was young.

While in line at the grill, Zoey teased, "Something tells me you didn't spend a lot of time making your own sandwiches."

"You're right." Dec hesitated. She didn't usually talk about her childhood, but this was Zoey. She didn't want to keep hiding what she didn't have to. "We had a housekeeper who sort of seconded as a babysitter, I guess. When my parents were both at work, she got stuck with me."

"I bet you weren't that much trouble."

"I had my moments of getting into trouble, but not when I was seven."

"Wild teens?" Zoey raised a brow.

Damn it. Dec could feel the blush. Blushing now? She was an idiot. Idiot or not, she liked the way Zoey smiled at her, clearly enjoying her discomfort. "Ah, maybe a little."

Zoey raised both brows. "Breaking hearts?"

Oo-kay. If she wanted to play...Dec leaned closer. "I don't kiss and tell."

Zoey's eyes widened, and *she* blushed.

Dec grinned.

The cafeteria worker cleared his throat. "Get you two something?"

"Ah...two cheesesteaks to go." She glanced at Zoey. "That good?"

Zoey said, "Perfect. Hey, Jerry, can you put mushrooms on mine?"

"Sure can."

A few minutes later they grabbed sodas, paid, and walked outside to a clear blue sky dotted with puffy white clouds. The park was a short block away, and Dec led Zoey down a wandering grassy path to a pond dotted with white-flowering lily pads in the center.

Zoey sighed. "Is this actually real?"

Dec took a deep breath and felt something very close to relaxation flooding through her. The tension she barely ever registered between her shoulders made itself known by its sudden absence. "It is, and it's easy how quickly we forget it's here."

"I know. God, it smells good out here." Zoey glanced at Dec. "Thanks for this."

"We got lucky," Dec murmured.

"Yeah, we did."

Zoey's soft voice flowed over Dec's skin like a warm hand. "A bench in the sun or bench in the shade?"

"Oh, definitely sun."

"Over here." Dec caught Zoey's hand and guided her around a small copse of trees to a wooden bench on the far side of the pond. A short grassy slope led down to the water's edge where a flock of ducks rested on the shore and swam in the shallows. She took off her lab coat and laid it over the back of the bench. Zoey did the same.

"So," Zoey said when Dec handed her a sandwich from the bag she'd been carrying, "what's your favorite thing to do when you're not at work?"

Dec laughed. "Are we doing the getting-to-know-you thing again?"

"Were we ever?"

"Well, I did ask you what your favorite color was, and I think we got through favorite movies."

"Then I guess we are," Zoey said with just a little hint of teasing.

"Well, I like to watch the ducks. What about you?" Dec said as they ate.

"You're gonna laugh."

"After the ducks, I don't think so."

"I like to knit."

"Aha." Dec pointed a finger. "You started knitting when you knew you wanted to be a surgeon, because it improves your dexterity."

Zoey's eyes widened. "How do you know that? No one else ever guesses."

"Because somewhere along the way, every medical student hears about a surgeon who knits."

"That's me." Zoey shrugged. "Not that I get all that much of a chance these days."

"So, what do you knit?"

"A lot of scarves."

"I'm glad I'm here and not in Texas," Dec said, "because then I wouldn't get a chance to ask for one."

"I'm glad you're here too." Zoey reached out as if to take Dec's hand before abruptly pulling back. "I'll put you on my gift list. So, tell me about the ducks."

"When I was a med student," Dec said, stretching her legs out and resting one arm along the top of the bench, "I used to sneak out here as often as I could during the day just to watch them for a while."

"Yeah?" Zoey asked, balling up the paper the steak had come in and sliding it into the paper bag. "How come?"

"I think they're pretty. I like to watch them swim. They're always so busy. And I love the way they hang together. Did you notice how they all walk around in a row, and if one heads someplace, they all have to follow."

Zoey laughed. "It's kinda like going on rounds. All the residents are like little ducklings."

Dec chuckled. "I never thought of it, but I think you might be right."

"Somehow, though," Zoey mused, "I can't see you sneaking away to do anything."

"Are you trying to say that you think I'm stodgy?" Dec said with mock insult.

"No, but, well...this is awkward...I heard you were a star. Stars usually don't break any rules."

"I don't know about being a star," Dec said, "and I don't think it's really rule-breaking as long as you're getting all your work done, right?"

"True. Although most of the time when anybody's got a spare minute, they find someplace to sleep." Zoey shifted on the bench until her gaze caught Dec's. "I bet you didn't tell anybody what you were doing."

"Oh yeah?" Dec murmured, watching the sunlight play through Zoey's hair. "Why do you think that?"

"Because it was private," Zoey whispered, "and I don't think you talk very much about private things."

"How come you know that?" Dec caught a strand of Zoey's hair as the breeze blew it across Zoey's cheek and tucked it back behind her ear. Her thigh pressed Zoey's. "As it happens to be true."

"I listen to what you don't say."

"That's a little scary." Dec's chest tightened. Fifteen minutes together and already she was in deep water, maybe over her head. And the weirdest thing was, she didn't care. Every time she realized Zoey was stripping off her layers of armor, one subtle move at a time, all she wanted was for Zoey to go faster. To finally touch her underneath the barriers that had kept her apart from everyone for so very long. Her heart hammered against her ribs. Zoey's face was inches away. "What else do you see?"

Zoey edged a few inches nearer until her shoulder bumped Dec's fingers. "Something hurts you. And I'm so sorry for that."

Dec shook her head. "It's not what you think."

"How do you know what I think?" Zoey asked. "Could it possibly be that I'm right, and you don't want me to know?"

Zoey's tone was gentle, but Dec wasn't fooled. Zoey could read her—and that left her half worried and half grateful. "You're very, very good at discovering what other people need."

"Is that a bad thing?"

"I wouldn't have said it was good for *me*," Dec confessed, "before..."

"Before?" Zoey asked.

"Before you." Dec checked that they were still alone in their section of the park before sliding her hand from Zoey's shoulder to cup her face. "You could probably make me change my mind about any number of things—except this. Right now, I'd very much like to kiss you."

"If you do," Zoey said, her warm breath brushing over Dec's fingers, "you'll have to finish what you start sometime very soon. But not now."

"Is that a challenge or an invitation?"

"Both."

"Accepted." Dec angled her head and brought her mouth to Zoey's. She kissed her carefully, reining in her desire to dive into the heat she knew was there, to immerse herself in the passion. She kept her other hand firmly on her own thigh, knowing if she touched Zoey anywhere else she wouldn't be able to stop. She slid her tongue over Zoey's lips, tempting her to open for her, teasing herself and Zoey at the same time.

Zoey made a soft whimpering sound in her throat, and Dec's stomach clenched. A drumbeat of need pounded lower, between her thighs. She groaned softly.

Zoey's palm settled between her breasts and pushed her gently away. "When you kiss me, I want more. It's all I can think about when I'm this close to you."

"Is that a bad thing?" Dec asked.

Zoey half smiled. "Turning things around, are you?"

Dec leaned her forehead against Zoey's. "Not if I confess that every time I'm near you, I want everything."

Zoey gasped.

"Are we even now?" Dec murmured, slipping in another kiss.

Zoey's fingers glided over Dec's throat and slipped behind her head, holding Dec still as Zoey deepened the kiss. Arousal, swift and sharp, shot to Dec's center, and she pressed closer until her body cleaved to Zoey's.

"Enough," Zoey gasped, breaking the kiss. "I won't be able to think of anything else if we don't stop, and I really do need to find my brain cells at some point soon."

"I've been thinking about making love to you since I kissed you the first time," Dec said, her breath coming in broken pants. "It's driving me crazy."

"Then we've been thinking the same thing." Zoey grasped Dec's hand, and their fingers linked again. She cradled Dec's hand between both of hers and drew them to her lap. "I'm not used to wanting anything quite that much."

"Why not?" Dec whispered, wanting to know as much as she wanted to kiss Zoey again. Which was with everything she had. She held her breath as Zoey gazed over the duck pond, a distant expression on her face.

"When I was nine," Zoey said quietly, "my mother left me with her sister to go on vacation with the man she was seeing then. Her boyfriend. There'd been a lot of them."

Dec gently squeezed Zoey's fingers, silently waiting.

"She never came back. I kept expecting her to come for me—everyone did, for the first few weeks, the first few months. My aunt—my mother's sister—and my uncle were young, early twenties, and they had two kids already. Four and six. They weren't happy about keeping me. I always knew that, but they did, and I'm grateful to them." She glanced at Dec. "They could barely support their own children, and adding me was a burden. I owe them."

"You didn't place the burden on them," Dec said quietly.

"I know, but I still feel it. They never treated me like one of their children, but they weren't unkind either. I just always knew they didn't want me there. When I got old enough to plan for college, I made sure I worked hard enough to get a scholarship. I don't owe them for that, or anything to anyone, really."

"You ever hear from your mother?"

Zoey's smile was sad. "It's funny, no one ever really came out and asked me that. But no, she never came back. We all assume she's alive somewhere, because no one's ever contacted us to say otherwise. It's possible, of course, that she isn't."

"I'm sorry," Dec said.

"I used to hope that I would hear from her, but I don't anymore." Zoey shrugged. "We would have nothing to say to each other."

"What about your aunt and uncle?"

"We send cards on holidays—sometimes. I don't go home."

Dec said, "So you're careful who you trust."

Zoey laughed humorlessly. "That's a nice spin on saying I don't want anyone to get close."

"How long have you lived with Emmett and...Hank, is it?"

"Ah, Emmett. Someone else's been listening to hospital gossip," Zoey said softly.

"Just the bits about people I'm interested in."

"Oh?" Zoey asked. "Who else?"

Dec chuckled, pleased at the little bit of fire in her voice. "Actually, let me think..."

"This could be dangerous, you know," Zoey said. "You don't know me all that well yet."

"Then in the interest of self-preservation, I'll confess that you're the only one I've been interested in hearing anything about." Dec leaned closer. "Or kissing."

"I'm a little worried what you might've heard," Zoey said lightly, but her eyes weren't laughing. "Emmett is a good friend and only a friend."

"Maybe we should agree not to listen to stories," Dec said.

"We could always just make our own." Zoey kissed her, drawing their joined hands upward until she pressed Dec's palm against her breast.

"You're killing me, Zoey," Dec groaned against her mouth.

"I'm determined not to die alone." Zoey stiffened suddenly. "God, that didn't come out right. I'm really sorry."

Dec drew back, meeting Zoey's gaze. "It's okay. You don't have to tiptoe around it."

"I'll try to remember that."

"We should walk back," Dec said, not moving a single muscle. "If we stay here, I'll kiss you again."

"If we stay here, I'm going to kiss you if you don't kiss me first."

"Call me when you're done in the OR?"

"It's probably going to be crazy late," Zoey said.

Dec grinned. "I'm a surgeon, remember?" She caught herself. "Well, I used to be. I know how it works."

Zoey released Dec's hand and brushed hers through Dec's hair.

"Twig," she murmured, drawing a tiny bit of leaf from her hair. "Why aren't you operating anymore?"

"My vision is impaired," Dec said, watching the clouds consume the shine in Zoey's eyes. She hated that. She hated knowing Zoey hurt for her, but that was Zoey. It was one of the things that made her so special. "The skull fracture on the left side extended into the orbit and damaged one of the extraocular muscles. My depth perception is off. I can't work under the microscope."

"But there are other procedures where you wouldn't need it," Zoey said, appalled to know that Dec's career had been cut short along with everything else that she'd lost in that accident.

"I can't get malpractice insurance. A neurosurgeon with a vision problem?" Dec laughed a little bitterly. "There are plenty of procedures I could do, but...my specialty was microsurgery. The ER would've been my second choice of residencies anyhow. I'm just thankful that I'm here, and that I can work."

"So am I." Zoey kissed Dec despite swearing she wouldn't until they were alone. She just needed so much to touch her, to soothe her, and to soothe herself at the same time. "I'm so very glad."

CHAPTER TWENTY-TWO

Dec walked Zoey up to the OR and paused outside the locker room door. "So, see you later."

"If you're sure—"

"Zoey," Dec murmured, "I'm sure."

She might not be sure about anything else she was doing, including what came after she saw Zoey next, but she was certain she did not want to spend another night lying awake, torturing herself with fantasies of touching Zoey when she could actually *be* touching her. And one way or another, unless Zoey said no, she was going to touch her as soon as they were both free of the hospital for a few hours. Even an hour would do. Not enough, but a start.

Just to make sure Zoey had no doubts, she lowered her head and whispered in Zoey's ear, "I am absolutely sure I want to kiss you again—for starters, and then I want my hands on you, and then—"

"I'll page you," Zoey said abruptly, a flush climbing her throat above the V of her scrub shirt.

"Good." Dec backed away a step, giving Zoey space to get her game face—and mindset—firmly in place. She wasn't worried about Zoey being distracted when it came time to work—the switch from anything and everything personal into surgeon mode was ingrained at Zoey's stage of training. When Zoey walked into the OR in another minute or so, she'd be ready. "Hope things go well in there."

Zoey blew out a breath. "Me too."

Dec lightly clasped Zoey's forearm. "I don't know exactly how you're feeling right now, but if my experience is any indication, I bet it feels like there's a little bit of a war going on inside you."

"That's a perfect way to describe it." Zoey grimaced. "I'm looking forward to the liver transplant—I've never scrubbed on one. But we're only able to do it because Tony is gone."

"Listen," Dec said quietly, "nothing you could have done would've changed this moment. Nothing *we* could have done in the trauma unit when he arrived and nothing anyone else could have done before he got to us. Everything that could have been done was done. This is the right decision, and it's...okay...to look forward to doing the best job you possibly can in there. That's part of what you're doing for Tony Ricci's family. Making sure that their decision helps as many people as possible. And if you take pleasure in doing that, that's okay too. That's why you're a surgeon."

Zoey nodded. "I know that, but it helps to hear it and to know that I'm not the only one who's felt this way."

Dec laughed softly. "You're not."

"And you know what else really helps?" Zoey said.

"What's that?" Dec murmured, running her fingers up and down the inside of Zoey's bare forearm. Even as they talked, she was aware of the softness of Zoey's skin, the heat of her body, just an inch away, the depth of Zoey's eyes as they held hers. So easy to get lost in everything that was Zoey.

Zoey's pupils flickered, growing larger, the blue deepening. "That you knew I needed to hear that. So many times, from the first moment standing out in the parking lot, you've known what I needed to hear."

"That goes both ways."

Zoey reached for Dec's hand and squeezed it. "I hope so."

"Believe it." Dec released Zoey's hand. "Now go, Dr. Cohen. I'll see you later."

Zoey smiled, nodded once, and disappeared inside the locker room. Dec took a deep breath, turned to go down the stairwell, and found Honor obviously waiting for her a little way down the hall. Not much point in pretending nothing was going on with Zoey now. Dec started her way and fell into step beside Honor.

"Hi," Dec said when she reached her.

"Hi, yourself. I'm on my way over to Labor and Delivery. Hollis called. She's getting ready to do Linda's section."

"Is she okay?" Dec asked.

"She's stable. Her blood pressure's still elevated, and her edema has worsened. The baby's all right for now, but Hollis says no more waiting."

"Good call," Dec said. "Is everything quiet downstairs?"

"Blessedly, yes." Honor slowed as the double doors from the main OR opened and Quinn strode out.

"Hey, I got your message." Quinn slipped a hand under Honor's elbow, a wholly automatic gesture. "Hi, Dec."

"Quinn." For just an instant, Dec envied them that easy familiarity. That unassailable connection.

"I didn't want you to break scrub," Honor said. "I know you're in the midst of things."

"That's okay—I just wanted to check on everyone," Quinn said. "Have you seen Robin?"

Honor nodded. "Earlier this morning. All the kids are covered. I'll stay with her during the delivery."

"Okay, good. You'll call me if you need anything?"

"The minute there's news."

Quinn squeezed Honor's shoulder. "All right. I ought to get back. Emmett's just finishing, and we've got another patient on the table."

"Go, go," Honor said.

"See you later, baby." Quinn spun around and hurried back to the OR.

"So," Honor said as they turned the corner and started for L&D, "how was lunch?"

"Ah," Dec said a little hesitantly, "good for hospital food?"

Honor shot her an *oh, please* look. "You did take Zoey to lunch, didn't you?"

"What, you're psychic now?" Dec snorted. "We ate lunch together, yes. I'd hardly call cheesesteaks in the park taking her to lunch."

"You took her to the duck pond?" Honor raised a brow.

Dec felt the blush. Damn it. "That's where the benches are."

"Uh-huh." Honor laughed. "Remember that time Annabelle was looking for you, and we were in the park? She actually thought—" She stopped abruptly. "Well, that was poor timing on my part, bringing that up now. I'm sorry."

"We can't rewrite our history," Dec said, "no matter how much I'd like to sometimes. I never brought Annabelle out there. She wasn't the outdoorsy type. There were no ghosts today."

"I'm glad," Honor said. "So, lunch…?"

"Lunch was fine," Dec said.

"And you're still not going to give me any more than that," Honor chided.

"Believe me, if I knew any more than that, I might."

"Well, as long as you're still working on it."

"I'm working on it." Dec let out a long breath as they reached the doors to L&D. "Call me when there's news?"

"You're officially on the phone tree," Honor said. "And Dec?"

"Yeah?"

"We can't rewrite our history, but we can learn to leave it in the past where it belongs."

Dec nodded, not sure at all she could grant herself that reprieve. "I'd better head down to the ER."

Honor shook her head. "I'd forgotten how stubborn you are."

"Stop reading my mind," Dec grumbled.

Honor laughed and disappeared into the delivery suite.

Forty minutes later, Dec's phone rang as she was listening to a resident present the case of an uncomplicated forearm fracture in a thirteen-year-old BMX rider. She yanked the phone out of her pocket, hoping to see Zoey's name on the screen even as she knew it wouldn't be her. When had irrational hope made a return appearance to her life?

Honor's name came up, not Zoey's. Just as she'd known. Still, for a second she was disappointed. Far more disappointed than she should be.

"Hold up a second," she said to the resident and stepped a few feet away. "Hi, Honor."

"It's a girl. Four pounds, eight ounces. Both mom and baby doing well."

"That's great," Dec said on a breath of relief.

"How are things down there?"

"Steady. Nothing maj—" Dec's trauma beeper went off. "Scratch that—better go."

"I'll be down in a minute," Honor said hurriedly and was gone.

Dec pocketed her phone and took off at a jog, calling over her shoulder to the resident, "Get ortho down here for that arm, and then come help out."

She didn't think about Zoey again until the last victim from a gang fight was stabilized and ready for transport to the TICU.

Almost five. Zoey wouldn't be done for another few hours.

And just like that, the taste of Zoey's kiss, the scent of her skin in the sunlight, the hazy want in her eyes came blasting back into Dec's awareness like a lightning strike. A drumbeat of anticipation pounded in her middle. Somehow she just had to hold on until she saw her again—just until she could touch her. Insane? Sure. Dangerous? Absolutely. Unstoppable? Completely.

❖

Zoey didn't let herself look at a clock until she'd gotten Bethany Giles, a thirty-five-year-old woman and new liver transplant recipient, settled in the intensive care unit, written her note, ordered the next set of labs, and talked to the nurses who'd be taking care of Bethany that night.

"Page me when her labs come in," Zoey said to the nurse.

"Sure," he said, "but we can just let the ICU resident know if you don't want to be bothered tonight."

"That's great," Zoey said, "but can you text me with anything relevant too?"

"Okay, no prob," he said and made a note in the patient's electronic chart.

Zoey finally turned and checked the big clock on the wall opposite the long row of patient cubicles. Most ICUs still had them, even though everyone had phones to check the time. Being able to see the time helped awake patients fight off the disorientation that came with days that had no beginning and no end in the always-on atmosphere of the ICUs.

Ten twenty-five. Late.

Too late?

Dec had said no matter what time. And Zoey really wanted to see her. The afternoon had started off hard—helping to bring Tony Ricci down to the OR after watching his parents say their last good-byes. While most of her mind was already on what she needed to do to assist the other teams in coordinating the organ recovery, a part of her wept for them. Once the case started, when the drapes went on and the scrub teams moved in, the emphasis shifted from the memory of the human being whose death made this possible to the living who were waiting for a chance at a new life. Death always bowed to the living when a choice must be made.

At the end of the case, all she felt was exhausted—physically and emotionally. What she needed right that moment was a reprieve from the pressure and the pathos. She needed to be away from everything the hospital demanded of her for just a few hours. She needed the searing sense of being alive that Dec stirred in her with barely a touch.

And she really needed a shower.

Not that she was necessarily contemplating anything, but...who was she kidding. She was hoping for a lot more than a kiss, and she wasn't even going to second-guess herself as to why. She could worry about that later. She was going to implode if she didn't do something about the churning unrest deep inside.

She ducked into the women's locker room, grabbed a towel off the rack by the showers, and shed her scrubs for a quick rinse. Five minutes later she was drying off in front of her locker when Dani came in.

"Oh hey," Dani said. "How did everything go?"

Zoey dropped the towel on the bench behind her and pulled on her jeans. "Good, so far. A couple of the teams are still working, but our part's done."

"Did Doolin let you do anything?"

"Yeah—most of the harvest and about half the venous hookup." Zoey paused, shirt in hand. Given a choice, she wouldn't do anything differently. She hadn't changed her mind about her career path. She just needed to feel...something beyond responsibility and duty. "It was awesome."

"Man, I'm jealous. Although I did get to do an aortic interpositional graft today." Dani leaned against her closed locker and eyed Zoey speculatively. "How come you're showering here and not at home?"

"Oh," Zoey said, "I just felt grubby."

"Uh-huh. And how is tonight different than every other night when you finish up in the OR and shower at home?"

Zoey pulled on her shirt, not bothering with anything else, and sat down to slip on her sandals. "I might be late."

"That's not exactly an answer," Dani said.

Zoey cut her a glance. "Maybe I have a date. Okay?"

"Okay." Dani grinned. "Should I guess?"

"Can I stop you?"

"Let me think." Dani waited a single beat, then said, "Where exactly are you and Dr. Black going?"

Despite the heat rising in her cheeks, Zoey grabbed her backpack and slammed her locker. "How do you know it's her?"

"Because you're not really much of a player, and you're interested in her. And if you're interested in her, you're not going out with anyone else."

"What do you mean I'm not a player? Everyone thinks I'm a player."

"They may think that," Dani said, "but they're not your best friend who knows better."

Zoey smiled. "Huh. You're right. You are."

"And I'm right about Dec, right?"

"Yes, I'm seeing her tonight. I don't know where we're going, and I really don't care. Maybe she'll just walk me home."

Dani snorted. "Oh yeah. That's probably why she's been waiting around since, what, two o'clock when you started that case?"

Heading for the door, Zoey said, "I'd better get going so she doesn't have to wait a lot longer."

"Wait! You're really not gonna tell me about it?"

Zoey laughed, punched in Dec's number, and let the door close behind her, Dani's question still hanging in the air.

"Hi," Dec said an instant later. "All done?"

"I am. Where should I meet you?"

"I'm outside in the ER parking lot."

"I'll be there in a minute." Zoey hurried down the stairs to the ground floor, bypassing the ER so she wouldn't see anyone who might delay her. She was done for the day. Done, done, done. She scooted out the side entrance adjacent to the ER and cut across the parking lot. Dec's Range Rover was easy to pick out, idling at the far end of the turnaround by the ER entrance. She climbed into the passenger side.

"When did you get your car?" Zoey asked. "I saw you running on the way to work this morning."

"It's a nice night for walking," Dec said without looking over at Zoey, "but I didn't feel like a long walk back, so I picked it up while I was waiting."

"Oh?" Zoey asked, her pulse picking up a little when Dec did *not* turn in the direction of her house. "Did you have something in mind?"

"I think I made that clear a little earlier today," Dec said as she deftly rounded the corner and pulled over in front of a three-story Victorian in a row of them on the quiet side street. She cut the engine and turned toward Zoey. "This is where I live. I was hoping you'd like to come upstairs with me."

Zoey's throat went suddenly dry. She'd done this before with women she knew less well than Dec, but this time she hesitated. This was what she wanted, what she needed. It didn't have to be more—wasn't likely to be more.

"You should know"—Dec leaned closer, her fingers sifting through Zoey's hair until her warm palm closed around the back of Zoey's neck. She drew Zoey effortlessly closer and kissed her—"if you come upstairs, I'm going to want to take you to bed."

"If I come upstairs," Zoey said, letting her hand drift down from Dec's shoulder over her chest until it rested on her hip, "it's because I want you to."

"Is that yes?"

Zoey kissed her, catching Dec's lower lip lightly between her teeth, tugging for a second before running the tip of her tongue over the silky surface and slipping inside. Dec's hips shifted under her hand, and the power surged within her. "Very much yes."

"Let's go." Dec pulled back, jerked her door open, and jumped out. By the time Zoey stepped down to the sidewalk, Dec was there, sliding an arm around her shoulders. Zoey circled Dec's waist, hooking a thumb in the waistband of her pants.

"My place is around the back," Dec said gruffly, guiding her rapidly down the stone walkway to a staircase in the back. As they started to climb, Dec took Zoey's hand as if afraid she might change her mind, and a minute later they were inside.

The door closed behind them, and Zoey had a quick glimpse of a neat kitchen, a small table with two chairs, and a stove with nothing on top—not even a kettle—before Dec gripped her waist and pulled her close. Dec's hands were strong and her body taut, as if she was holding herself on a tight leash. Zoey slid her arms around Dec's neck and lifted her face to the kiss she knew was coming.

Remembering Dec's promise earlier to do more than kiss her the next time they were alone, she whispered, "Time to pay up."

"I plan to."

Dec's lips were firm and smooth, the kiss possessive and demanding. Dec's hands skimmed up and down her back, one settling on her ass and cradling her closer until their hips fit together, heat to heat. Zoey gripped Dec's shoulders, reveling in the taut muscles that grew even tighter everywhere she touched. Dec's body vibrated, her kisses more and more feverish. Zoey tightened inside, her skin buzzing, her nipples tingling. Every inch of her electrified, clamoring for more.

"Where's the bedroom?" Zoey pulled away to take a deep shaky breath. "I want your hands on me."

Dec shuddered, and for an instant, Zoey feared she might back away.

"Dec," Zoey said gently. "If you don't—"

"No," Dec said hoarsely, the word almost a groan. "Please. I need you."

The words slashed through her, more powerful than she could've ever imagined. More daunting than *I want you.* Another time, she might have run from them, but she wanted, needed, this moment too much.

"Show me."

Dec grabbed Zoey's hand and tugged her quickly down a narrow hallway that opened into a large bedroom occupying the entire rear of the apartment. Big bay windows let in moonlight that illuminated a room dominated by the bed and not much else. Zoey didn't care what was there or even where they were. All that mattered was they were alone, and she hungered. She stepped to the side of the bed and pulled her shirt off.

Dec was on her in an instant, her hands closing over Zoey's breasts, her mouth at her neck, voracious and demanding. Zoey arched, the pleasure piercing through her breasts, down into her belly, and driving lower into her sex. Dec's mouth was molten. Her touch was fire. Zoey shivered, her thighs trembling. Her pulse throbbed between her legs.

Dec backed her up, still kissing her, still fondling her breasts, until Zoey's legs hit the bed and she fell onto it. She pulled Dec with her, opening her legs for Dec to straddle. Dec leaned over her, one thigh pressed hard into Zoey's sex, her kisses traveling lower, covering Zoey's breasts, finding her nipple, closing around it.

"Oh God." Zoey clutched the back of Dec's neck, pressing herself harder against Dec's mouth. Dec's teeth grazed her nipple and her clitoris spasmed. "Wait!"

Dec went still, her tense body shuddering. "What—did I hurt you?"

"No, no. I want to be naked. I need your skin against me. Hurry, God. Hurry."

Dec pushed herself up and yanked at her clothes while Zoey shimmied out of her jeans and threw them on the floor. Naked, she parted her thighs and reached for Dec, grasping her shoulders and dragging her down until Dec settled between her legs, her weight pressing against Zoey's clit.

"Oh fuck. That feels so good. I'm not going to last." Zoey arched up to kiss Dec's throat, found her mouth, and dove inside. Dec kissed her back, rocking into Zoey's sensitive flesh until Zoey couldn't wait another second.

Clinging to Dec with both arms around her shoulders, Zoey wrapped her legs around the back of Dec's thighs and pressed her belly into Dec's. Their bodies cleaved, and she set the rhythm, rocking, pressing, pushing herself higher and higher.

"I want to come," Zoey gasped when every inch of her screamed.

Dec framed her face with both hands, staring down at her, her face tense in the moonlight, her eyes blazing.

"Let me be inside you," Dec said hoarsely. "I want to make you come."

"Yes, yes," Zoey cried.

Dec levered up to her knees, her hand instantly between Zoey's thighs, and then she was inside her, stretching her, filling her, gliding in and out, faster and faster and faster.

Zoey lifted her hips to take her deeper, a hand to her breast, teasing a nipple in time to the pulsations building, building, building between her legs.

She kept her eyes open as long as she could, but the spiraling pleasure, the agonizing pressure, finally erupted and forced all sensibility from her consciousness. She threw back her head with a startled cry and came, pulsing around Dec's fingers with each endless surge of release.

Dec braced herself on her free arm, her heart skittering in her chest, her breath long gone. Zoey abandoned to pleasure, her features starkly beautiful in the silvery moonlight, stopped her heart. Zoey's cries trailed off into small, broken whimpers that struck Dec deep inside. She quivered, so close, so close, so agonizingly close.

"Zoey," she gasped, "touch me."

Zoey's hand streaked down the center of her abdomen and cupped her, her fingertips finding her unerringly.

"Don't stop." Dec reared upright and straddled Zoey's hips, all the while watching Zoey's hand stroke between her legs. Watching Zoey make her come. When the orgasm hit, her mind blanked, an explosion that wracked her body and rent her soul. As she collapsed beside Zoey, Zoey rolled into her and wrapped an arm around her waist.

"God, you're amazing," Zoey muttered.

"Not through," Dec gasped.

Zoey laughed a little unsteadily. "Good. I think. I *might* live to do that again."

Dec laughed and kissed her. "Take a minute."

Zoey moved in a little closer, one leg thrown over Dec's hips, and nibbled at her earlobe before whispering, "Maybe I want to take more than a minute."

"You can take whatever you want," Dec murmured.

"You don't know what I might want," Zoey warned, only half teasing. She was almost afraid to ask herself the same question.

"I don't care what it is." Dec's face appeared perfectly composed, completely sure. "Not when you make me feel this good."

Zoey rolled on top of her, already wild for the taste and feel of her, and stopped thinking. Later, later she could wonder just what she'd done.

CHAPTER TWENTY-THREE

Dec hadn't slept next to anyone for two years, and the slight shift in the mattress as Zoey got out of bed roused her from her light doze. Streetlights still on. Sky outside the window black but not inky. She mentally calculated the time. Somewhere around four a.m. Had she slept? More like unconscious, in a good way. Exhausting sex was a great sedative—as she recalled from the distant past—and the sex last night was better classified as superlative. Zoey had been passionate, inventive, demanding, and unexpectedly take-charge. Dec smiled to herself. That had been nice.

The raspy slide of a zipper brought her out of the haze of sexual memory and back to the reality of the next day in her life, one of many, and one that bore little resemblance to the unchained emotions of the night before.

"Are you leaving?" Dec said, the heaviness of sleep and lingering arousal abrading her voice.

"I've got to check on the transplant patient," Zoey said from the shadows, "and I want to stop home first."

Dec pushed the light sheet aside, rose, and searched for her pants. "I'll walk you."

"It's only a few blocks," Zoey said. "Don't get up yet."

"It's still dark, Zoey," Dec said. "Are you always this resistant to a little help?"

"I'm not afraid of the dark," Zoey said lightly.

Dec grabbed a T-shirt out of the dresser drawer and pulled it on. "I used to be, but after a while, when nothing comes to get you, you stop being afraid."

"Maybe," Zoey said quietly and disappeared down the hall.

The early morning predawn streets lay still and quiet. The temperature hadn't dropped much from the nineties of the day before. A sluggish, heavy breeze did little to cool the faint sweat that broke out on Dec's bare arms. No one passed by on the silent five-minute walk to Zoey's. Dec shouldered the silence patiently—she'd made the first move the night before, and now, obviously, Zoey was planning the first move of the morning.

Zoey stopped in front of the walkway to the darkened twin.

"I needed last night," Zoey said. "And you were…great."

Dec smiled wryly. "Thanks. I needed it too."

She could've said she needed *Zoey*, not just mind-blowing sex, but that would take them in a direction neither of them, it seemed, wanted to go. Neither of them had been playing a game. She'd been honest with her intentions—with what she wanted and what she needed. Zoey had been too. There'd been no rules, restrictions, demands, or promises on either side. Now she had a choice, just as she'd had a choice to follow the inescapable pull of her attraction to Zoey these past few days. Now she could choose to accept the amazing night they'd had for what it was, a convergence of their mutual need in a single moment of exquisite connection, or she could go somewhere she'd already decided she wasn't going to go again.

"I should go," Zoey said, seeming to have already decided.

"I hope your patient does well," Dec said. "Let me know what you decide about talking to Doolin."

"I will." Zoey hesitated, then leaned forward and kissed Dec fleetingly on the mouth. "I'll see you, Dec."

"Yeah," Dec said softly as Zoey turned and walked away. She disappeared inside the house without looking back. "I'll see you."

Zoey took a deep breath as the front door closed behind her. She'd made the right decision, she was sure of it, despite the heaviness that settled around her heart. One thing being with Emmett had taught her, after it was all over, was that friends-with-benefits wasn't as much of a benefit as she'd thought at the time. Dani had called it. She wasn't all that good at casual, and nothing about Dec had been casual from the beginning. If she kept seeing Dec in any kind of relationship way, she'd keep sleeping with her. She couldn't *think* about her, let alone be anywhere near her, without wanting to climb inside her—or have Dec inside her. Her whole body still hummed from the night before, ready for more. Freaking screaming for more. Any more nights like the last one, and she'd be in deeper than she was now. And she was afraid she was already in too deep.

She climbed the stairs, trying hard not to wake whoever might be sleeping, and hoped the shower would dampen the riot in the core of her. It didn't. Still jittery with pent-up arousal and skittering emotions, bouncing from relief to misery, she pulled on a clean pair of scrubs from the stack she kept at home. No point putting on street clothes that she was going to change in half an hour. After jamming clean underwear and other essentials into her backpack, she went downstairs. A light burned in the kitchen, and she smelled coffee.

"Thank God," she said as she entered the kitchen.

Dani looked over her shoulder as she pulled cups from the cabinet. "Are you early or late?"

"I think, at this point, they're one and the same." Zoey stumbled forward with her hand out. "Coffee."

Grinning, Dani poured her a cup and handed it over. "How was your night?"

Zoey fashioned her answer while taking her time getting the milk for her coffee. "It was good." Really, Dec deserved more than that. She'd known what she was asking for—and what she would be getting. "No, actually, it was great."

"Woo-hoo. Somebody's getting some."

And so, so much more than Zoey had dreamed. She turned away, pulling out the peanut butter and bread.

"Um," Dani said cautiously, "why am I not seeing wild, ecstatic, satiated joy all over your face?"

Zoey put on a smile. "Hey, I said it was great, right?"

"I'm not going to be crass—"

Zoey snorted.

"*Or* ask for details," Dani went on as if she hadn't heard, "but my definition of great might be different than your definition of great. So perhaps a teeny bit more detail would be helpful."

"While great may be relative, I think you can safely assume they're close." Zoey hoped Dani would read her reticence as just her wanting to keep special things private.

"So what's wrong," Dani said, sipping her coffee. "She blow you off this morning?"

"No." So much for Dani not reading her silence as anything but avoidance. "It was mutual."

Dani grabbed the toast when it popped up in the toaster and took a bite, not even bothering with butter.

"Hey! That's mine." Zoey pretended offense. "You could've asked for a piece."

"Oh, I thought this was for me." Dani grinned, leaned over, and put another piece of bread in the toaster. "Mutual what? Mutual *oh hey, it was nice, but let's not do it again*?"

"That pretty much sums it up," Zoey said.

"Okay." Dani shrugged. "You've done that before. We've all done that before. One night with some people is plenty. No strings, everybody goes about their life."

"Exactly."

"Why do I get the feeling this isn't that?" Dani said, spooning peanut butter out of the jar onto her toast in messy globs.

"It is," Zoey said with finality.

"Who said it first?"

"Nobody exactly. We just didn't say anything else."

"Neither of you mentioned the big what-next elephant sitting on the end of the bed?"

"It sort of…didn't come up." Dec hadn't even hinted she wanted to see her again, and Dec'd been totally up front about everything else she'd wanted, in and out of bed, up until then. So as far as Zoey read things, silence was as good as saying they were one and done.

"So why aren't you going for it?" Dani said. "We both know it's different this time."

"Don't you ever quit?"

"I might if I didn't have to play dentist and extract every last little bit of information out of you with a shovel." She frowned. "You know what I mean."

Zoey dropped into a chair at the kitchen table with her coffee and the toast she didn't really want. "It *is* different, and that's the problem.

I'm already twisted up about her. I don't want to get so tied up, I can never get the knots out."

"How do you know you would? Get tied up, or need to get unknotted?"

"Because she's not over her wife."

"How do you know?" Dani blew out a breath. "People move on, Zoey. It's human nature."

"Maybe. But you know the story. The high-powered perfect partner. Somebody so special that Dec changed her whole life for her. Have you ever really looked at her? Because I have. She hasn't moved on from that."

"Okay," Dani said, nodding slowly. "We're done with her, then."

"Damn right. Done."

Zoey grabbed her backpack and headed for the hospital. She'd made the right decision, and eventually she'd stop hurting over it.

Dec had no reason to go home after Zoey went inside. She could shower and change into scrubs at the hospital, and she still had plenty of time. Too much time she didn't want to spend reliving the night before or second-guessing what she should have said to Zoey and why she didn't.

Instead, she watched the sunrise over the duck pond, slouched on the bench where she'd sat with Zoey, where she'd kissed her. Where she'd decided—no, she'd never really decided anything—she'd just followed her instincts because she hadn't been able to find a way not to. Zoey unlocked parts of herself that had been closed long before the accident, places that she'd closed off bit by bit as she'd adjusted her life to fit with Annabelle's. And after Annabelle was gone, she'd sworn not to open those doors, and for a long time, she hadn't wanted to. Hadn't needed to.

But Zoey—Zoey had walked into her life like the sun coming out after a long, dark winter, hot and bright and filled with promise. She'd awakened Dec's desire, her need, her hope. Like a prisoner with their first taste of unexpected freedom, she knew she'd never be able to go back. She could live with knowing that, but she couldn't risk Zoey discovering she had nothing left to give.

At dawn she walked to the hospital and took the stairs to the OR locker room to avoid the ER night shift and their curious stares when she was early, again. She showered perfunctorily, realized she'd left her clean scrubs on the bench by her locker, and walked naked into the locker room as she toweled off. She expected the place to be empty like it was when she came in, but Zoey stood a few feet away, opening her locker. Zoey's face registered surprise as her gaze swept down Dec's body. Her nostrils flared and her lips parted before she abruptly turned away.

"Morning again," Dec said briskly, opening her locker and tossing in her street clothes. She toweled off her hair, aware that Zoey's back was still turned, and pulled on her scrubs and running shoes.

"Morning," Zoey said without looking her way. A few seconds later, Zoey walked toward the door. "Have a good one."

"Thanks," Dec called as the door swung closed. She closed her eyes, but she could still see the ice in Zoey's eyes as the chill flowed over her and settled around her heart.

Zoey slowed outside the locker room. Her heart jackhammered behind her ribs. Her stomach clenched down into a small hard ball, and the rest of her burned. Damn it, did Dec have to be so beautiful? And did every one of her traitorous cells have to ignite just from looking at her? Every single memory she'd been trying to avoid came crashing back. Dec above her, her gaze voracious. Dec, stroking her breasts, stroking inside her, murmuring her name as she pushed her and pushed her and pushed her to the edge and over.

The locker room door behind her scraped open, and she hurried away down the hall. Time, she just needed a little time to get herself back together. To get her body under control and her sanity restored. She just needed to find the old her. The Zoey who never risked too much or needed too much. The Zoey she'd been before Dec walked into her life.

CHAPTER TWENTY-FOUR

Psychiatry department," a young man announced when Dec's call was answered.

"This is Dr. Declan Black in the ER. I have a consult for you."

"Hmm. It's just now five, and I'm not sure any of our people are still in-house. I could check, or if there's no rush, I can page the resident on call."

Dec said, "The patient is pretty agitated and probably needs admission, so anything you can do to get someone down here in a hurry would be appreciated."

"Hold on. I'll see what I can do."

"This is Dr. Kelly," Bridget Kelly announced in her sultry alto when Dec's call was transferred from the receptionist.

"Dr. Kelly," Dec said, "Dec Black. Sorry to catch you just when you were about to leave."

"Dec, of course. No problem. And it's Bridget. Now, what can I do for you?"

"We've got a twenty-five-year-old male down here in the ER who made a pretty convincing suicide attempt with a vacuum cleaner hose plugged into his car exhaust. I think he needs to be admitted, but that's your call."

"First attempt?" Bridget said.

"According to his mother, who is on her way from Reading and should be here in an hour, this is the first as far as the family knows. Apparently, though, he hasn't been himself since his girlfriend bailed on him a few months back."

"All right, I'll be down."

"Thanks."

Bridget arrived less than five minutes later and, after a quick look at the chart, went to see the patient. Twenty minutes later she joined Dec at the nursing station.

"You're right—he needs to come in to get on a med regimen and started in therapy. His car ran out of gas, or he'd be dead now." She sighed as she input notes in his record. "I'll call the unit to let them know."

"Thanks for getting down here so quickly."

Bridget slid the tablet away, leaned on the counter, and smiled at Dec. "Part of the job. And how's the new job going for you?"

"Fine," Dec said. "The first few weeks with new residents are always challenging."

"Well, of course, you're not new to the place," Bridget said, "but it's got to feel a little different than when you were here before."

"Sure, but a lot is still the same." Dec shrugged. "Of course, I've got a different job now."

"One you seem to be pretty well-suited for. How is it for you?"

"It's good. I like the pace, and the patients, and the people I work with." Dec grinned. "Is this an employee health interview?"

Bridget laughed and lightly rested her hand on Dec's forearm. "Not at all. Just interested, and I'm very glad to hear things are going well. Actually, I've been looking for an opportunity to ask you if you'd like to have dinner."

"Ah," Dec said, "thanks. I appreciate the offer, and I might take you up on it sometime later."

"All right," Bridget said graciously, "I hope you do. I'm easy to find."

Dec couldn't imagine a scenario in which she might call Bridget Kelly for a date. Bridget was attractive and bright, but she also had that glint of cold steel at her core. A chill Dec recognized and wanted nothing to do with. "When the patient's mother arrives, I'll see that she gets upstairs."

"Good." Bridget turned to go. "'Night, Dec."

"Good night," Dec called as Bridget walked away. She grabbed the next chart and turned around. Zoey regarded her from ten feet down the hall.

"Hi," Dec said, heat blooming in her midsection. Zoey must have just come from the OR—she still wore scrubs under a drab green cover gown, scuffed tennis shoes, and a mask dangling around her neck. A few stray strands of hair clung to her neck. She looked a million times more beautiful and twice again as sexy as the perfectly coiffed, designer-attired psychiatrist who'd just left.

"Dec," Zoey said, her tone clipped. "You called for a consult?"

"Yeah," Dec said. "Room five. Roger Torres—one of your kidney patients waiting for an organ. His shunt isn't working, and he's skipped dialysis twice in a row. That, and his numbers are crazy out of whack. I can get him admitted to medicine for stabilization, but I thought you'd want to see him for—"

"You're right." Zoey skirted around Dec and strode over to the rack where the electronic charts were lined up. "He can go to medicine, but I'll take care of the shunt problem."

Zoey half turned away to study the chart. After a minute Dec joined her.

"How's the service going?" Dec asked.

"Fine," Zoey said without looking up.

"I heard the liver transplant patient did really well."

"Yes—she's about ready to go home."

"That's great."

Zoey closed the chart. "I'll go see this patient. Medicine can have him anytime."

"I'll call them," Dec said, a spike of frustration clawing at her throat. They'd barely spoken in weeks, and now they couldn't even exchange a few words across the chasm between them. "Zoey—"

Zoey looked up, her eyes flat, her expression blank. "Everything's fine, Dec."

"Right," Dec said, watching Zoey walk away.

Nothing felt right. The last few weeks, she'd seen Zoey in the cafeteria, in the ER, occasionally in passing in the locker room, but they hadn't talked. Every time she saw Zoey, she wanted to stop her, find out what she was doing, how she was feeling, hear about her day, anything to rekindle that connection they'd had so effortlessly before. Her days had been busy, but her nights had been empty and restless. She was pretty sure Zoey was intentionally avoiding her, and she wasn't entirely certain why. Zoey hadn't been any more eager to take things further than she had. Except, why had everything changed?

Anger warring with disappointment, she headed for the break room to give Zoey the space she obviously wanted. Honor joined her a couple minutes later.

"So," Honor said, pouring a cup of coffee and sitting down opposite Dec. "Don't forget our traditional summer barbecue for the surgery residents and staff. It's this weekend."

"I'm not surgery," Dec said darkly.

Honor ignored her mood and went on, "Your name is in the directory under neurosurgery. That makes it official. Besides, you work as much with the surgery residents as most staff. *And* I want you to come."

Dec sighed. She couldn't fight it. "All right."

"One o'clock. Be prepared for volleyball."

Dec winced. "You know, I sorta suck at volleyball."

"I sorta remember that." Honor laughed. "But you're tall and can block a lot of shots."

"No way I can get a rain check on the sports thing?"

"'Fraid not," Honor said. "The staff versus residents game is tradition, and I'm always busy, you know, doing something important like making potato salad."

"I can make potato salad."

"Can you?"

"Not really. But better than I can play volleyball."

"Stop complaining. You've been moping around here doing extra shifts for a month. You need a challenge."

"I haven't been moping."

Honor gave her a look. "You have, and I've exercised great restraint in not pushing you on it. Are you all right?"

"Yes." Dec rubbed her face and blew out a breath. "No. But I will be."

"Are you sure?"

"I…" Dec looked past Honor, remembering the cold, distant look in Zoey's eyes. Eyes she didn't recognize. That was not the Zoey she'd come to know and…care about. "I'm not sure, no."

"So?" Honor drew out the question.

"So maybe I should do something about that."

"Good idea." Honor rose. "I'll see you Saturday."

"Right. Okay. What should I bring?"

"You could bring a date."

Dec sucked in a breath. "What are my other choices?"

"Never hurts to bring beer."

"I can handle that."

She wasn't so sure she could handle an afternoon of socializing, especially if Zoey was going to be there. Somehow she'd have to manage not to be watching her every second, when Zoey was the only one she wanted to see. Maybe it really was time to do something about that.

❖

"When am I going to get my new kidney?" Roger Torres asked, the deep circles under his eyes making his brown irises appear even darker and more haunted. His pale skin, stretched so tightly over his bones, added decades to his thirty years.

"You're near the top of the list, Roger," Zoey said, "and as long as dialysis keeps all of your blood chemistries in line, we've got some time to find you a great match."

He grimaced and stared at his right forearm where the sinuous bulge of his A-V shunt distorted the thin silhouette. "As long as this thing keeps working next time."

"I know it's frustrating," she said, "but ignoring it and skipping dialysis is not the answer. We'll get it fixed and get you back in order again. It's hard to wait, but you've got to try."

He sighed and closed his eyes. "Okay. I guess I don't have any other choice."

Choices.

How many choices did anyone really have, when what they *thought* they were choosing was really only the culmination of so many other forces in their lives that drove them in a certain direction? That molded people without their even knowing. Zoey considered the choices she'd made—freely, she'd told herself at the time—but were they really? All her life she'd been driven by one singular need. To never let anyone know how much it hurt to be discarded. To be the reluctant obligation. If it seemed like she didn't care, if everything she did was exactly what she wanted, and everything she had was all she desired, then she never had to admit it wasn't enough.

Zoey clutched the tablet to her chest, over the spot where her heart ached. "We'll get you upstairs to medicine, and I'll talk to Dr. Doolin about when we can schedule the repair."

"Thanks," he said faintly and closed his sad, dark eyes.

Steeling herself, Zoey left the cubicle and walked back to the nursing station. Dec was gone, and she pushed aside the disappointment. She was glad. She could choose to be glad, couldn't she? Could she?

She left before she might run into her again, letting the ER resident know the patient would be admitted. With a few minutes left before she needed to be back in the OR, she went to the cafeteria for a fast lunch. She'd just sat down by herself with a burger and a helping of steamed broccoli as penance when Emmett slid a tray across from her and dropped into a free seat.

"How's transplant going?" Emmett said.

"Good," Zoey said. "How's being chief resident?"

Emmett grinned wryly. "It's a lot of work, and at least once a day somebody's mad at me."

Zoey laughed. "Remind me not to covet that."

"You've probably got a good shot. Everybody loves you."

Zoey looked away. "Yeah, right."

After a beat of silence, Emmett said, "I haven't seen you much."

"Well, you know how it is. New service, new juniors, and…well, you kinda *have* changed houses."

Emmett stared down at her plate for a second, then met Zoey's gaze. "Yeah, I know. And I should've talked to you about it."

"Why? You're still paying your part of the rent. Although we're going to have to do something about that. You *are* moving in with Syd, right?"

"Yeah." Emmett couldn't hide her smile of pleasure, and seeing it, Zoey didn't resent it. She was glad for her. If Emmett'd found what she needed, why wouldn't she be happy?

"Do you regret it, Zoey?" Emmett said after a moment.

Zoey didn't pretend she didn't know what Emmett was saying. "No, Emmett, I don't. We're friends still, right?"

"Of course."

"What we had going for us, it worked...at the time. Then it didn't work anymore, at least not for you."

"I know, but that's the point, isn't it? Just because we didn't make any promises doesn't mean, you know, it might not have hurt."

Zoey sighed and destroyed a spear of broccoli. "I can't say I wasn't pretty upset at first, but I wasn't mortally wounded. And I'm not hurt now." She paused, thinking of Emmett and the intimacy they'd shared. They'd always been good friends, but they'd been cautious too, or at least she had. Never letting down her guard, never letting Emmett too close. Why had everything been so different with Dec? Not just making love with her, but the quiet moments, the things she'd somehow wanted so much to say when she never had before, the way she'd ached to soothe the sadness in Dec's eyes. She had never been cautious with Dec, until she'd dropped every one of her barriers and let Dec into her heart. "What we had was enough then, but it wouldn't be anymore. So we're good."

"I'm glad," Emmett said, her grin returning. "Oh, Dani's gonna move over with you, right?"

Zoey forced herself back to the present. "That's the plan. Actually, I think it's a done deal at this point. What about Jerry? Is he going to be staying over there with you and Syd?"

Emmett nodded. "For the time being. I think he and Sadie might be cooling."

"Can't imagine why," Zoey muttered.

Emmett laughed again. "Yeah, Sadie is an acquired taste."

Zoey raised a brow. "And you would know this how?"

"Come on. Don't go there."

Zoey's spirits lifted. She'd missed Emmett. "You know what, I don't even want to."

"So we're good." Emmett gathered her tray. "I gotta get going. I'm taking one of the juniors through triple tubes. See you this weekend, if I don't catch up with you before then."

"This weekend?" Zoey said.

"You know, the barbecue at Quinn and Honor's. Saturday afternoon."

"Oh, right. The resident-staff thing." Zoey wondered how she'd get out of it.

"You need to be there, Zoey," Emmett said. "You know—make nice with the staff, get to know the newbies—chief resident slot next year."

"I don't want your job."

Emmett grinned. "Sure you do—admit it."

"I'll be there," Zoey grumped. At least Dec probably wouldn't be, so she'd be safe. She jumped up and called to Emmett, "Hey, wait up. I'll walk up with you."

CHAPTER TWENTY-FIVE

Zoey served a rocket into the far rear corner of the opposing team, feeling the winning point as her fist connected with the leather. Her heart raced, adrenaline surging, as the cry of victory rose in her throat. Somehow, as the ball speared toward the boundary line, Quinn Maguire dived under it and lofted a loopy return.

"Emmett," Zoey shouted as Emmett, at the net, launched herself upward, an arm flexed to block. "Spike, spike!"

Emmett uncoiled with the snap of an overwound spring and soared head and shoulders above the net, slamming the ball at its apex and driving it straight to the ground. No way would anyone get to it.

"Yes, yes, yes!" Zoey's fists clenched as the ball shot downward on a vertical path. Out of nowhere, Dec flew into view, body almost parallel to the ground, both arms outstretched for the save. Zoey screamed, "Nooo!"

Dec missed the ball by an inch.

The ball struck the ground, and Zoey's team erupted in jubilation.

Emmett yelled, "Yeah, residents two, staff zero," and did a little victory dance.

Syd grabbed Dani and kissed her on the mouth. Dani grinned.

Jerry looped an arm around Zoey's waist and spun her in a circle, her feet flying in the air. "Great serve, babe."

For a moment the world swirled, but as soon as Jerry set her down, Zoey ran for the net, the victory cry long gone, and fear gripping her throat. Dec hadn't gotten up.

Just as Zoey went to duck under the net, Bridget Kelly cut into her line of sight and knelt next to Dec. Where the hell had she come from? She wasn't even a surgery attending.

Dec rolled over onto her back, coughing.

"Dec, are you hurt?" Kelly asked, a hand on Dec's shoulder.

Zoey backed up a step, edging sideways to see Dec's face.

"Winded...not...hurt," Dec asked. "Fine."

Kelly reached out and brushed the hair off Dec's forehead.

Zoey's fear turned into a growl. She took a step, and Dani's hand landed on her shoulder.

"Hey, good game," Dani said.

"Yeah."

Dani's grip tightened. "It's never a good idea to kill attendings at the resident–staff party."

"She's not a surgery attending," Zoey gritted out between clenched teeth. "Besides, I'm not going to kill her. Only hurt her."

"Might you need a moment to find your sanity?" Dani said, laughter coloring her voice.

"No. And if she doesn't stop touching Dec, I just might change my mind about homicide." Zoey had the strangest urge to swat the hand Bridget Kelly kept running over Dec's body. Looking for injuries, her ass.

"Really?" Dani asked with just a hint of glee.

Zoey spun around and turned her back. "No, not really. Fuck it."

"Okay, that's one way to handle it."

"Shut up."

"Come on. We won." Dani laughed a little. "Hey, I got a kiss."

"Yeah, from Syd, who's practically married."

"True, but she's hot."

Zoey burst out laughing, and some of her misplaced fury drained away. "Sometimes, I fear for you."

"Yeah, sometimes I do too. Come on, let's go get a beer."

"Great idea." Zoey refused to glance at Dec and Bridget as she slung an arm around Dani's shoulders and walked away.

❖

Dec pushed to her knees and wiped the dirt off her cheek before Bridget could do it. "I'm fine. A little embarrassed."

"Why should you be?" Bridget said, kneeling next to her, her hand on Dec's hip. "That was a great move. You got closer than anybody else would've."

"Thanks...nice of you to say, but I know I'm a lousy volleyball player."

Bridget's smile could have melted the ice in the beer coolers. "I think you're a great volleyball player. You looked very good doing it too, which is even better."

"Unfortunately, looking good isn't quite enough in sports." Dec rose and brushed herself off. Thankfully she hadn't worn shorts, which really weren't her thing anyhow, and the knees of her jeans were completely covered with grass stains. Bridget edged a little closer, and Dec looked desperately around for a polite escape. Quinn and several of the other staff members stood nearby, and Dec caught Quinn's eye. "Great return back there, Quinn. Sorry I couldn't finish it out for you."

Quinn ambled over. "I got lucky, and just barely. I'm sorry I set you up for that one, though. Not much you could do once Emmett got to it."

Dec shrugged. "No problem. At least we didn't have to play another game."

Quinn laughed. "Buy you a beer?"

"I'll pass for now, but thanks," Dec said.

Quinn slapped her on the shoulder just as Omar Mahar, one of the new ENT attendings, walked up to Bridget. "I snagged us a couple of spots in the shade. Are you hungry?"

Bridget's smile brightened as she turned from Dec to Omar and slipped her hand in the crook of his elbow. "Famished. I'm definitely ready for something."

Dec didn't bother watching them walk away but turned to search the residents still milling around on the far side of the net and straggling toward the food. Zoey wasn't there. Again. The crowd at the party wasn't all that big, and Dec had run into almost every other person there at least once. Except Zoey. Zoey was always somewhere Dec wasn't. The annoyance of knowing she was being consciously avoided had been simmering inside her for weeks, and the proof she wasn't imagining it finally ignited her temper. She threaded her way through the crowd until she found Dani Chan.

"Have you seen Zoey?" Dec asked.

Dani studied her for three probing seconds and said, "She said she wanted a break and took a beer out front. She's probably sitting on the porch."

"Thanks."

"Good luck," Dani called.

Dec didn't look back. She wasn't sure if she needed luck. Probably. She wasn't even sure what she was going to do, but she was done pretending that whatever was going on with Zoey was okay with her.

As Dani predicted, Zoey sat on the top step of the porch, her back against the round white column, her feet down on the stair below, a bottle of Corona nestled in her lap.

Dec sat beside her. "I don't think I ever told you that I hate volleyball."

Zoey said, "I guess that was one of the areas we missed in our getting-to-know-you conversations."

"Since we've been through most of those topics already, why don't we skip the rest," Dec said mildly. "How about we talk about why you're so angry at me."

"I'm not angry at you." Zoey pointedly did not meet her gaze.

"Okay. Then maybe you'll tell me why you're angry at yourself?"

Zoey's gaze snapped to Dec's. "What makes you think I'm angry at myself?"

"You don't want to talk to me, but you say it's not me you're angry at. It's got something to do with me, and the anger's coming from somewhere, so that leaves you."

"You know what, Dec," Zoey said, heat in her eyes now, "you're right. I *am* angry. I'm angry that I can't get you out of my head."

"Zoey," Dec said softly. She hadn't known until just that moment what she wanted to hear, but like so many times before, Zoey said exactly what she needed to hear. Exactly what she couldn't pretend didn't matter. "I've missed you."

"Dec," Zoey said, "I can't do this."

"Do what?" Dec's frustration and need boiled over in her voice. "Talk to me?"

"Get involved with you."

There it was again. Exactly what Dec needed to hear, plain and simple and clear, the opening to get up, walk away, and stick to all the vows and resolutions she'd made. The silence stretched, and finally Zoey looked away.

"I didn't have any plans to ever get serious with anyone again," Dec said.

"I know," Zoey said, a catch in her voice.

"I was wrong."

"I don't want to hear that." Zoey looked at her. "I can't do it, Dec. I wish I could, but I can't be second-best. I'm sorry."

Dec frowned. "What are you talking about?"

"Your wife, Dec," Zoey said, "I can't be with you and know you're still in love with her. I just can't. I'm sorry."

For a second, Dec could only stare. "That's what you think? You think I'm in love with Annabelle? Zoey, Annabelle's dead because of me. I might as well have killed her myself. I'm not in love with Annabelle."

"I don't understand," Zoey said softly.

"Look, can we walk? This might take a while, and this isn't exactly private out here."

"All right," Zoey said slowly. "If you're sure you want to."

"I'm sure. I need to tell you this," Dec said. Until that instant, she'd never realized just how much.

"And I need you to." Zoey set the bottle on a small table on the porch. "Come on, let's walk over to my place. Nobody's there."

I'm not in love with Annabelle. I'm not in love with Annabelle.

The words kept echoing in Zoey's head. She should have been happy but heard the pain beneath the words. Something was very wrong. "I thought—"

"I know what you thought." Bitterness laced Dec's voice. "I know what everyone thought. *Still* thinks, everyone except Honor. She sees more than she says, and she doesn't push."

Zoey snorted. "Dani's opposite number."

Dec almost grinned. "Dani's something. She sent me after you."

"Did she." Zoey shook her head. "Maybe I'll thank her later."

Dec glanced at her. "I hope so."

"Let's go inside," Zoey said as they approached her Victorian twin.

"I should've told you something a lot sooner," Dec said as Zoey led her down the hall to the kitchen. "I'm sorry that I made you think that I…that I would have slept with you if I…" Dec dropped into a chair at the table and rubbed her face. "What a mess I made of this."

"It's all right," Zoey said quietly. "Do you want something to drink?"

"I'll take a beer now if you've got one," Dec said.

Zoey found two bottles of microbrew in the refrigerator and opened them, passing one to Dec. She sat opposite her at the table. "You didn't have to tell me about your past. What we had—have—is about now. It's my fault for thinking I knew what you felt, when I didn't."

"How could you, when I didn't tell you? I wanted to keep all of that away from you—from us," Dec said, "and that was stupid. As if I could ever really start all over again."

"Why can't you?"

"My past is part of me," Dec whispered.

"Just like mine is. Just like everyone's. But we get to make the future what we want, or at least we can try. Dec," Zoey said gently, "tell me about Annabelle."

"Yeah, that's the missing piece, isn't it." Dec blew out a breath. "I was a resident when we met. Annabelle was finishing her business degree at Wharton. You know that, right?"

"I heard that, yes."

"You probably heard the part about us getting involved, and me leaving here to go to Texas too, right?"

"That's kind of common knowledge," Zoey said, mildly embarrassed to admit she'd heard the gossip.

"Well, that's what everybody knows. The part they don't know is that when I met Annabelle, I'd never had a serious long-term relationship. My goal, my whole focus, had been studying, achieving, making it to the top. That's what my parents taught me mattered most. Then Annabelle came along and told me exactly the same thing, only she rewarded my achievements with attention and…well, you know."

"I get the idea." Zoey wasn't jealous that Dec had had a relationship. How could she be? Still, hers were in the past.

"I became dependent on her rewards, without even realizing it," Dec said. "When she was happy with me, when I achieved what *she* wanted, she made me feel special. So I performed as directed. I'm not proud of that."

"Dec, those things happen between people. And you weren't in that relationship alone."

"Yeah, well, I pretty much gave up doing anything I wanted if it wasn't what Annabelle wanted, for years. She wanted to bring home a doctor for her daddy's hospital, and I was the one. I fit nicely into his plans for expansion too, and before I knew it, I was specializing in an area I'd never planned to work in. But Annabelle wanted it." Dec turned the bottle on the table, rubbing the moisture streaming down the neck with her thumb. "And she rewarded me for it. When she was unhappy, she took away the rewards, and I lived in a freezer in the middle of Texas."

"That sounds…lonely. Lonely and hard."

Dec glanced at Zoey. "Maybe you can understand why I didn't want to tell you this. I'm not the person you thought I was."

"Of course you are. The Dec I know is sensitive and strong and caring. You supported me at work while letting me make my own decisions. You wanted to know me and made it safe for me to tell you things I've never told anyone else. You made love with me, and every minute you did, you *gave*, Dec. You gave me the freedom and security to say what I wanted, what I needed, and you gave me *you*." Zoey shook her head. "I spent a big part of my life hiding who I was and what I needed so no one would ever know that I wasn't strong and independent and sure. I didn't have to hide with you."

"You *are* all those things," Dec said, reaching to touch Zoey's cheek. When she drew back, Zoey caught her hand and linked their fingers.

"If I was, I wouldn't have walked away from you."

"No," Dec said. "You should have. You deserve to know me, and I was afraid to let you."

"And you think I've been completely honest with you?" Zoey shook her head. "You know why I left? Because I wasn't brave enough to fight for you. I was afraid of a ghost. I was afraid that I would always be looking over my shoulder for Annabelle, or that Annabelle would always be sitting at the table with us. And I wasn't big enough or brave enough or strong enough to make room for that, if that's what *you* needed." She paused. "I'm not Quinn Maguire."

"Well, thank God for that," Dec muttered.

Zoey smiled, relieved to hear a bit of Dec's fortitude creeping back. "I can't do casual with you, Dec. I can't. It's already too late."

"Zoey," Dec breathed, "it's never been casual for me. The first time I kissed you, you felt like the last woman I wanted to kiss ever again."

"Finish telling me the rest," Zoey said, fighting the desire, the need to touch Dec. If she started, she would never stop. Not tonight, not ever again.

"The chairman of my department—the neurosurgery department— was embroiled in a huge malpractice case, and Annabelle's father wanted to get rid of him. His politics didn't agree with Annabelle's father's. They needed an expert witness with a big name to testify against him. Annabelle's father wanted it to be me."

"Oh man," Zoey said. "That's ugly."

"Yes, and unethical. I didn't agree with the charges. Annabelle was furious, and as punishment, she shut me out of the bedroom and everywhere else." Dec shrugged. "I finally realized I didn't care. That's when I knew I wanted a divorce."

The words took a moment to register. "You...were leaving her?"

"Yeah, not the fairy-tale ending everyone's talking about, is it?" Dec tilted the bottle and drained it in two long swallows before setting it down with a hollow-sounding thud. "So you see, if this is about Annabelle, you've got the wrong idea."

"Then maybe," Zoey said, tightening her grasp on Dec's hand when Dec started to pull away, "it's time I had the right idea. Starting with why you think it's your fault Annabelle is dead."

"I didn't kill her," Dec said quietly, "not intentionally, but it was partly my fault."

"How?"

"I let my self-loathing get the better of me."

"That's a harsh word. You seem to be blaming yourself for an awful lot that sounds like two people were involved."

Dec gazed at their arms stretched out across the table between them, hands linked as if across a wide chasm, feeling that if she let go, she would truly fall. The only way to save that link, maybe to save herself, was to confess.

"I don't know how much you know about what happened," Dec said.

"I know what everyone knows," Zoey said. "Annabelle died in a car accident. You were terribly injured."

"The night of the accident, we were at a big gala. Of course I had to be there because Annabelle was being feted. Another award for some super business achievement. There were so many I lost track. She always spent most of her time at these things with her father and the other movers and shakers, planning or plotting." Dec shrugged. "She wanted to impress him that night by letting him know that I'd be delivering on their investment."

Zoey winced. "The malpractice case?"

Dec nodded. "Yes. She wanted to tell him that I was going to testify, and in all likelihood if I did, the outcome would be foreseen. Her father, or the board—her father's voice in these things—would get rid of him, and I would take his place."

"You told her you wouldn't do it," Zoey said with certainty.

"Oh, I did, right after I toasted her on her latest achievement. She was furious. She told me she was going to tell her father what he wanted to hear, no matter what."

"I can't believe she still couldn't see you."

"I told her she could tell him anything she wanted, because I was moving out the next day. Filing for divorce." Dec smiled wryly. "She told me I couldn't do that. That I'd be nothing without everything she'd done for me. That all those rewards I'd been given all these years, I couldn't live without."

Zoey squeezed Dec's hand. She couldn't hate a dead woman, but she could dislike her an awful lot.

"I told her I'd have to find out, because the rewards, as she called them, weren't worth it."

"I'm glad," Zoey said. "You deserve a great many things because of the amazing woman you are and not because of anything you have to earn."

"We fought in the car," Dec went on, needing to get it all out. "She was driving. She might've had a little more to drink than I realized when I got in the car with her too." Dec shut out the sounds of the squealing brakes, the shouts, the twist of metal, and the wail of sirens that surged at the edges of her consciousness. "She lost control, and we crashed. You pretty much know the rest of it."

"I'm so sorry. I'm sorry for what you went through with Annabelle, and I'm sorry that Annabelle's dead. No one deserves that, but that's not your fault. None of it is your fault."

"Why does it feel that way?" Dec whispered.

"Because you are a good and decent person, because you take responsibility for yourself, and probably because you loved her at one time in one way, or you wouldn't have married her."

Zoey edged her chair around the corner of the table and cupped Dec's face. Leaning close, she said, "It's time you forgave yourself. You are not the same person who married her. You proved that the night you told her you were leaving. But the person who married her wasn't at fault either. We can only learn from our mistakes and try to do better." She laughed shakily. "Listen to me—I'm just figuring that out myself. I was so afraid that I might not be enough for you, I didn't even try."

"Not enough?" Dec grasped her shoulders, the intensity in her eyes so fierce Zoey shivered in her deepest reaches. "You're so much more than I ever dreamed, Zoey. So much more than I deser—"

Zoey pressed her fingers to Dec's lips. "Don't say that. Never. You, Declan Black, have shown me I could be braver than I ever imagined I could be. That I matter for who I am. That's a gift that you've given me. I love you for that and so much more."

Dec's eyes widened. "Zoey."

"No, it's true. How could I not, when I can feel you every second of every day. When I want you more than anything or anyone I've ever wanted. When thinking of you makes me excited, and being with you makes sense of the world."

"If…" Dec kissed her, the kind of assured, demanding kiss that always set Zoey on fire. "If we're together, there'll be no one else. Not for me, not ever."

Zoey gripped Dec's shirt with one hand and thrust her fingers through her hair with the other. "Kiss me again."

Dec pulled Zoey onto her lap, one arm around her waist and the other cupping her cheek. Her kiss deepened into a darker, more commanding kiss. When she finally drew back, her voice was gravel. "Zoey?"

"Only you for me, Dec. Only you, from here until forever." Zoey stood and tugged Dec to her feet. "Starting now."

CHAPTER TWENTY-SIX

Dec followed Zoey through the silent house, up the stairs, and into a room on the second floor still awash with early evening sunlight. Somewhere, someone had just finished mowing, and the scent of fresh-cut grass wafted through an open window. She pulled on Zoey's hand, turning Zoey to face her, and lightly clasped her waist.

"I feel like I've taken a step back in time," Dec said. "Only this time, I'm beginning at a new place. You're the only one I see, Zoey. I see the strong, determined, beautiful woman who makes me feel like anything is possible. Who makes me feel like I'm not alone."

Zoey framed Dec's face, her thumbs brushing Dec's cheekbones before cradling the back of her neck. "I see you, Declan Black. Brave, compassionate, steady and sure."

When Zoey leaned into her, her breasts firm against Dec's chest, Dec slid her arms farther around Zoey's waist, molding them, melding them. "I want you. More and more, every time we touch."

Smiling, Zoey rested her forehead against Dec's and kissed her gently. "And did I mention, sexy as hell?"

Dec's heart thundered, the drumbeat echoing through her blood and pounding in her depths. "I want you like this and so much more. I want tomorrow, every one of them. Is that too much?"

"Never." Zoey reached between them and tugged Dec's shirt from her jeans, her fingers sliding unerringly beneath, her palm warm against Dec's middle. "I'm here. Right where I want to be. Right where I plan to be every one of those tomorrows."

"Zoey." Dec breathed her name like the benediction it was. "I love you."

Zoey's eyes widened, and she kissed Dec again, her lips whisper soft, winging across Dec's mouth with just a tease of silky warmth brushing the inside of her lip. Dec tightened her grip and took the kiss deeper until Zoey's heat erupted, a flare burning bright between them.

With a moan, Zoey tugged Dec's shirt upward. "Off. Off, off, off. God, I have missed you. Every time I saw you and didn't dare go closer because I wanted to touch you so much, I died a little inside."

"We're together now, and you can touch me whenever you want, any way you want. I'll always need you to touch me." Dec ripped the shirt off over her head and tossed it behind her. Naked except for her jeans, she carefully, as if handling a precious work of art, eased Zoey's shirt off her shoulders, down her arms, and dropped it. Tenderly, she cupped Zoey's breasts and brushed her cheek against Zoey's nipple. Zoey jerked with a tiny cry.

"I don't want to hurry," Zoey murmured, "but God, I need you so much."

"Come lie with me," Dec urged, her mouth against Zoey's breast, her lips tracing Zoey's nipple with her tongue. "Come let me touch you everywhere."

"Only if you promise never to stop," Zoey said.

Dec went to her knees, clasping Zoey's hips, and looked up. "I promise—I am yours."

Zoey unbuttoned her shorts, pushed them down along with her panties, and kicked them away. "And I'm yours."

Dec guided Zoey closer and kissed the gentle curve of her belly, the valley along the crest of her hips, and, slipping a hand between her thighs, guided them to open. "Let me show you how much I want you."

Zoey steadied herself with both hands on Dec's shoulders and closed her eyes. When Dec's mouth found her, she bit her lip, her thighs trembling as the pressure built and the pleasure cascaded. "Go slow. I'm close."

Her words a plea and a command.

Dec took her up, stroke by tender stroke, almost to the edge... almost...and then eased her down, back up again, and down, over and over until Zoey couldn't bear the need.

"Dec, Dec, I can't...I have to come."

"Wait." Dec surged to her feet and tumbled them onto the bed. Zoey landed on her back, and Dec settled between her legs and took her again, faster and deeper, her mouth pulling her in, a whirlwind unmooring her.

"Oh," Zoey cried in surprise. "You're making me come."

Dec closed her eyes, holding Zoey tightly to her, awash with Zoey's scent, the taste of her, the sounds of her pleasure. She stayed with her through every shuddering peak, the beat of Zoey's heart pulsing against her lips, until Zoey, laughing breathlessly, twisted away.

"Get away from me. I'm done."

Chuckling, Dec rested her cheek against the inside of Zoey's thigh. "Are you certain?"

"Positive. Except"—Zoey gripped a handful of Dec's hair and tugged—"I want you. I can't move, but I want you. Come to me."

Dec stretched out next to Zoey, sliding an arm behind her shoulders. Zoey turned to her, her hand sliding down the center of Dec's chest, burning a trail wherever she touched. "Can you wait until I can move a little bit?"

Dec kissed her. "I'll wait as long as you want."

Zoey took a long breath, put both hands on Dec's shoulders, and pushed Dec down onto her back. "Well, I can't wait."

"Thank God," Dec muttered. "You make me so fucking hot I'm about to explode."

"Oh, then maybe I should wait a little longer. I like you when you explode."

"Zoey," Dec groaned, and Zoey laughed.

She kissed Dec's mouth, her throat, the soft curve of her breast, and the long tight plane of her belly, and then took her as she had been taken. Slowly at first, then insistently as her hunger rose and the need to devour, to take, to claim, overtook her. She wanted more than she'd thought possible. Hungered like she'd never hungered before. She needed to be inside Dec, and she was. She needed to hold her as deeply as possible, and she did, and when Dec came with her name on her lips, Zoey rejoiced.

❖

"The beer's gone, the food is gone, and Robin is in charge of trash pickup and corralling the kids," Quinn said as she walked into the kitchen. "We're pretty much wrapped up out there."

"Oh no," Linda said from her seat at the table, "does that mean there's no leftovers?"

Laughing, Honor slid a plastic container onto the table next to the baby bag. "Would I let you go home without leftovers?"

"I certainly hope not," Linda said, "after I made a special trip over here with all this baby paraphernalia, and I didn't even get any good gossip out of it."

"Don't worry," Honor said, "there'll be more for you to catch up on when you get back to work. And besides, you know you wanted to show her off to everyone. There was practically a receiving line winding around to your chair."

Linda shifted the baby from one shoulder to the other, patting her back with the unconscious rhythmic movements of mothers the world over. "She did seem to get a lot of attention for someone who isn't even able to focus her eyes yet."

"And how is little Lucy getting on at home?" Quinn asked.

"*Princess* Lucinda," Linda said with false archness, "is well on her way to being spoiled, and she's not quite a month old."

Quinn grinned. "I take it her sibs are solely responsible for the spoiling?"

"Oh, not at all. Everyone—from neighbors to babysitters to the family dog—adores her."

"And that's as it should be," Honor said. "After all, she is the baby of the family."

Linda said, "Honestly, I'm ready to get back to work. I love her, she's amazing, but I'm not cut out to be a stay-at-home mom."

The kitchen door swung closed as Robin walked over to Linda. "Good thing I am, then, huh?"

"Better than good. I'm fantastically lucky." Linda tilted her face back, and Robin kissed her upside down.

"You ready to herd the brood home?" Robin asked.

"Whenever you are. Honor's feeding us dinner."

Robin grabbed the leftovers and the baby bag. "Praise be."

Linda hugged Honor good-bye. "I'll see you in the ER soon."

"It will be good to have you back. Whenever you're ready."

"'Night," Quinn said.

Robin held the door for Linda and the baby, and a moment later, the kitchen was empty.

Quinn slipped her arm around Honor's waist and kissed her temple. "I didn't see Arly for most of the afternoon. She looked like she was having a serious conversation with you there for a bit. Problem?"

"No, she just wanted to let me know that she and Janie were going out with Claudio and Eduardo. Either Claudio's mother or Janie's father will be doing the driving."

"Double date sort of thing?"

"I don't think so—more the group friend thing." Honor pulled a half-full bottle of wine from a collection of open bottles on the counter and lifted it in Quinn's direction. "Yes?"

"Sure."

As Honor poured, she said, "Arly also said her friends want her to take over running the gay-straight group at school. Some of the other members graduated, and there appears to be a lack of leadership."

"Ah—hence the discussion. She wanted your opinion?"

"Probably, but you know, at her age it's not totally cool to come right out and ask your parents for advice."

Quinn laughed. "So what did you say?"

"The truth. She'd be good at it—everyone likes her, she's got a mind for organizing, and if she's passionate about it, she definitely should consider it."

"You know," Quinn said, leaning back against the counter and pulling Honor in tight against her, face-to-face, hip to hip, "I wonder sometimes if she's going to be a doctor or lawyer, but I get this persistent feeling she's going to end up in politics."

"Whatever she does, she'll be good at it," Honor said.

"Yeah—we have great kids. Speaking of which," Quinn said, "Lucy is pretty cute."

Honor braced her palms against Quinn's chest and kissed her. "Have you got the baby bug, Dr. Maguire?"

"Well, I *was* thinking that Arly will be leaving home for college in a few years, and that's going to leave Jack without a sibling at home when he's still pretty young."

"I know. It would be nice for him to grow up with a sibling near his age," Honor said, "but I've been thinking about it since we talked, and I'm pretty certain my baby-making days are over."

"We've got alternatives," Quinn said.

"Mm. So what do you think, infant or older? Boy or girl?"

"No preference, really," Quinn said.

Honor ran her fingertips beneath the edge of Quinn's T-shirt, tracking along the ridge of her collarbone. "I was thinking it might be a good idea to bracket, a couple years younger than Jack and a couple years older. What do you think about two at once? Then we don't have to decide on gender either."

Quinn tightened her arms around Honor's waist and kissed her throat. With her lips against Honor's ear, she murmured, "I think that's a great idea. We've got plenty of love to go around."

Honor tilted her head, murmuring encouragingly, "We do indeed. I think right now it would be a good idea, since Jack is with Phyllis for the night, that we practice a little bit of that love right here at home."

Quinn picked up the wineglasses and said, "A little practice is always a good idea."

❖

Zoey stretched and let out a long, contented sigh. Dec's shoulder and thigh rested against her, and she braced for the fear to hit, for the urge to back away, to run—but it never came. Nothing had ever felt so right. She found Dec's hand and pulled it to the center of her chest, over her heart. "Do you have to be anywhere in the morning?"

Dec rolled toward her and skimmed her hand down Zoey's middle to the curve of her hip. Goose bumps broke out along Zoey's skin despite the heat that lingered in the room a half hour after sunset.

"I'm off tomorrow," Dec said. "You?"

"Same."

"Plans?"

"I'm making some right now," Zoey said, turning to face Dec. She kissed her and toyed with the damp curls on the nape of her neck. "Those plans include a lot more of what we've just been doing."

Dec grinned. "Funny, I was kind of planning the same thing."

"If there's something else you want to do—" Zoey began.

"Oh, there is," Dec said, and for an instant Zoey struggled not to appear disappointed.

She *did* want to spend time with Dec doing ordinary, couple-y type things. Just not right away. She said brightly, "Okay, sure."

"There's a million things...no, ten million things I want to do with you," Dec murmured, "to see, to share, to learn. But tomorrow, mostly what I want is my hands on you. And a lot of skin on skin."

Zoey laughed with the burst of relief. "I don't think I've ever heard anything more romantic."

Dec's brows winged up. "Oh, it's romance you want. Well then, how about—"

Zoey stopped her with a kiss. She'd meant the kiss to be light and casual, but the instant the heat of Dec's mouth met hers, arousal shot through her. And though she would've sworn she couldn't possibly go again, she felt herself awakening.

Dec pulled back a fraction. "Again?"

"Soon," Zoey said, resting her forehead against Dec's. "I might need a break to get something to eat."

"I could go out—"

"No. Not a chance. You're not going anywhere."

"I already told you that." Dec cupped her cheek. "I'm here for the long term."

"I believe you. But for the rest of this weekend, I don't want you farther away than the length of my arm so I can touch you whenever I want to." Zoey's throat tightened, and she didn't try to hide it. She didn't have to hide what she needed from Dec. "Whenever I need to."

"Always, Zoey. Anything."

Zoey forced herself up and ran both hands through her hair. "I really should get us something to eat. Peanut butter or leftover pizza?"

"Pizza for sure."

"I'll run down to the kitchen and nuke it. Five minutes."

"You need me to do anything?"

"Kiss me." Zoey leaned over, instantly distracted when Dec cupped her breast, her thumb brushing over her nipple. Zoey sucked in a breath. "Do not do that if you want something to eat."

"I can't help it."

"Good." Zoey kissed her quickly and moved back out of touching range. "Just stay here and think about all the things I'm going to do to you after we eat." She pulled on the cutoff sweatpants she wore as shorts around the house and a raggedy sleeveless tee and backed up a few more steps. "And all the things you want to do to me."

Dec groaned. "Come on. Are you sure you're hungry?"

Laughing, Zoey ran barefoot down the hall, took the stairs two at a time, and skated into the kitchen.

Dani turned from the open refrigerator door. "Oh hey, I didn't know you were here."

"Oh," Zoey said, "yeah, I'm here."

"That's cool. There's nothing in the refrigerator. I'm going to nuke the—"

"Dibs on the pizza," Zoey said instantly.

"Really?"

"Really. Can you order cheesesteaks or something? My treat."

"Yeah, I could do that. Don't you want me to get you one too?"

"Ah, no," Zoey said, sidling around Dani and grabbing the pizza box out of the fridge. "I'm just gonna have the pizza."

"Okay, you're being weird," Dani said. "Did something happen? Did Dec do something?"

A kaleidoscope of images crashed through Zoey's brain. She couldn't have stopped the heat rising in her face if she'd wanted to. "Um."

"Um?"

"You could say that. She's upstairs."

Dani's mouth literally dropped open. She recovered in an instant. "You're kidding me."

"No. Serious."

"She's upstairs in your bed?"

Zoey laughed. "Well, she's not upstairs in the broom closet."

"You...She...Okay. Who started it?"

"I suppose I did?"

Dani raised her clasped hands over her head in a victory salute. "Go, Zoey. So, what, you're eating pizza in bed so you can go another couple rounds?"

"Shut up."

Eyes sparkling, Dani pointed a finger. "You are. You're having marathon sex. Oh my God. Is she amazing?"

"Shut up." Zoey started the microwave and tried very hard not to think about sex. It wasn't working. Maybe pizza wasn't going to be enough to get them through the night.

"And you're totally good with it, right?" Dani said. "You know what you're doing."

Zoey turned so Dani could read her eyes. "I'm more than totally good with it. She's everything I've ever wanted."

Dani's face took on a wholly uncharacteristic expression. Slowly, in the gentlest voice Zoey had ever heard from her, she said, "I'm really happy for you."

Zoey grabbed her by the shoulders and yanked her into a hug. With her cheek against Dani's, she whispered, "Thank you."

Dani gave her a squeeze and stepped away. "Go back upstairs. I'll deliver the pizza."

"Oh yeah, see if you can get a look at Dec with no clothes on?"

"I had thought about that," Dani said.

"No doubt. I'll wait right here for the pizza."

"So does this mean we're going to have another vacancy?"

Zoey halted in midstep. "No. Well, not right away, for sure. I want a long courtship and an even longer engagement. So you don't have to worry about finding a new roommate for quite a while."

"Good. I'm not ready to give you up yet."

"Hey," Zoey said, "that's never going to happen. You're my best friend, remember?"

"I'll remember." Dani brightened, her solemn expression fading. "Hey, I think your pizza's done."

Zoey stacked the slices on a plate and grabbed a few paper towels. "I'll see you in the morning. Try to stay out of trouble if you go out tonight."

"Me? No worries." Dani grinned.

"See you tomorrow," Zoey called on her way back upstairs. She edged the bedroom door open with her hip and carried the plate toward the bed. Dec sat up against the pillows, naked, her hair tousled, and her gaze devouring Zoey as she moved closer.

"Miss me?" Zoey asked, forgetting she was hungry as the need grabbed her.

"I got very, very hungry waiting," Dec said, her voice low and dangerous.

Zoey set the pizza on the bedside table and pulled off her T-shirt. "How do you feel about cold pizza?"

"Love it." Dec grabbed Zoey's hand and pulled.

Laughing, Zoey tumbled on top of her, free at last to love without fear.

About the Author

Radclyffe has written over sixty romance and romantic intrigue novels as well as a paranormal romance series, The Midnight Hunters, as L.L. Raand.

She is a three-time Lambda Literary Award winner in romance and erotica and received the Dr. James Duggins Outstanding Mid-Career Novelist Award by the Lambda Literary Foundation. A member of the Saints and Sinners Literary Hall of Fame, she is also an RWA/FF&P Prism Award winner for *Secrets in the Stone*, an RWA FTHRW Lories and RWA HODRW winner for *Firestorm*, an RWA Bean Pot winner for *Crossroads*, an RWA Laurel Wreath winner for *Blood Hunt*, and a Book Buyers Best award winner for *Price of Honor* and *Secret Hearts*. She is also a featured author in the 2015 documentary film *Love Between the Covers*, from Blueberry Hill Productions. In 2019 she was recognized as a "Trailblazer of Romance" by the Romance Writers of America.

In 2004 she founded Bold Strokes Books, one of the world's largest independent LGBTQ publishing companies, and is the current president and publisher.

Find her at facebook.com/Radclyffe.BSB, follow her on Twitter @RadclyffeBSB, and visit her website at Radfic.com.

Books Available From Bold Strokes Books

A Woman to Treasure by Ali Vali. An ancient scroll isn't the only treasure Levi Montbard finds as she starts her hunt for the truth—all she has to do is prove to Yasmine Hassani that there's more to her than an adventurous soul. (978-1-63555-890-6)

Before. After. Always. by Morgan Lee Miller. Still reeling from her tragic past, Eliza Walsh has sworn off taking risks, until Blake Navarro turns her world right-side up, making her question if falling in love again is worth it. (978-1-63555-845-6)

Bet the Farm by Fiona Riley. Lauren Calloway's luxury real estate sale of the century comes to a screeching halt when dairy farm heiress, and one-night stand, Thea Boudreaux calls her bluff. (978-1-63555-731-2)

Cowgirl by Nance Sparks. The last thing Aren expects is to fall for Carol. Sharing her home is one thing, but sharing her heart means sharing the demons in her past and risking everything to keep Carol safe. (978-1-63555-877-7)

Give In to Me by Elle Spencer. Gabriela Talbot never expected to sleep with her favorite author—certainly not after the scathing review she'd given Whitney Ainsworth's latest book. (978-1-63555-910-1)

Hidden Dreams by Shelley Thrasher. A lethal virus and its resulting vision send Texan Barbara Allan and her lovely guide, Dara, on a journey up Cambodia's Mekong River in search of Barbara's mother's mystifying past. (978-1-63555-856-2)

In the Spotlight by Lesley Davis. For actresses Cole Calder and Eris Whyte, their chance at love runs out fast when a fan's adoration turns to obsession. (978-1-63555-926-2)

Origins by Jen Jensen. Jamis Bachman is pulled into a dangerous mystery that becomes personal when she learns the truth of her origins as a ghost hunter. (978-1-63555-837-1)

Unrivaled by Radclyffe. Zoey Cohen will never accept second place in matters of the heart, even when her rival is a career, and Declan Black has nothing left to give of herself or her heart. (978-1-63679-013-8)

A Fae Tale by Genevieve McCluer. Dovana comes to terms with her changing feelings for her lifelong best friend and fae, Roze. (978-1-63555-918-7)

Accidental Desperados by Lee Lynch. Life is clobbering Berry, Jaudon, and their long romance. The arrival of directionless baby dyke MJ doesn't help. Can they find their passion again—and keep it? (978-1-63555-482-3)

Always Believe by Aimée. Greyson Walsden is pursuing ordination as an Anglican priest. Angela Arlingham doesn't believe in God. Do they follow their vocation or their hearts? (978-1-63555-912-5)

Courage by Jesse J. Thoma. No matter how often Natasha Parsons and Tommy Finch clash on the job, an undeniable attraction simmers just beneath the surface. Can they find the courage to change so love has room to grow? (978-1-63555-802-9)

I Am Chris by R Kent. There's one saving grace to losing everything and moving away. Nobody knows her as Chrissy Taylor. Now Chris can live who he truly is. (978-1-63555-904-0)

The Princess and the Odium by Sam Ledel. Jastyn and Princess Aurelia return to Venostes and join their families in a battle against the dark force to take back their homeland for a chance at a better tomorrow. (978-1-63555-894-4)

The Queen Has a Cold by Jane Kolven. What happens when the heir to the throne isn't a prince or a princess? (978-1-63555-878-4)

The Secret Poet by Georgia Beers. Agreeing to help her brother woo Zoe Blake seemed like a good idea to Morgan Thompson at first…until she realizes she's actually wooing Zoe for herself… (978-1-63555-858-6)

You Again by Aurora Rey. For high school sweethearts Kate Cormier and Sutton Guidry, the second chance might be the only one that matters. (978-1-63555-791-6)

Love's Falling Star by B.D. Grayson. For country music megastar Lochlan Paige, can love conquer her fear of losing the one thing she's worked so hard to protect? (978-1-63555-873-9)

Love's Truth by C.A. Popovich. Can Lynette and Barb make love work when unhealed wounds of betrayed trust and a secret could change everything? (978-1-63555-755-8)

Next Exit Home by Dena Blake. Home may be where the heart is, but for Harper Sims and Addison Foster, is the journey back worth the pain? (978-1-63555-727-5)

Not Broken by Lyn Hemphill. Falling in love is hard enough—even more so for Rose, who's carrying her ex's baby. (978-1-63555-869-2)

The Noble and the Nightingale by Barbara Ann Wright. Two women on opposite sides of empires at war risk all for a chance at love. (978-1-63555-812-8)

What a Tangled Web by Melissa Brayden. Clementine Monroe has the chance to buy the café she's managed for years, but Madison LeGrange swoops in and buys it first. Now Clementine is forced to work for the enemy and ignore her former crush. (978-1-63555-749-7)

A Far Better Thing by JD Wilburn. When needs of her family and wants of her heart clash, Cass Halliburton is faced with the ultimate sacrifice. (978-1-63555-834-0)

Body Language by Renee Roman. When Mika offers to provide Jen erotic tutoring, will sex drive them into a deeper relationship or tear them apart? (978-1-63555-800-5)

Carrie and Hope by Joy Argento. For Carrie and Hope, loss brings them together but secrets and fear may tear them apart. (978-1-63555-827-2)

Detour to Love by Amanda Radley. Celia Scott and Lily Andersen are seatmates on a flight to Tokyo and by turns annoy and fascinate each other. But they're about to realize there's more than one path to love. (978-1-63555-958-3)